The Young Unicorns

MADELEINE L'ENGLE

· · · · · · · · · · · · ·

The Young Unicorns

· · · · · · · · · · · · ·

SQUARE
FISH

Farrar Straus Giroux

☐
SQUARE
FISH
An Imprint of Macmillan

Square Fish and the Square Fish logo are trademarks of Macmillan
and are used by Farrar Straus Giroux under license from Macmillan.

Library of Congress Catalog Card Number: 68-13682

ISBN: 978-0-312-37933-9

Originally published in the United States by Farrar Straus Giroux
Square Fish logo designed by Filomena Tuosto

First Square Fish Edition: 2008

10   9   8   7   6   5   4
mackids.com

AR: 6.5 / F&P: Y / LEXILE: 820L

For

*all my friends at the Cathedral Church of St. John
the Divine, who are as the stars of heaven
for multitude and brightness,*

*and with the affectionate reassurance that with the exception of Canon
Tallis and Rob Austin all the characters in this book are figments of my
imagination. The Sub Dean of the Cathedral reminds me that, in the
author's note to* Murder Must Advertise, *the late Dorothy Sayers
wrote: "I do not suppose that there is a more harmless and law-abiding
set of people than the Advertising Experts of Great Britain. The idea
that any crime could possibly be perpetrated on Advertising premises is
one that could only occur to the ill-regulated fancy of a detective nov-
elist trained to fasten the guilt upon the most Unlikely Person," and
suggests that I might substitute* Ecclesiastical *for* Advertising, *and
the* United States of America *for* Great Britain, *and thus have my
own author's note for* The Young Unicorns. *I would also like to remind my friends that the action takes place not in the present but in
that time in the future when many changes only projected today may
have become actualities.*

". . . in their early days they were like the unicorn, wild and uncommitted, which creature cannot be caught by the hunter, no matter how skillful. Nay, but he can be tamed only of his own free will."

FROM THE APROCRYPHAL WRITINGS OF ST. MACRINA

Introduction

"Who are you in this book?" we would constantly ask our grandmother, Madeleine L'Engle, about every book that she wrote. Her books have protagonists that many people can identify with, generation after generation, whether it is the brave and clever, gawky and frustrated Meg Murry, or the vulnerable and awkward, but at the same time, sensitive and intuitive Vicky Austin. Madeleine also strongly identified with her characters, and said many times that she was both Meg and Vicky. There was so much that was recognizable as her and her life in her stories, and we wanted to be able to map her fiction to her biography, thereby fixing and understanding her place, and by extension, ours, in the family and the wider world.

Most children want to be told stories about themselves. We were no different, and so, reading the Austin books was always a special thrill, because the narrative is peppered with incidents and details that also featured in family lore, like the adorable malapropisms of Rob Austin and Vicky's bicycle accident. The Austin family house in the quiet New England village of Thornhill (as described in *Meet the Austins*) is ever-present as a touchstone of their domestic peace, and is modeled on Crosswicks, a pre-Revolutionary War farmhouse in northwestern Connecticut where our grandparents and their children lived in the 1950s. The cross-country road trip in *The Moon by Night* copies the Franklin family itinerary of 1959, during which Madeleine started writing *A Wrinkle in Time*. In *The Young Unicorns*, the Austin kids unravel a mystery at the Cathedral of St. John the Divine, where our grandmother was the librarian and writer-in-residence for more than forty years.

There is enough similarity of detail in the books to have caused us some confusion: If our grandmother is Vicky, how can she have the bicycle accident that left our own mother with a Y-shaped scar on her chin? If some of the details confounded our sense of reality, we never questioned the underlying truth of the characters and our grandmother's relationship to them. If Madeleine were Vicky, then we felt understood. Because we were Vicky, too.

People would joke that *Meet the Austins* could have been called *Meet the Franklins* (Madeleine's married name), and yet, we knew that Vicky and the Austins couldn't be a simple translation of our grandmother's life, because of the family tension and pain surrounding these books about this family. Madeleine's own children were often shocked at how their own lives were appropriated and rewritten for publication, and felt judged against this very happy and practically perfect family. The line between fact and fiction can sometimes be blurry for writers, and the temptation to inscribe a certain version of and authority on events is strong.

All of Madeleine's writing, fiction and nonfiction, was an example of how all narrative is fiction, and all fiction can be true. She wrote and lectured extensively on the difference between truth and fact, arguing that it is through story that we human beings approach the truth, not through facts, which can only get us so far. As her granddaughters, this was both liberating and confusing, but we happily suspended our disbelief, and some of our best-loved stories are ones that are culled from her real life, from her days in the theater, from her early years with our grandfather, and the mysterious decade of the fifties.

The five books that are now presented as The Austin Family Chronicles were written over a period of thirty years. A prolific writer of more than sixty books in a variety of genres, Madeleine created a web of characters that grew, changed, and surprised her. As we re-read these books over our lifetime, what strike us are the very different responses we have to this family. At eleven, we thrilled to the references to things that our mother or aunt or uncle would confirm were true. At seventeen, we were cynical about the blur between fact and fiction, and thought we could read our grandmother as if she were a book. In our mature adulthood, we recognize how rich and complicated our grandmother was, and that fact can be the springboard for fiction, and fiction can inform who we are and tell us about ourselves.

Charlotte Jones Voiklis and Lena Roy
March, 2008

One

Winter came early to the city that year. Josiah Davidson, emerging from the subway, his arms loaded with schoolbooks, shivered against the dank November rain which blew icily against his face and sent a trickle down the back of his neck. He did not see three boys in black jackets who moved out of a sheltering doorway and stalked him.

Uncomfortable, unaware, he hurried along the street until he came to a run-down tenement. Here he let himself in through the rusty iron gate that led to the basement apartment.

The three boys went silently up the brownstone steps and took cover in the doorway, listening, waiting.

The one room was dark and cold and smelled of cabbage; Josiah Davidson dumped his books on the table, sniffed with displeasure, and left. He stood for a moment on the wet sidewalk, looked downhill towards Harlem, uphill towards the great Cathedral which dominated the area, its multicolored Octagon of stone and glass glowing brilliantly against the rain-filled sky.

The three boys in the doorway waited until Josiah Davidson started up the hill, then followed. He climbed quickly and
it was not easy to keep his pace. They began to run as he pulled
a key ring, heavy with keys, from his pocket and fitted one into
the wrought-iron gate at the bottom of the Cathedral Close.

As he opened the gate he swung round and saw them.

"What's your hurry, Dave?" one asked.

"No!" he said sharply, pushed through the gate and slammed
it in their faces.

They laughed mockingly, banging against the gate but not
really trying to get in.

Dave ran up the hill past the choir buildings, through the
Dean's Garden, November-sad in the downpour, and climbed a
flight of concrete steps that led into the Cathedral itself. The
small side door was already closed for the night; he unlocked it
and went into the ambulatory, a wide half-circle off which seven
chapels were rayed like the spokes of a wheel. He could hear the
high voices of the choirboys singing Evensong around the full
length of the passage in St. Ansgar's chapel. He had once been a
Cathedral chorister himself, but for the past few years the Cathedral had been mainly a short cut for him. He hurried down the
echoing nave, past the soaring beauty of the central altar. Above
it, the great Octagon seemed to brood over the Cathedral, pro-
tecting it for the night. One of the guards, strolling up the center
aisle, saw the boy and waved: "Hi, Dave."

Dave waved back but did not slacken his pace. From the
chapel came the clear notes of the Nunc Dimittis: Lord, now
lettest thou thy servant depart in peace, according to thy
word . . .

—That's all I want, the boy thought, —a little peace. And to have my past leave me alone.

He pushed out the heavy front doors and ran down the steep flight of stone steps that led to the street.

Josiah Davidson walked quickly along Broadway, stepping out in the street to avoid a cluster of darkly beautiful women looking cold in their saris, too delicate for the November air. He brushed by a group of men in native African dress, pushed through strolling Columbia students in assorted eccentricities of clothing. He was so accustomed to the conglomerate and colorful crowd on the Upper West Side of the city that it would have taken someone beyond the bounds of the merely unusual to have made him pause and take notice.

He halted at a large school building. Its bright lights spilled warmly onto the street; the heavy rain had slackened, was only a fine drizzle, but he felt cold. He turned up the collar of his coat and blew on his fingers. He looked up and down the street, but the three black-jacketed boys were nowhere to be seen. He leaned against the school building and watched boys and girls of all ages begin to straggle out the side door; classes had been dismissed an hour before, but older children had stayed for orchestra rehearsal, for detention, for club meetings; younger ones with working mothers had remained for supervised play until they could be called for. Some carried violin or clarinet cases, some satchels of books, and some, despite the icy wind blowing in from the Hudson, were eating ice cream. One of the senior boys, about Dave's own age, called, "Emily'll be along in a minute, Dave. She's helping that little kid get his boots on."

"Okay. Thanks." Dave shoved his cold hands into his pockets, slouched against the cold wall of the school building, and waited.

Across the street a man in a dark overcoat and a foreign-looking fur hat stood in the doorway of an apartment building, watching the school, watching Dave.

"We're here, Dave!"

Dave turned to the opening door; a little boy in a navy-blue pea jacket and a bright red woolen cap appeared. Behind him, one hand on his shoulder, came a tall, long-legged girl; her dark hair fell loosely on a wine-colored velvet coat which was in marked contrast to the plain navy blue everybody else was wearing.

"Emily!" Dave demanded. "Do you know what you have on?"

She bristled. "My good coat. My school coat's still sopping."

"Okay. So how was orchestra rehearsal?"

She relaxed. "Horrendous. Ear-splitting. Cacophonous. And if they don't get the auditorium piano tuned I'll have to do it myself. Hurry, please, Dave. I'll be late for my piano lesson again and Mr. Theo'll slaughter me."

The man in the fur hat left the shadows of the doorway and followed the oddly assorted trio: the dark, shabby boy; the definitely younger and rather elegant girl; and the fair little boy who couldn't have been more than seven or eight years old.

They reached the corner and turned down Broadway. The bitter wind whipped a few brown leaves and bits of soiled newspaper across the sidewalk. Strands of Emily's fine, dark hair blew across her face and she pushed it back impatiently. As they passed a shabby little antique shop with a gloomy bin of oddments on the sidewalk in front of the dusty windows, Dave paused.

"It was here," Rob said. "Right here."

8

Emily pulled impatiently at Dave's arm, but the older boy stood, looking at the shop window, at the door with the sign PHOOKA'S ANTIQUES, then moved on, more slowly.

Shortly before they reached 110th Street the man with the fur hat pulled ahead of them and merged with a group of people clustered about a newsstand. He held a paper so that he could look past it at the children as they came by.

The little boy, who had made friends with the crippled man who owned the newsstand, looked up to wave hello. His mouth opened in startled recognition as his eyes met those of their follower. He didn't hear the news vender call out, "Hi, Robby, what's up?"

The man in the fur hat smiled at the small boy, nodded briefly, rolled up his newspaper, and turned back in the direction of the Cathedral.

Dave and Emily had gone on ahead. Rob ran after them, calling, "Dave! He's the one!" He tugged at the older boy's sleeve.

"Who's what one?" Dave pulled impatiently away from the scarlet mitten.

"The man we saw yesterday, the one who talked to Emily!"

Dave stopped. "Where?"

Rob pointed towards the Cathedral.

"Wait!" Dave ran back round the corner.

"Emily, he was the one," Rob said. "I'm sorry, but I know he was."

"I don't want to talk about it." Emily's face looked pale and old beyond her years. She was just moving into adolescence, but her expression had nothing childlike about it. "It couldn't have been the same one," she whispered.

"But he *was* real," Rob persisted. "It *did* happen."

9

Dave returned. "I didn't see anybody. Anyway, how do you know he was the one?"

"Because he had no eyebrows."

Emily gave a shudder that had nothing to do with the cold. "I don't want to think about him. I don't want to think about yesterday. Come on. Let's hurry." She took Dave's arm.

Rob backed along excitedly in front of them. "He was right under the light. And he recognized me, too. He did! He looked right at me and nodded."

"Rob!" Emily said sharply. "Not now! Not before my lesson."

Dave steered her away from a group of jostling boys and hurried her down the street, past the light from the shops, from the street lamps, from buses crowded with people coming home from work. "I suppose your lesson's going to be a knock-down drag-out fight all the way as usual?"

"Mr. Theo'll be furious if I'm late, but I know that fugue inside out. As a matter of fact—" Emily relaxed again and burst into a pleased, expectant laugh.

"What?" Rob asked. "What's funny?"

"Nothing. At least not yet. If you come along to my lesson you'll see."

"Anything for a laugh," Dave said. "Give me your key, Emily."

As they turned towards the Hudson, Emily reached inside the collar of the velvet coat and tugged at a chain with a key on it, tangling it in her hair as she pulled it over her head. "Here."

On the corner of Riverside Drive stood a large and dilapidated but still elegant stone mansion. Dave opened the heavy blue door that led into a hall with a marble floor and wide marble stairs. At the back of the hall, double doors were open into a great living room dominated by two grand pianos. By one of the pianos stood a small old man with a shaggy mane of yellowing hair.

If he had been larger he would have looked startlingly like an aging lion. He let out a roar. "So, Miss Emily Gregory!"

"So, Mr. Theotocopoulos!" She threw each syllable of his name back at him with angry precision.

"Three times in a row you come to me late."

Emily flung her head up, simultaneously unbuttoning her coat and letting it fall to the floor behind her. "How late am I?"

The old man pulled out a gold watch. Temper matched temper. "Remember, Miss, that I come personally and promptly to you, instead of making you come to my studio—"

"So I'll come to your studio—"

"In my declining years I must still work like a hog. One minute too late is too many of my valuable time—"

"I couldn't help it, orchestra rehearsal—"

"No alibis! And kindly pick up your coat and hang it up—"

"I'm going to!"

"—like a civilized human being instead of a spoiled rat."

Emily reached furiously for her coat. "I'm not spoiled!"

"You are disrupted and disreputable!"

"Then so is Dave!"

"Emily! Be courteous or be quiet!" The old man sounded as though he himself were no more than Emily's age. "I am fit to be fried."

Emily grabbed the coat and rushed towards the hall, bumping

11

headlong into the doorjamb. She let out a furious yell, echoed by her music-master.

"If you knock yourself out you think that will make me sorry for you? Hang up your coat and come sit down at the piano. And do not move without thinking where you are going."

"Do I always have to think!" Emily shouted.

Rob, who had started automatically to help Emily, turned back to the room and sat on a small gold velvet sofa in front of a wall of bookshelves, the lower, wider shelves filled with music. "Do you mind if I stay?" he asked politely. "Sort of to pick up the pieces, you know, if there are any left."

"Mr. Theo," Dave said, holding himself in control, "there is a difference between mollycoddling her and—"

"Sit down!" Mr. Theo bellowed. "You are talking about a twelve-year-old girl, and I am talking about an artist. I will not let her do anything that will hurt her music. Now sit still and listen—if you have ears to hear."

Shrugging, Dave stalked over to his favorite black leather chair by the marble fireplace.

Out in the hall by the coatrack, Emily managed to get her coat to stay on its hook; then, walking carefully but with the assurance of familiarity, she came back and sat down at one of the pianos. "Then why don't you let me give a concert if you think I'm a musician?"

Mr. Theotocopoulos took her hands in his. "Why could you not come straight home from school? Cannot that so-called orchestra get along without you? And your hands are too cold to be of any use for music at all." He began to massage her fingers. "You are too young for a concert. You would be not only a child prodigy, you would be a blind child prodigy, and people would say, 'Isn't she marvelous, poor little thing?' and nobody would have heard you play at all. Is that what you want?"

"No," she said.

He rubbed her hands for a moment more in silence, then asked, "What is bothering you?"

"Nothing. I don't want to talk about it."

"Something at school?"

"No."

"But there is something. Yes. Bigger than something at school. I can feel it in your hands. All right. Play, and we will see what you tell me."

"I won't tell you anything."

"You think you can hide yourself from me when you play, hah?"

"We'll see." Emily sounded grim, then gave an unexpected giggle. "Shall I start with the G minor fugue?"

Mr. Theo looked at her suspiciously. "If you think your fingers are limber enough."

She adjusted the piano bench carefully, then held her hands out over the keyboard, flexing them before starting to play. Rob sat straight on the little gold sofa. Dave slouched on the end of his spine in the leather chair and put his feet on the brass fender. Mr. Theo scowled and waited.

Emily began to play. After less than a minute Mr. Theo roared, his yellowed mane seeming to rise in rage from his bulbous forehead, "And what in the name of all I treasure is *that*?"

She stopped, turning her face towards his voice with an expression of wounded surprise. "You told me last week that I was to learn that fugue backwards and forwards. That's backwards."

Mr. Theotocopoulos's roars of rage turned into roars of

laughter and he grabbed Emily in a huge hug of delight. "See?" he asked, more to an imaginary audience than to Rob and Dave. "See what I mean? All right, child, let us hear. Play it backwards all the way through."

Whenever Emily was pleased with herself and her world she had a deep chuckle that gave somewhat the effect of a kitten's purr. Pleasure in her accomplishment, and it was indeed an accomplishment, made her purr now. She reached for a moment for a cumbersome sheet of Braille music manuscript, concentrated on it with a furious scowl, then grinned again and turned back to the piano. "I really rather like it this way. I wonder Bach never thought of it."

Dave turned to ask Rob, "Your family know where you are?"

"They knew I was going to wait after school for Emily. If anybody wants me they'll guess I'm here and come downstairs and get me."

"Quiet!" roared Mr. Theotocopoulos.

"The trouble with you," Emily said to her teacher without a fraction's hesitation in her playing, "is that you can't concentrate." She raised her hands from the keyboard. "It's rather splendid backwards, isn't it? Shall I do it forwards now?"

Dave closed his eyes and listened, merged, submerged in counterpoint. Rob tugged at his red overshoes until he got them off, dumped his shoes on the floor beside the boots, curled up on the gold velvet of the sofa and, listening, slept.

So no one noticed when a blond, curly-haired girl, about Emily's age, appeared on the threshold. The big double doors were open wide and she stood, center stage, conspicuous in a quilted bathrobe that was too long for her, and with a large piece of red flannel tied round her throat. "Hi," she croaked.

Nobody paid any attention.

"Well, even if you can't hear me I should think you could smell me. I reek of Vicks." She crossed to the sofa and shook Rob. "Mother just happened to see you coming in with Emily and Dave. If you don't check in with her when you get in from school, you won't be allowed to walk home alone again."

Rob woke up, almost falling off the sofa, and yawned like a puppy. "But I wasn't alone, Suzy," he said, reasonably if sleepily. "I was with Emily and Dave."

Suzy blew her nose noisily, getting a glare from the old music teacher. "That's not the point," she whispered, her attempt at quietness almost louder than her croak. "You're still supposed to check in, you know that. Hasn't it penetrated that the Upper West Side of New York City is not a safe place for little kids to wander about in?"

"The whole world isn't a safe place," Rob said. "Anyhow, be quiet. I'm listening to Emily. How's your cold?" he added as an afterthought.

"*It* flourishes." Suzy pulled a fresh wad of tissues from the dressing-gown pocket. Her small nose looked red and sore from much blowing. She shuffled in her huge, fuzzy slippers over to the fireplace and sat across from Dave in a wing chair with sagging springs. "Anyhow, you weren't listening to Emily. You were sound asleep." Music apparently meant less to Suzy than it did to Rob or the older boy; she wriggled in the chair, bounced on the creaking springs, blew her nose, wriggled, sniffled, bounced,

15

until Mr. Theotocopoulos shouted at her: "Either keep your not-listening to yourself, Miss Austin, or go upstairs to your own apartment."

"I'm *not* not-listening, Mr. Theo," she protested hoarsely. "Anyhow, that's not music, what you're making Emily do now."

"But it will lead to music. Sit still and kindly keep your germs to yourself. Burn your used tissues. Don't leave them around to spread the plague. Emily and I have only another fifteen minutes."

Suzy sighed, heavily, then gave a choked sneeze.

Emily, paying no attention to this contretemps, had continued to work.

"No!" Mr. Theo bellowed. "Seven against four has to be absolutely precise."

"Stinky old Papa Haydn," Emily muttered. "I don't like this sonata anyhow." But she went on working.

At the end of the lesson Mr. Theo sat on the piano bench beside her and gave her a rough hug. "Tired?"

"After a lesson with you?" She leaned against him affectionately. "Good tired, though."

"Josiah." Mr. Theo was the only one Dave allowed to call him by his first name; with the old man he had little choice. "You will sing for us now, yes?"

"I will sing for you now, no." Dave opened his eyes and glared at the old man.

But the three children began begging him, please, Dave, please, until he got up, ungraciously, and went to the piano.

Mr. Theo moved back to the long windows, covered by dusty gold velvet curtains.

Dave bent down and whispered something to Emily. She nodded and began to play, and the two of them started to sing, with mock self-pity, *"Sometimes I feel like a motherless child . . ."*

Suzy stood up, stamping. "Stop! I hate you, Dave! Stop!"

Emily took her hands from the piano, slightly shamefaced, but Dave sang on alone, mellifluous voice throbbing with assumed sentimentality, while Mr. Theo said, "That threatens you, eh, Suzy? It shakes your safe, cozy, little world? All right, let us keep it safe for a few minutes more at least. That is enough, Josiah."

At the quiet authority in the old man's voice, very different from his excitable shouting, Dave shut his mouth.

"I don't think it's very safe," Suzy said in a small voice, and blew her rosy nose.

Mr. Theotocopoulos came over to her and took her hands in his. "You are thoroughly unsterilizing me," he said, "and I am too old and fragile ["Ha!" Emily snorted] to come in such close contact with germs. And you smell revulsive." But he continued to hold her hands, looking down at her. "So. Whatever is upsetting Emily is upsetting you, too. Where did you get this so-blossoming cold?"

He held her gaze and she looked at him reluctantly. "I already had a cold. Then yesterday it poured—remember? and we got soaked. Emily's school coat wasn't even dry enough for her to wear today. And Mother and Daddy kept me home from school."

"But you are not upset because you got wet, I think."

"Mother and Daddy were furious, and at school they don't take kindly to people not wearing their school coats."

17

Emily jumped in quickly, "Which is more than enough to be upset about. I have three days' detention, which means three hours' practicing missed, unless I manage to get out of the library and to the horrible piano in the auditorium. Sing something decent now, Dave. We really can't wallow in being motherless while Mrs. Austin's around. Let's do 'Sleepers, Wake.' Rob likes Bach." She was very definitely changing the subject.

Rob nodded, got up from the small velvet sofa and lay down, flat on his back, on the floor in front of it.

"Child," Mr. Theo asked, "what are you doing?"

Rob explained patiently. "I like to feel the music. Dave showed me about it the first day he took me to hear you play the organ in the Cathedral. He had me lie down in the choir stalls so I could feel the music through the wood."

"Josiah, of all the paradoxical people I have ever known, you take the biscuit." Mr. Theo flung out his hands, palms up, in one of his characteristic gestures. "Sing. And properly."

Dave's voice had finished changing; it was a warm, true baritone, deep and rich, in contrast to the prickly roughness that often came to his speaking voice, or to the overlush velvet he had brought to "Motherless Child." When he sang he stood straight and tall, rather than with his characteristic slouch; his long, lean body was relaxed and easy; his restless eyes were at peace. When he had finished and the last notes of the Chorale Prelude came to a close under Emily's strong fingers, he put his hand gently on her shoulder. "If you've got much homework for me to read to you, Em, we'd better get at it."

"But it's time for dinner," Suzy protested. "It's spaghetti and we have loads, so do stay, Dave. Mother said I could ask you. And you, too, Mr. Theo, and don't forget you're all un-sterile and have to wash."

Mr. Theo held his hands stiffly in front of him, demanding of Emily, "Where is your father?"

"He had a chance to go to Athens for a week. One of his pals there, a Greek archpriest or something, is having a ninetieth birthday party, which is really quite a thing, so Papa took off."

Mr. Theo raised his bushy brows. "Leaving you as usual for the Austin family to cope with?"

"They can cope." Emily grinned. "Even with me."

"Someone, then, must be giving them superhuman strength and patience." He continued to hold out his unsterile hands and sniffed as loudly as Suzy. "It is enough to make one believe in God, or, at the very least, guardian angels. Even if I find these Austins a noisy group who keep you from practicing," but he looked with affection on Suzy and Rob as he said this, "in less than three months they have had a distinctly civilizing influence upon you. They are, to say the least, an improvement over the Oriental gentlemen who were your father's last tenants and who failed singularly to take care of you."

"Mr. Theotocopoulos," Emily said, with ominous calm. "It didn't have anything to do with Dr. Shasti or Dr. Shen-shu. It wasn't their fault."

"Who is accusing them?"

"You are! You're prejudiced because they're—because they're *different!*"

"You mean because Shasti is Indian and Shen-shu Chinese? Idiot."

"I'm not an idio—"

19

"Everybody is different," Mr. Theo roared, cutting her off. "As we should be. This does not mean that I understand the Oriental mind, granted. Nor did they understand my ways of thought. But we were very good friends. I do not fall into the common error of thinking we all need to be alike and comprehensible to each other. In a way your Austins are equally foreign to me, but they, too, are my very good friends. Yes, Suzy, tell your mother that I will stay for dinner. Out of curiosity if nothing else."

"Mother's a very good cook!" Suzy defended.

"I do not question your mother's cooking, having already received on innumberable occasions of her bounty. Your mother, like many good women, works on the theory that whenever there is trouble, put the kettle on. What I question is the fact that you and Emily and, I think, Rob here, are hiding something, something at which you keep giving timid glances over your shoulders."

"Maybe we are," Suzy said. "But if we told you what it was you wouldn't believe it. Dave didn't."

"I am not as much of a skeptic as Josiah."

Emily spoke sharply. "Suzy is imagining things. And she talks too much, like the rest of her family."

"That is better than keeping things in the dark."

Emily snapped, "I didn't choose the dark."

Mr. Theo snapped back, "Stop that kind of talk and take me to some hot water and soap. Suzy, go dispose of your soiled tissues." He followed Emily out.

Suzy put her used tissues in a corner of the fireplace and looked around for a match. "I suppose Dr. Gregory took them all to Athens with him. Got a match, Dave?"

Dave produced a matchbook and she lit the tissues. "That Mr. Theo can make me so mad." She scowled at the flames.

"Forget it. His bark is worse than his bite."

"Don't you mean his Bach?" Rob asked.

Dave ignored this. "And he'd die for Emily. Well, maybe not for Emily as Emily, but for Emily as a musician."

"Is there a difference?" Rob cocked his head on one side questioningly. "I mean, aren't people what they are?"

"What're you talking about?" Suzy asked impatiently. "Don't be such a baby, Rob. Emily's Emily and the piano is something else."

But Rob shook his head, putting his shoes back on and struggling with the laces. "What about Daddy? He's Daddy and he's a doctor, and that's Daddy. If he were a scholar, like Dr. Gregory, or a musician, like Mr. Theo, he'd be a different person. He wouldn't be himself, he'd be somebody else."

"For heaven's sake talk sense, Rob," Suzy said.

"Hey." Dave gave an unexpectedly warm and gentle smile. "You're too young to tie your shoelaces properly and you're already talking like Dr. Gregory. Give me your foot."

"Well, I like Emily's father." Rob stuck his foot in its untied shoe out to Dave. "He wanted to take me to Athens with him and I wanted to go."

"Why didn't he, then?" Dave tied the laces in a double knot. "He usually does whatever he wants. Let me have your other foot."

Suzy said, "Daddy said no, for one thing."

"What he said," Rob corrected her, "was, not this time."

"Listen." Dave continued holding the little boy's foot,

though he had finished tying the shoelaces. "You really going to tell your parents? Everything?"

Rob looked directly at him with wide, blue eyes. "Emily told you."

"That's different."

"Why?" Suzy asked. "You don't understand it any more than we do. Maybe Mother and Daddy will."

"They aren't omnipotent."

"What's that mean?" Rob asked. "Oh, hi, Mr. Theo, are you antiseptic again?"

Mr. Theotocopoulos stood in the doorway, one arm about Emily's waist. "I doubt it. Don't surgeons have to wash their hands for twenty minutes? Emily allowed me a bare five. I must ask your father before eating dinner. Suzy, if you will get me that enormous and idiotic dog of yours I will walk it over to Broadway and procure a bottle of wine as my contribution to the meal."

As she left the room Suzy whispered to Emily, "I've got to tell Mother and Daddy. Don't you and Dave try to stop me."

Two

Rob walked to Broadway with Mr. Theotocopoulos, both of them looking very small beside the beautiful Great Dane who pranced along beside them, slowing his enormous stride to the smaller steps of the little boy and the old man.

"We have another dog besides Rochester," Rob confided. "Her name's Colette, but she's getting old so she stayed in the country with the people who're in our house there."

"I suppose," Mr. Theo said, "that it would be taking advantage of your youth to ask you what has upset everybody so?"

"Suzy'll talk at dinner," Rob said positively, "because she doesn't believe it happened. She's a scientist."

"Do you, then, believe that it—whatever it is—happened? Does Emily?"

From up the street came the loud voice of a woman singing "The Old Rugged Cross," exhorting the city to reform, hiccuping, almost falling, and bursting into a string of oaths. She wore a man's coat and shoes, and her eyes were bloodshot; she staggered as she walked. But as she saw Rob she pulled herself up, saluted in military fashion, and gave him a great, jagged-toothed smile. Rob returned both the salute and the smile, paused as Rochester lifted a leg to a hydrant, and answered Mr. Theo.

"About Emily, Mr. Theo: you see, she didn't *see* what was happening, and all she *touched* was the lamp." He caught himself from speaking further, and carefully changed the subject. "In the country we had lots of cats, but they stayed there, too. I don't like having everything be changed, and having John go off to M.I.T. I don't like being the only boy in the family. With John around, he and I were 'the boys,' but now I'm only 'the youngest.' Well, John'll be home from college for Thanksgiving and that's not too far off now. I wonder what Thanksgiving in New York will be like?"

"You will all be together," Mr. Theotocopoulos said, "and that's what matters, isn't it?"

"And you'll come, too, won't you, Mr. Theo?"

"Thank you." The old man accepted the invitation promptly. "I would like that. Who else will be there?"

"Oh, Emily and Dr. Gregory, of course. I don't know who else. We usually have lots of people."

"Will Dr. Hyde be there?"

"Daddy's boss? I don't know. We don't see much of him. He never comes for dinner. Daddy says he isn't used to children, and anyhow he's awfully busy."

"He wasn't too busy to arrange for all of Emily's training when she lost her sight." Mr. Theo gave Rob a curious look and asked, "What do you think of him, child?"

Rob considered this, pausing while Mr. Rochester sniffed at a corner phone booth. "I don't know what to think." He pulled

Mr. Rochester away from what was evidently a delectable canine odor. For a moment the big dog resisted, letting Rob tug helplessly at his chain. "Mr. Rochester!" Rob ordered, and the dog sighed and followed the little boy. "Everybody in the country thought we were silly to bring Rochester to New York, because he's so big, but we *had* to bring him. You do see that, don't you?"

"Yes, of course," Mr. Theo assured him. "He's a protection for you, anyhow."

"I wish he could walk to and from school with us," Rob said, "the way he used to walk us to the school bus. One of the cats usually came along, too. Oh, hi, Rabbi Levy." He stopped, pulling Rochester up short, to greet an elderly, grey-bearded man standing in front of a synagogue. The liquor store towards which Mr. Theo was heading to buy the wine was on Rob's route to school, and he had made many friends going back and forth each day, of which the closest was the Rabbi. The synagogue had fascinated Rob. It was the first one he had ever seen, and it was completely different from the other buildings on Broadway, being of pink stone, with ornamental arched doorways, brass scrollwork, and an Oriental dome. It was, to the little boy, a mysteriously beautiful building, completely unlike the great Gothic Cathedral which also drew him, yet sharing the same feeling of soaring heavenwards, of being built on light. Each day on the way home from school he had stopped to stare at the Hebrew lettering above the entrance:

עדת שומעי אל

And the Rabbi, seeing his interest, had translated for him: Adath Shomai-el, Congregation of the Ones Obeying God.

"Hello, Rob," the Rabbi said, now. "Good evening, Mr. Theotocopoulos. Is all well with you?"

Mr. Theo simply smiled and nodded, but Rob studied the question seriously. "Not entirely," he concluded finally. "May I come talk to you some day after school? I'll bring Rochester."

"By all means," the Rabbi said. "I enjoy our discussions, Rob."

Mr. Rochester pulled at his chain, so they said goodbye and moved on. "You talk too much," Mr. Theo told Rob. "You must not air all your affairs to everybody you meet."

"I don't!" Rob was indignant. "Rabbi Levy is my special friend."

"How many special friends have you? Every drunk and fanatic on the street?"

"They're not! They're my friends! But they're not all the kind of special friends you tell things to and have discussions with, the way I do with the Rabbi. He reminds me of my grandfather. My grandfather is a minister. Well, you met him when he was visiting us, didn't you, Mr. Theo?"

The old man sighed. "Yes, Rob. He is a fine man, and so is the Rabbi. I do see that they have much in common. But you must be a little more discreet, nevertheless."

"What does discreet mean?" Rob asked as they came to the liquor store. "Oh, here we are. Rochester and I will wait outside while you go in for the wine."

Emily and Dr. Gregory occupied the first two floors of the mansion; the Austins rented the third and fourth. When Rob and Mr. Theo came up the marble stairs into the living room the record player was on, full blast, a Frescobaldi sonata which Emily and Dave were accompanying on two battered recorders. Mr. Theo, bulbous forehead pink from the cold, turned down the volume as Mrs. Austin shouted from the kitchen, "Come help set the table, Dave. I don't want Suzy's germy fingers touching anything."

Mr. Theo snapped off Rochester's leash and handed it to Rob to put on the bookcase. Suzy offered the old man the most comfortable chair. "Getting out of household chores is the only advantage of being repulsive."

In the dining room a tall girl with short brown hair was setting out place mats; she nodded to Dave as he came in.

"Thanks, Dave. You know where the silver is. If everybody wants milk you'd better use the jelly glasses in the pantry."

"Well, Mr. Theo brought wine, Vicky."

Vicky paused by the enormous mahogany table which Dr. Gregory had loaned the Austins; light from the crystal chandelier brightened her hair. She called into the living room, "It's just for you and Mother and Daddy, I suppose?"

"It is not a feast day as far as I know, Victoria," Mr. Theo said, "and it is a very small bottle." He rose and came to stand in the open archway between living room and dining room. "And you, Miss Vicky? Do I sense that this is one of your days to be a defiant adolescent?"

"Hi, Mr. Theo," Mrs. Austin called from the kitchen. "If Vicky is being rather fifteen tonight, I often think that a small amount of defiance is necessary to survive the fifteens."

"Thanks, Mother," Vicky called back. "Maybe I'll be more bearable when I'm as old as Dave."

"Just wait until you are," Dave told her. "I'll pour the milk."

Mr. Theo leaned against the archway. "I have known Josiah since he was not much older than your little brother and sang in a pure sweet treble with the other little animals in the Cathedral School. It did not take adolescence to make Josiah rebellious. Josiah, you have let your father know you will not be home till late, yes?"

"I have let my father know, no." Dave came in from the kitchen with milk.

Mr. Theo gave an annoyed grunt. "Nothing should excuse *you* from courtesy. Once you had left the Alphabat gang I hoped that you would have learned that."

Dave spilled some milk on the table in his rage and stalked out to the kitchen for a cloth to wipe it up. "Mr. Theo," he said in a low, angry voice as he came back, "I'm not one of your choirboys any more. I haven't been a choirboy since eighth grade. I do not run with any gang, Alphabats or any other kind of bats. My father is probably the worst bum they've ever had on the Cathedral maintenance staff. I wish some kind of sentimentality wouldn't keep them from firing him."

"When your father wishes to be," the old man said, "he is the best craftsman they've ever had in the shop. And I doubt if they've ever kept any employee out of sentimentality."

"Dinner's ready," Mrs. Austin called. "Come help me serve, Vicky. Suzy, go tell Daddy we're ready. Rob, have you and Emily washed your hands? If not, please do." She came into the dining room, untying the apron that covered her dark kilt and yellow sweater. With one hand she pushed a loose lock of hair back from her forehead; she wore her hair pulled back

28

from her face and knotted neatly at the nape of her neck, but it gave an impression not of severity but of comfort.

Dinner proceeded in its usual noisy, haphazard, and pleasant fashion. They started with an Elizabethan grace which they sang in canon, as a round, first Mr. Theo and Dave, then the girls, and lastly Rob, who was supposed to be joined by his parents but who ended singing alone because Emily inadvertently knocked over Dr. Austin's wineglass. Doing anything clumsy made her furiously angry, and Dr. Austin had to calm her down rather sharply while Mrs. Austin cleaned up.

Mr. Theo, ignoring the fracas, listened to Rob's light, sweet treble. "You ought to be in the choir next year." He sounded cross, which was always his reaction to being moved.

"I wouldn't mind if you were still organist," Rob said. "But as long as you're retired I think I'd rather stay with Vicky and Suzy and Emily."

"I am around a good deal," Mr. Theo assured him, "and I still play for a number of services. I would see to it that no one ate you."

"If Dave were back in the choir, now that his voice has finished moving down . . ." Rob said.

"I will sing grace for Mr. Theo," Dave growled, "and that's all."

"That's disgraceful," Rob said, very pleased with himself.

"He's only seven." Vicky's voice was tolerant. "We must excuse him."

"Listen, everybody," Suzy cut in. "I have something to tell you. I'm sorry, Emily, but I have to. You told Dave, and you've got to let me tell my family."

"If you like, I will leave," Mr. Theo said stiffly.

Emily flashed, "You know perfectly well wild horses couldn't drag you away."

But Mr. Theo did not fight back as he did during the piano lessons. "I am concerned about you, child. You are not yourself. Something is wrong."

Dr. Austin, at the head of the table, looked around at the children, his wife, the old man, said nothing, waited. He looked tired. His brown hair was going very grey. Fatigue made dark lines around his gentle hazel eyes.

"Daddy," Suzy said, "it's going to sound funny. I mean funny peculiar, not funny ha-ha."

"Go on, Suzy."

She took a deep breath. "Yesterday after school Rob and Emily and I were walking home together. Vicky stayed for play rehearsal, remember? It was pouring and we thought maybe if we stopped and had cocoa or something the rain would let up."

Mrs. Austin interpolated, "They called from the drugstore. It seemed a perfectly reasonable request, particularly with Suzy's cold."

"You know that junk shop next to the drugstore?" Suzy asked. "Phooka's Antiques, it's called, but they're not my idea of antiques. I mean it's really junk. Old clothes and votive candles and bleeding hearts. There's a table outside, usually mostly books and dented pots and pans and egg beaters and stuff like that. And every once in a while something good. Vicky's found books there, and you found a piece of your favorite Minton china, remember, Mother?"

"I remember," Mrs. Austin said. "We all know the place, Suzy. It gives me the horrors for some reason. Go on."

30

"Dave—" Emily started, licking her lips nervously. Her strong, square hands held the table edge.

"What is it, Emily?" Dr. Austin asked. "Would you rather tell it than listen?"

"You go on, Em," Suzy said. "I'm losing my voice. I think I'm getting laryngitis on top of everything else."

"At night," Emily said vaguely, "we've been reading—Mrs. Austin has, you know, the way she usually does, and the last time it was Rob's turn to choose, the book he chose was *Arabian Nights,* and I like *Arabian Nights* even if Suzy thinks she's too big—"

"The trouble is she's not grown up *enough*," Vicky said.

"Anyhow, one night the story was about Aladdin and the lamp, remember?"

Her voice trailed off and Rob picked up. "And yesterday I saw a lamp like the one in Aladdin. It was out on the table in front of the junk shop, all tarnished, and looking just like the lamp in the picture, sort of like a gravy boat. So I picked it up."

"This was when we'd finished our cocoa," Emily added. "It'd stopped raining."

Suzy, despite her creaky voice, could not keep out of the story. "So I said, and of course I was kidding, I wonder what would happen if we rubbed it? And Rob took me seriously."

"Somebody has to," Rob said.

"Stop being a sibling."

"I am a sibling."

"Don't start arguing, for heaven's sake," Vicky said.

Rob stuck his tongue out at Suzy, quickly, so his parents wouldn't see. "I rubbed it and nothing happened."

Dave asked, "What did you expect to have happen?"

"I don't know, Dave. Everything's so peculiar in New York, you get the feeling almost anything *can* happen. So I gave the lamp to Emily, and she took off her gloves to feel it, and I said rub it, so she did."

For a moment there was utter silence around the table. Mr. Rochester, the Great Dane, who was not allowed in the dining room during meals, lay on the threshold breathing heavily. Mr. Theo cut into the silence, asking calmly, "I suppose you called up a genie?"

Dave made an angry noise, but Rob answered, "Yes. She did."

They had been standing around the lamp, looking at Emily holding it in her strong fingers, rubbing it. Certainly none of them, not even Rob, expected to hear a sepulchral voice behind them.

"You called me?"

They swung round.

Standing, looking down on them, was a tall, powerful figure in long smoky green robes and a pale blue turban. He repeated, "You called me? I am the genie Hythloday, the servant of the lamp."

"You can't be!" Suzy cried. "There isn't any such thing."

"Then why did you raise me up?"

"We didn't. At least we didn't expect to. At least I didn't."

The voice of the genie, if that is what he was, was as smoky as his robes. "But you have called me up, my dear, and perhaps now that you have done so, there is something I can do for you? Is there anything you could wish to command of your servant?"

Rob asked, "Are you our servant?"

"I am the slave of the lamp, my dear, and since you have raised me up, I am at your service. What would you?"

Rob put his red-mittened hands on his hips and stared at the figure. "What about wishes? Do we get three wishes?"

"Rob!" Suzy scolded. "This isn't a fairy tale. Come on. Let's go home. Mother'll be——"

"But don't genies grant wishes?" Rob asked.

"In moderation, my dear. Your servant will grant wishes within reason."

For the first time Emily, who had been scowling and listening, spoke. "Why within reason? Genies aren't reasonable."

"What will you, my dear? Ask me and we shall see what the slave of the lamp can do for you."

"Make me see again."

Suzy knocked the lamp out of Emily's hand.

Emily gave an angry, anguished wail.

Suzy burst into tears. "Emily, you can't ask that! It's wrong!"

"Why? What's wrong about it?"

"I don't believe in genies and I don't believe in magic. It's wrong, I know it's wrong!"

"Why?" Emily asked again. "How could it be wrong?"

From behind them came a clear voice, crisp and completely unlike the genie's hollow-toned speech. "I think, child, that you are beyond that kind of wishing."

Again the children turned. The genie was gone, and in his place stood a man under a huge black umbrella.

"Sorry to interfere," he said, "but I couldn't help hearing

while I was putting up my umbrella. I rather think, you know, that I'd be suspicious of a twentieth-century genie." He nodded at them and left.

Nobody laughed at the children's story. Dr. Austin asked in a tone of detached scientific interest, "Can you describe the genie a little better?"

"He was just—huge," Suzy said. "I mean really. Remember I'm not given to flights of imagination like Vicky."

Normally Vicky would have risen angrily to this, but as she looked across the table she saw that Emily was struggling to hold back tears, and it was the first time in the three months that the Austins had known Emily that anyone had see her cry—except tears of rage.

So Suzy, uninterrupted, continued, "Honestly, Daddy. I'll bet he was even taller than Dr. Hyde."

"But where did he come from?" Dave asked.

"Well, that's just it," Rob answered. "We don't know. He just sort of appeared."

Suzy the scientist was scornful. "Next thing you'll be saying you saw smoke coming out of the lamp and he materialized. The thing is that we weren't really looking. I agree with the man under the umbrella. I'm extremely suspicious of a twentieth-century genie."

"This man with the umbrella—tell me: what did he look like?" Mr. Theo asked.

"Bald," Suzy said. "I mean really bald."

"And his voice. Emily, describe to me his voice."

"English," Emily said. "But not the kind that spits out all its

34

teeth with its consonants. Clear and clean. Not old and not young. It was a Bach kind of voice, Mr. Theo, if you know what I mean."

"Yes, child. And bald? Completely bald?"

"Bald as Humpty Dumpty," Rob said, "but not as fat. And he didn't have any eyebrows."

Mr. Theo gave a small puff. "That is strange. That is extraordinarily strange. What's Tallis doing in New York?"

"What's that?" Dr. Austin asked.

But Suzy was saying, "It doesn't make sense. I still don't believe in genies."

Dr. Austin asked, "Are you sure it wasn't just another neighborhood character? There are plenty around."

"Yeah, and Rob picks them all up. No, Daddy, this was different."

Mrs. Austin suggested, "Halloween was just last week. Maybe it was someone's idea of a joke."

"Joke indeed." Mr. Theo indicated his empty plate. "Mrs. Austin, this spaghetti bears no relationship to the pink pasta one is usually given. I would like some more to go with my wine. When I am with you Austins I am a convulsive eater."

She took the old man's plate. "Anybody else? Dave?"

"Yes. Please."

"Emily?"

"But I'm afraid I'm making a mess."

"It doesn't matter. The blouse goes into the wash tonight." She had not noticed that Emily's voice was shaking.

"It's just that I'm all over spaghetti. . . . If you'll excuse me, I'll go wash up." She pushed out of her chair.

Rob started after her, but Dr. Austin stopped him. "Leave her alone, Rob."

"But she's—"

"I know, Rob. That's why she needs to be alone for a few minutes. Anybody's love right now, even yours, would just upset her more. All right, Suzy, let's get it clear. Emily asked the genie to give her back her eyesight and this made you angry. Why?"

"Daddy," Suzy sounded desperate because her father would ask her to explain such a thing. "We've talked and talked about it, I mean when we first came to New York, and Rob kept praying for a miracle, that Emily would wake up in the morning and be able to see, and I didn't want that kind of a miracle, I wanted something real. I wanted doctors to be able to operate and do something."

"That's right." Mrs. Austin returned with the spaghetti. "And you told Suzy that would be even more impossible than Rob's miracle."

"Suzy wants science to be able to do everything," Vicky said.

Dr. Austin looked stern. "There isn't any operation that can help Emily."

"But with the laser, with the Micro-Ray," Suzy started.

"Even the Micro-Ray can't replace an optic nerve."

"Don't you see, then, Daddy?" Suzy's voice strengthened, though her hoarseness was hindering her. "Don't you remember the way I kept asking why it had to happen to Emily? And if God is good, how can he let things like that happen? And you said Emily wasn't asking that question, and if I kept on asking it, even if not out loud, I'd be making things harder for her when she's doing so well. . . . So when she asked the genie yesterday I just sort of burst."

"You were right," Mr. Theo murmured.

"But why didn't you tell us last night, Suzy?" her mother asked.

"You and Daddy had company for dinner and Emily made me promise not to, and I wanted to think about it some more before we said anything anyhow."

Mr. Theo growled, "And have you?"

"I've done nothing else all day, except blow my nose."

"And?"

"Mr. Theo, I don't know! Maybe one reason I got so mad at Emily was I was so scared, and if you get mad enough at something it helps you not to be so scared." She sighed, heavily.

Emily came back to the table. Her face showed traces of tears, but she was quite composed.

"Let's have dessert now," Rob suggested.

His father nodded. "Start clearing the table. Okay, kids. It's quite a tale. But I don't think you three are the kind to go in for mass hallucinations. Or to make up tall stories for our dinner-table amusement. I agree with your mother in wishing you'd mentioned it to us last night, though I really don't see what we could have done."

Mrs. Austin, holding the salad bowl, paused in the doorway to the kitchen and looked across the table to her husband. "*Is* there something we can do, Wallace?"

"I'll make it my business to pass Phooka's Antiques some time tomorrow," he said, "though I don't really expect to find anything. When we told you New York was a colorful city, kids, I don't think we expected it to be quite this colorful. Genies, forsooth. Dave, if you wouldn't mind walking everybody home from school tomorrow, I'd appreciate it."

"*I* can walk everybody home tomorrow," Vicky said.

"You *and* Dave. I don't think there's really anything to worry about. It's probably, as your mother suggested, some kind of post-Halloween prank, maybe somebody from Columbia with a peculiar sense of humor."

A note of hope came into Emily's voice. "I wouldn't put it past some of Papa's students."

Mr. Theo did not look convinced. He mumbled to himself something that sounded like, "Not if Tallis is here," then looked anxiously at Emily. "In these parlous times it is as well to take precautions."

Vicky looked at the old man affectionately. "But isn't it fun to live in parlous times? I wish I'd been there yesterday."

"I wish you had, too," Emily said.

Three

After dinner, when Mr. Theotocopoulos had gone home, Vicky took his place in the creaky rocking chair in her father's study. "Daddy."

She rocked for a moment, looking at him. He seemed to her older, his hair greyer, thinner, than when they had come to New York. The laugh creases in his face were still there, but they had been joined by deeper lines of worry: about what? She spoke tentatively.

He looked up from a page of formulas he was rechecking. "What's up, Vicky? Where's Mother?"

"Putting Rob to bed. And steaming Suzy and rubbing her chest."

"Emily?"

"Dave's still reading her schoolwork to her. She thought she'd lost her Braille stylus and they had a fight because Dave wouldn't find it for her."

"Where was it?"

"On the floor, under the dining-room table."

"What happened?"

"She found it. But she was furious because he made her get down on her hands and knees and feel all over the floor for it when she knew perfectly well he could see it and just pick it up for her and save all that time and trouble. But he was right, wasn't he?"

"Yes, and Emily knows it. That's one reason she's so fond of him."

"Usually she won't *let* anybody find anything for her or help her. It's only after her piano lessons with Mr. Theo, when she's tired, that she asks any of us for anything."

Dr. Austin pushed his papers aside and leaned back in his desk chair. He had been forcing himself to ask questions, to assume an interest that a few months earlier would have been spontaneous. His fingers were cramped from writing and he flexed them, much as Emily did over the piano. Both his desk and his chair were discards from Dr. Gregory's office at Columbia and were functional, ancient, and comfortable. The rest of the furnishings had been left by Dr. Shasti and Dr. Shenshu. Rob's favorite object in the study was a small Hsi-Fo, a white laughing "Buddha" that reposed on the desk, benevolent, forbearing. Dr. Austin let his eyes rest on the wise and amused ivory face and relaxed, letting accumulated tensions and unanswered questions lie less heavily on his shoulders.

The rocker across from him in which Vicky sat was an ancient one of wicker which Dr. Shen-shu had painted saffron yellow. Mrs. Austin had added cushions, and it was extremely comfortable if rather creaky. Dr. Austin's red leather chair answered in a lower voice, and father and daughter rocked thoughtfully together in counterpoint.

"Daddy . . ." Vicky asked tentatively, "is it all right if I ask you about something?"

"Of course, Vicky. What?" He put the pencil he had been twirling down on the desk.

—It isn't "of course," Vicky thought, looking across the desk at him. Their father was in the house far more than when he had been a busy country doctor, but the children saw less of him. He shut himself up in the study and made it clear that he didn't want to be disturbed. "It's something I've been wanting to ask you for a long time," she said finally.

"Okay. Fire ahead."

"Why did Dr. Shasti and Dr. Shen-shu go to Liverpool right after their papers were stolen and Emily was blinded?"

Her father picked up the Buddha and frowned at it. The Buddha smiled back. "It didn't have anything to do with it, Vicky. They were here on a foundation grant, their time was up, and they'd already accepted the position in the lab in Liverpool."

Vicky considered this. "Then maybe whoever was after the papers wanted to get them before Dr. Shasti and Dr. Shen-shu left?"

"Very likely."

"You liked them, didn't you?"

"Very much. I wouldn't have taken their place in Hyde's lab if I hadn't."

"You're really doing the work of both of them, then, aren't you?"

"Not really. As we've come to know more about the laser and to control its power, the formulae have become simpler. As a matter of fact, Dr. Hyde tried to manage alone for almost two years, but the work got too heavy for him, so he offered me the job."

Vicky looked carefully at her father. "I don't think Mr. Theo liked Dr. Shasti and Dr. Shen-shu, and that sort of makes me wonder."

Dr. Austin put the Buddha down and picked up in its stead a small, ugly clay paperweight and turned it over in his hands. It was infinitely precious to him, having been made by Rob from clay dug out of the fresh-water pond near their house in the country. "It isn't that Mr. Theo didn't like them, Vicky, but he isn't very objective where Emily is concerned, and he holds them responsible for her accident."

"Were they?" Vicky demanded.

"Only in the sense that we're all responsible for one another, I think. I imagine you'll find that Mr. Theo's equally prickly about Dr. Hyde in spite of all he's done for Emily."

"Why did he? Dr. Hyde, I mean."

"Because whoever attacked Emily was trying to steal papers that belonged to his laboratory, and he felt a sense of personal responsibility. Emily's father isn't very practical once he leaves Attic Greece, you know, so it's a good thing somebody took care of Emily's training, or she'd be a much sadder child than she is today."

"But, Daddy, why were the papers here instead of at the lab?"

Dr. Austin's usually friendly, open face closed. He put the

paperweight down on the desk with a bang. "I imagine Dr. Shasti and Dr. Shen-shu had their reasons."

Vicky looked at him in shock. He never spoke curtly to his children without cause. But she had started this and she was determined to finish. "Please, Daddy, one more thing: whoever hit Emily wasn't just an ordinary thief, was he, looking for money for dope or something?"

"Why do you ask that?" His voice was sharp.

"Suzy says it must have been someone who knew a lot about physics, and about microwaves and coherent radiation. Is she right?"

"Suzy thinks she knows far too much." But he made no denial.

"But what about Emily?" Vicky pursued. "Why would he have wanted to hurt Emily?"

"Nobody knows, Vicky." Dr. Austin spoke in his normal, quiet way when answering his children's questions. Usually he encouraged them to ask, to stretch their minds. "Presumably because she walked in on him stealing the papers."

"So he hit her on the head and pushed her downstairs."

"That's what it seems like. All Emily remembers is coming up to the study as usual—"

"Right here," Vicky said, "this very room," and gave a deep shudder.

"Yes. Somebody came at her so quickly that all she got was an impression of someone masked and huge rushing at her, and then there was a blinding light and darkness and that's all she remembers."

"Why would a fractured skull have hurt her eyes?"

"This is really the problem, Vicky. Nobody knows. It may possibly have been the angle at which she was hit, the placement of the blow. But what it really seems like, medically speaking, is an optic nerve damaged by powerful radiation, such as might come from an uncontrolled laser beam or Micro-Ray."

"I don't understand."

"You know how, whenever there's an eclipse of the sun, I warn you never to look at the eclipse directly, or even through dark glasses, because of the intensity of the radiation. Or do you remember those kids I told you about who were brought into the hospital after they'd been looking at the noonday sun under the influence of LSD? One said he was having a religious conversation with the sun. He was totally blinded; he'd burned out his optic nerve. Two had their reading vision destroyed by their psychedelic fantasies because they'd burned the macula, which is a small part of the cornea. The others got off without serious trouble; they were just lucky idiots. Anyhow, the damage to Emily's optic nerve was very much as though it had been burned by overexposure to radiation." He broke off as there was a rap on the door.

Emily stuck her head in, scowling with her listening look. "Are you in the middle of something?"

"We'd finished," Vicky said. At last her father had talked to her in the old way, as though she were a reasonable human being capable of learning something. She sighed, deeply, relieved.

Dr. Austin went to Emily and took her hands. "Homework done?"

"Not really. I couldn't concentrate tonight. Dave said I've done enough to get by. But he was cross at me for not being able to—what did he call it?—retain properly. I don't know what's the matter. I'm tired or something. Have you done your homework, Vic? Could we go to bed, please?"

Vicky had not finished her homework, but after a look first at Emily, then at her father, she said, "Okay, as long as you don't mind if I set the alarm and finish up before breakfast."

Postponing work was something she hated to do. Just as she had always found it impossible to go to bed angry (unlike Suzy, who could go to sleep happily nursing a grudge), so she hated to go to bed with studying still to be done. Her time for daydreaming was the few minutes before she went to sleep, and unfinished algebra equations or untranslated Latin phrases were apt to poke at her mind and interrupt her reveries.

Suzy, smelling strongly of Vicks, had come to stand in the doorway. She demanded, cross and hoarse and stuffy-nosed, "What about reading tonight? We're right in the middle of the biography of Mendel and it's my turn. We never skip when it's anybody else's turn."

"We do, too," Vicky said. "We missed my turn three times in a row. Anyhow, Rob's gone to bed."

"Rob wouldn't mind. He doesn't care about genes and chromosomes and how we inherit things." As Emily opened her mouth to speak, Suzy cut her off. "Don't say 'neither do we.' I listen to the things *you* choose."

Vicky looked from Emily to Suzy, caught Suzy's eye and nodded in Emily's direction. "We're all tired tonight, Suze. Let's skip reading. Daddy, will you and Mother come downstairs and say good night to Emily and me?"

"You think you're so big," Suzy muttered.

Emily spoke through Suzy's words. "Yes, please, Dr. Austin. And thanks, Suze."

"For what?" Suzy asked ungraciously, and blew her nose.

Dr. Austin regarded her sternly. "Put your cold to bed, Suzy. You two girls go downstairs. Mother or I will check on you later."

As they descended the marble stairs Emily said, "I know you don't like leaving homework, Vic, and I'm sorry about Suzy, I know she's mad at us, but I thought maybe we could talk . . ."

Vicky nodded, forgetting Emily couldn't see, then said, "Yes. Okay. You're still upset about what happened yesterday, aren't you?"

"Wouldn't you be?"

"Probably. Mother and Daddy say I let myself get upset about things. Suzy's not. Very upset, I mean. It's not bothering her any way nearly as much as it's bothering you."

"Suzy always thinks everything can be explained."

"Don't you?"

Dr. Gregory had read Shakespeare, Sophocles, and Aeschylus aloud to his small daughter, who now quoted. "There are more things in heaven and earth, Horatio, than are dreamt of in your philosophy—or Suzy's science. Anyhow, Vic, I can't talk with the others around. It sounds so nutty."

But they undressed and got ready for bed in silence.

When Dr. Gregory had left for Athens, Mrs. Austin planned to have Emily come upstairs to sleep, but Emily had begged to have Vicky come down and sleep with her; she wasn't as familiar with Suzy's and Vicky's room and bath, she would bump into things, and she and Vicky never, never had a chance to talk, and please, please, couldn't they, after all Vicky was fifteen . . .

"Just," Mrs. Austin had said.

"Yes, but she's very responsible, you know she is, and we'll be all right, and do anything you say and we promise not to talk all night—"

"You'll hurt Suzy's feelings," Mrs. Austin had said. "After all, the two of you are the same age."

"I know, and I love Suzy, but we're always together at school, and anyhow I'm ever so much older than she is, centuries older, you know I am, Mrs. Austin, and it's Vicky who's really my friend, oh please!"

"All right," Mrs. Austin had agreed. "I know you're more mature than Suzy is, Emily, but Suzy doesn't. In any case, you and Vicky are to include her as much as possible and not go off to your room and make her feel left out." —And, Mrs. Austin thought to herself, —our apartment cannot be just our apartment to Emily. It is also Dr. Shasti's and Dr. Shen-shu's; it is their rooms she must still *see*.

Emily's bedroom was on the Drive and faced the river. Under her windows was a long seat covered with a deep blue cushion. There Vicky established herself to wait while Emily finished in the tub. Despite a storm window, there was always a leak of cold air in the winter when the wind blew from the river; Vicky pulled her bathrobe close around her. It was a new one; she had grown two full inches during the summer, so Suzy had inherited her old one, and Mrs. Austin had put most of Vicky's other clothes away for a year to see if Suzy was ever going to grow into them. In a tall family, Suzy was going to be much the smallest and, with her golden curls and gentian-blue eyes, by far the most conventionally beautiful; her looks were what made many people underestimate her acute scientific intelligence.

In the bath Emily was singing. Vicky had learned that Emily did two kinds of singing: when she was happy she invented her own melodies; when she was angry or upset she picked more formal themes from the composers she was studying. Bach always indicated deep and serious thinking, coming to terms with some kind of problem. Chopin or Schumann were indications of self-pity, but were seldom heard. A purely intellectual problem, like trouble with her studies at school or memorizing from the unwieldy Braille manuscripts, was apt to be approached with Beethoven or, by contrast, Scarlatti.

Tonight the music that came from the tub was Bach, not a theme from one of the fugues, but one of the more introspective chorale preludes.

—What would I be singing, Vicky wondered, —if I sang out my moods?

If Emily had been one of her friends in the country, Vicky would have blurted out, 'I'm scared. Something's wrong with my father. Always, always he's wanted to work in a big hospital where he could concentrate on his research, and now that he's got exactly what he's always wanted something's wrong. It isn't just tonight, but the way he snaps at Mother for no reason. And I went into his study once and he was just sitting there with his head in his hands.'

But she couldn't wail in front of Emily. If she thought for even a moment about all the problems Emily had to face, then

48

a complaint even about something as fundamental as a change in her father, who had always seemed perfect, wasn't possible.

Emily came out of the bathroom, wrapped in a large, white towel, her long fine hair dark against it. "Vicky——"

"Yes. I'm here."

Emily moved towards the voice and sat by the older girl on the window seat. Vicky turned from the river, from watching the lights across in New Jersey, a barge crawling up the river, cars streaming north and south on the West Side Highway, the lights of the park baring the dark branches of the trees, and looked at Emily. ——I wonder, she thought, ——if Emily used to sit here this way, looking out and dreaming . . .

"Vicky," Emily said, "I love your mother, you know."

"I know."

"I don't even remember my own mother, not really. I was only four when she died. Sometimes I think I remember things, but I'm never sure whether or not it's something Papa's told me. All I've really known have been housekeepers, and some of the teachers at school. Oh, Vicky——" Emily spread out her arms and Vicky dodged to avoid being hit on the nose, "when Mrs. McTavish went back to Scotland to live, and you all came to stay in Dr. Shasti and Dr. Shen-shu's apartment, I thought I'd absolutely hate it when Papa arranged with your mother to have me eat with you and everything. I thought I was going to lose my freedom. I even talked to Dave about running away with him. But it's been——splendiferous."

"It's been pretty splendiferous for us, too," Vicky said. "Not just financially, but getting to know you and Dave, and being friends."

Emily gave a small sigh. "Mr. Theo thinks my guardian angel arranged it. He says it's about time it started paying some attention to me. Vic, I know Suzy was right to knock the genie's beastly old lamp out of my hands yesterday, but it's you I want to talk to about it."

Vicky said nothing, simply sat there on the window seat, waiting. The small boat moved on up the river under the delicate pale green lights of the George Washington Bridge, and slid out of sight. The wind moved the trees on the Drive back and forth across the street lamps so that light and shadow mingled and intermingled. She wanted to touch Emily for comfort, as she would have Rob, but she kept her hands in the lap of her bathrobe and looked steadily out over the river. The arch of the great bridge seemed to sway lightly in the wind. She shivered.

As though she had seen, Emily said, "It's cold tonight." She put her arm out and spread the palm of her hand against the window glass. "Well . . . when I could see, and I was practicing the piano, and I'd forget something—and the funny thing is that the pieces you forget are the ones you've had memorized the longest—well, what would happen would be that if I tried to think what the notes were, I couldn't, or if I tried to think with my mind which was the fingering Mr. Theo and I had worked out, I couldn't. My mind just wouldn't remember. You've had piano lessons. Do you know what I mean?"

"Yes," Vicky said. "And just the way you say, always with the pieces I'd known by heart best. I'd get my fingers mixed up and get stuck."

"So what did you do then? Look it up in the music?"

"Not always," Vicky said slowly.

"Well, what did you do?"

Vicky spoke reluctantly. "I closed my eyes and thought about something else. If I sort of went into a daydream, or made plans about something or thought about homework—then, usually I'd remember the notes."

Emily's strong fingers closed about the cushion on the window seat. "But it wasn't your mind that remembered, was it? Your fingers would remember for you?"

"Yes. It always struck me as sort of funny, how my fingers could do it when my eyes or my mind couldn't. But I'm not a musician, Emily. I love music, all our family does, but Mother's the only one who really might have been good at it if she hadn't married Daddy. I love to fiddle around at the piano, but I used to goof off on my practicing."

Emily frowned, turning the subject back. "I hated to have to look something up in the music after I'd memorized it. I used to make my fingers remember for me, when my mind had forgotten, and they almost always would. I think it's called kinesthetic memory or something. Anyhow, I always had it, you see. And that made things easier, I suppose. I mean about what was most important. Even so, I've never quite believed it. Being blind. I know it with my mind. I mean, I do understand that there isn't going to be a grand and splendid operation the way there is in TV or the movies. But I don't know it with *me*. I don't suppose I ever will, no matter how used I get to it. I still dream seeing. I dream seeing all of you. I wonder if you really look the way I dream you? I know your mother has purply-blue eyes like Suzy's, but I *see* them as grey. And your father's a brown person. So're you, but not as dark a brown."

51

"Mouse," Vicky muttered rather bitterly.

"And I can see your apartment. Your mother described all the colors and furniture to me one day, and I can *see* it. I used to be afraid to go back up, but now the apartment is you, all of you, the Austins. . . . Well. I forgot to brush my teeth. Be right back." She hitched the towel around her like a Roman toga and left the window seat. From the bathroom she called over the sound of running water, "You know the Englishman—"

"What Englishman?" Vicky asked vaguely. This was the first time Emily had ever talked about her blindness, or had referred, even indirectly, to the accident that had caused it.

But Emily had moved far beyond her last thoughts. She sounded impatient. "Oh, you know, Vicky, the one who spoke to me after I called the genie up. The one Rob said had no eyebrows. Do you suppose we'll ever see him again?"

"I doubt it."

"I don't," Emily said.

Four

The following afternoon after school Vicky took Mr. Rochester for a walk in Riverside Park. Dave was reading Emily's social-studies homework to her, and making her memorize the names of South American rivers and mountains. Both of them were in bad moods, Emily insisting that it was a waste of time to burden her memory with useless facts when she needed to keep it clear for important things. Dave could not produce a logical argument, so was reduced to yelling. Suzy in turn told them to shut up so that she could work. She was still nursing her cold and was cross about the math work the others had brought her home from school and which she did not understand. Rob was lying under the dining-room table playing a private game with his battered wooden trains.

Vicky went out into the kitchen, where her mother was starting dinner. "Is it all right if I walk Rochester? Somebody has to."

"Somebody usually does," Mrs. Austin said. "But you may if you want to. Anything wrong?"

"Nothing special." Vicky looked into a pot simmering on the stove and sniffed at its contents. "Everybody else seems to be in a stinky mood so I suppose it's okay for me to be in one, too."

Mrs. Austin was briskly beating eggs in a small earthenware bowl. "A mood's not quite like measles. You can try not to catch it."

"You can try not to catch measles, too," Vicky said, "but it doesn't always work. Anyhow, I'm the only one who likes walking Rochester in this weather. It makes me feel like Emily Brontë."

She left the house, crossed Riverside Drive, and walked along the upper level of the park. Even with the protection of Mr. Rochester she was not allowed down in the park proper after dusk, and shadows deepened early on these cold November evenings. The street lamps were beginning to come on, and a soft fog was rolling in from the river so that the Jersey shore was obscured and the jeweled span of the George Washington Bridge no more than a faltering glow. Across the Drive, the houses and apartment buildings faded into the mist.

She was isolated in a small world of swirling fog and soft drops of moisture blowing against her face. At first she walked rapidly for the dog's sake. She would have liked to dawdle dreamily along by the wall, pretending to be Emily Brontë looking out over the trees and shrubbery where the fog was rolling softly in from the river, but Dave had warned her that rats lived in the park wall and that they were dangerous. What kind of wild animal might Emily Brontë have had to watch out for on the moors?

She always felt a sense of magic in the park when it was foggy or rainy and not many people were out. Forgetting Rochester, forgetting rats, she leaned her elbows on the stone wall. Even the trees close to her were blurred by soft tendrils of fog. A twitching dark shadow startled her, but it was only a squirrel who ran along the wall, saw her, jumped down, and rushed in terror up a tree. Rochester barked in frustration because he couldn't chase it as he would have done in the country (though he had never come near to catching one), jerked roughly at his leash to remind her that the walk was supposed to be for his benefit, and pulled her on up the pathway.

Occasionally they met another dog walker; some of the dogs they knew, and she would pause while Rochester sniffed and wagged. One amiable collie had already become an old friend, and the two dogs were allowed off their leashes for five minutes of wild and joyous romping. Vicky called Rochester back as a snarly little Pomeranian approached, straining ferociously at the safety of his leash and barking imprecations.

"Quiet, Rochester," Vicky said. "Behave." She held him on a tight leash and walked rapidly up the path, leaving the Pomeranian yapping something extremely rude.

While they walked, the fog thickened, so that the few other strollers seemed to appear out of smoke. She was so absorbed in the beauty of fog and solitude that she almost bumped into a man who was walking a great, jowly brindle bulldog. She let out a small gasp.

"It's all right," the man said with quick reassurance, putting out a hand to steady her. "He just looks ferocious. He's really utterly amiable." He had a low and pleasant English voice.

The two dogs were already sniffing. "So's Mr. Rochester," Vicky said. "He'd defend any of us to the death if he had to, but he'd never start a fight."

"Who's us?" the man asked.

"Me and my family."

"Do you live around here?"

"Yes. Down a few blocks. Do you?"

"I'm in New York on a bit of a visit. Cyprian belongs to my host. He's a charmer, isn't he?"

The two dogs were trotting companionably along together. Cyprian paused to investigate a lamppost and Rochester halted, following suit. In the small yellow circle of light that pushed at the white and swirling fog Vicky was able to observe her companion. He was a tall, middle-aged man in a dark overcoat and hat. He had penetrating eyes and a relaxed, easy expression. Vicky regarded him casually; then something in her clicked: the man had no eyebrows.

"Something wrong?" he asked her.

She stuffed her hands into the pockets of her navy duffel coat. "No. Why?"

"You look as though you'd just seen some kind of apparition."

"Well," Vicky said cautiously, "you sort of looked like somebody."

"Oh? Friend of yours?"

"Not exactly . . ."

"Enemy?"

"Oh, not that, either. I don't know him." Then, on an impulse, she blurted out, "May I ask you something?"

"What?"

"Do you believe in genies?"

They were in the foggy shadows between lampposts, but he stopped, holding the big brown dog on a short leash, and peered at Vicky. "What an odd question."

"Yes, I know." She gave an embarrassed laugh. "But do you?" She looked at him as he paused to answer. He was surrounded by swirls of fog, and in its smoky movement he seemed far more of an unearthly apparition than the exotic person who had told Emily, Suzy, and Rob that he was a genie. Nevertheless Vicky, waiting for a response, felt a reassuring sense of solidness and reality coming to her from the man.

"It all depends. I rather fancy that if I rubbed a lamp and a genie appeared in the middle of New York City I might be a bit suspicious. Would you mind telling me why you asked?" When she was silent he said, "I answered *your* question."

She hesitated; but she had gone so far that to stop now made even less sense than to have started this ludicrous conversation at all. "My little brother and sister and a friend of ours— they're very responsible, all three of them—they don't make up silly stories just for jokes or to get attention—" she blundered into silence.

He prodded, "But they told you they saw a genie?"

"Yes."

"What do you think?"

"Well—I'm from the country and I'm not very sophisticated and when I trust people and they tell me something, even if it sounds as peculiar as something I know they couldn't have seen— well, I do think they must have seen something, or someone, and it wasn't just ordinary . . ."

57

"I understand," he said. "That is not at all unsophisticated of you, by the way. Now I must ask you another question." He started down the path again, walking after the two dogs, who were gamboling along together. "Have you met other people out dog-walking this evening?"

She looked at him in surprise. "Yes. Of course. This is a very dog-owning neighborhood."

"Did you ask anybody else what you've just asked me?"

"You mean about the genie?"

"Yes."

"Of course not!"

"Why of course not?"

"It's not the kind of question you go around asking people."

"But you asked me."

"Look," she said, though in the fog neither of them could look very far, "I know maybe this will sound silly, but I trust you."

"Are you in the habit of making snap judgments about people?"

She couldn't tell him that she had asked him because he was the Englishman who had spoken to Emily. "No. But Rochester does. If his hackles rise I wouldn't trust the person he was reacting to with my mother's marketing list. But he likes you."

"Are you sure it isn't Cyprian?"

"Mr. Rochester is not just indiscriminately fond of dogs the way some people are of babies," she said with dignity. "If he'd thought there was something wrong about you he wouldn't have paid any attention to Cyprian at all."

"Vicky," he said, "don't talk about this to anybody else, will you, please?"

Vicky.

Now she was frightened.

Perhaps if it hadn't been for the fog enclosing the park in gentle and fairylike beauty she wouldn't have spoken. Despite the tangible bulks of Mr. Rochester and Cyprian, Vicky had felt a sense of unreality, of moving in a dream world where it was not only possible but logical to do the unusual. But now the fact that she had told this stranger about the genie seemed enormous and awful and terrifying. "How did you know my name!" she cried.

"You told me."

"No, I didn't! It was the one thing I was careful about! You're never supposed to tell your name to strange men——"

"Vicky," he said, quickly, reassuringly, "I won't hurt you. I'm a friend. I promise you. I'm staying——" Then he stopped as both Rochester and Cyprian raced back to them. Barely visible in the fog they could see three leather-jacketed youths, cigarettes dangling from lips and giving out a small glow. Rochester growled. So did Cyprian, who no longer gave the slightest impression of being amiable.

"I'd just as soon they didn't recognize me," the man said. "Go home, Vicky. You're all right with Rochester. I'll be in touch. Cyprian!" His voice was sharp, commanding. He turned and strode off into the fog, the dog at his heels.

Vicky picked up Mr. Rochester's leash. The big dog stayed close beside her as the youths approached, emerging from the fog, and strolled on past. As Vicky walked back towards the Gregorys', she had the unpleasant feeling that they were staring after her. "Let's run, Rochester," she said, and panted along the path, her heart thumping from fear and exertion. Without waiting for the light she crossed Riverside Drive and ran up the steps, two at a time, and across the street to the house, pounding on the blue front door. Mr. Rochester, catching her unusual excitement, barked noisily and protectively. She began to fumble in her pocket for her key, but before she found it Dave had opened the door.

"What on earth——" he asked as she rushed into the big hall, Rochester bounding after her but not galloping on upstairs as he usually did.

She tried to catch her breath. "I'm still not used to having a key. We didn't even *have* a key in the country. Where's everybody?"

"Your family's all upstairs, more or less where they belong. Emily and I are in the music room in front of the fire trying to do Latin. We came downstairs to get out of the zoo for a few minutes."

"Very funny," Vicky responded automatically. Then, "Dave, I've got to talk to you." Dave was not in any way like her brother John; she would have given anything to be able to talk to John at this moment. But Dave was a boy, and older, yet not in the grown-up world. If he could possibly help her she was sure that he would.

He turned and went back into the music room, and she followed, Rochester still sniffing close behind her.

"What's the matter with the d-o-g?" he asked. He had picked up the Austins' habit of spelling when they didn't want Mr. Rochester to know what they were saying. 'Though if you think Rochester doesn't understand when you spell dog,' Rob had said, 'you think wrong. He spells better than I do.' To which Suzy had replied, 'That wouldn't be difficult.'

Emily was sitting in the wing chair, her long legs in black knit stockings stretched out to the fire. On her feet were pink ballet shoes. The light from the cannel coal glowed softly over her. Her eyes were closed and her long dark lashes accentuated the contrast between skin and hair. "Vicky?"

"Yes. And Rochester."

"What's wrong?" Emily opened her deep grey, almost black eyes. Her expression was strained as though she were trying to see.

Dave sat down in the black leather chair. Vicky, still in coat and gloves, stood on the hearthstone, holding her hands out to the blaze. Mr. Rochester tramped heavily across the parquet floor and thudded to his haunches beside her.

"I'm not sure whether or not I've done something awful. . . . You're sure the little ones aren't going to come down?" It infuriated Suzy to be referred to as a "little one" when Emily was not.

"I told them to leave us alone," Dave said. "Emily may not care about getting a decent academic record, but I promised her father—"

"Shut up," Emily said. "Vicky, what happened?" She sat forward, her hands out, feeling Vicky's tension.

Vicky closed her eyes and saw herself in the park again: if she could visualize the tender streamers of fog twining in the trees, if she could see the reassuring bulk of the man with the dog, then it did not seem quite so incredible that she could have talked to him as she had . . .

Emily listened quietly, seriously, with the intent expression

61

with which she listened to music. Dave lurched out of the black leather chair, started to speak, clamped his jaw tight shut, shoved his hands into his pockets, and paced.

"Dave," Vicky said, "you look like them, walking up and down that way—the boys who made the man leave so suddenly."

"Nobody ever pretended I was all sweetness and light. I'm an ex-hood. Remember that. And the Englishman was quite right. You were an idiot to have told him."

"He didn't say I shouldn't have told him. He said not to tell anybody else."

Emily asked, "Did he touch you—I mean, did he shake hands or anything?"

"No."

"That would have been important. You can tell a lot from shaking a person's hand."

"I can't tell as much as you can."

"I know, but you can still tell something. I used to, even before."

"Now listen, Vicky," Dave said, "we know you have a great imagination and all that . . ."

"No," Vicky said vaguely, instead of getting angry. "That's not it, Dave. It was all right to talk to him. I have a feeling. That's all."

"Vicky," he said heavily, "aren't you old enough yet to know that you can't go around trusting feeling? You can't go around trusting people. Not anybody. Not in New York City. Not today."

"As Papa would murmur," Emily said, "it's a naughty world. Listen, Vicky, did you tell him you recognized him?"

"No."

"Then he'd have thought you were just talking about the genie to a stranger, any stranger, wouldn't he?"

"Why'd you shut up about that?" Dave asked. "You seem to have told him everything else."

Vicky silently pulled off her gloves and shoved them into one pocket, yanked off her red beret and stuck it in the other, then went out into the hall and hung her coat up on one of the pegs. "I'd better let Mother know I'm home," she said stiffly.

Five

Dave frequently stayed for dinner with the Austins, but he was so annoyed at Vicky's indiscretion that as soon as he finished reading to Emily he left. He walked rapidly, jingling his keys. Dean de Henares knew that he had a gate key to the Cathedral Close; even though his choirboy days were almost four years behind him he was still considered by the Cathedral Chapter as one of the family, particularly since his father was on the Cathedral maintenance staff. What neither the Dean nor any of the Canons knew was that Dave had managed to collect keys to every gate and door on the Close. He himself did not know quite why they were so important to him, or why they gave him a sense of security.

He hurried in through the front gate, head down against the wind that was rising and dispersing the fog. The wind was never, in any event, as heavy a few blocks inland as it was down by the river. To his left the west towers of the great building raised themselves into an evening sky that had the pinkish tinge that always stains the night when clouds are low over the city. Light, stretching from one end of the spectrum to the other, shone through the slender lancets of the Octagon; the twenty-four delicate flying buttresses were visible and living bones shaping and defining the pulsing color.

Around the Close, light fell in warm yellow pools from the lamps scattered about the grounds, illumining the bare branches of trees and shrubs. Dave had been around the Cathedral most of his life, and the beauty was so everyday a part of his comings and goings that he seldom noticed or acknowledged it. He was in a hurry to get back to the cluttered room which he shared with his father, so he broke into a half trot, veered aside to avoid a man who was heading towards Cathedral House, walking the Dean's large brindle bulldog.

Brindle bull—

Hadn't that idiot Vicky said that the man in the park had been with a bulldog?

Dave looked up, into the man's face.

How many men can there logically be in New York with no eyebrows and who walk bulldogs—

"What are you doing with the Dean's dog?" Dave demanded.

At this piece of rudeness the man stopped, an alert and slightly startled expression on his pleasant face. "Walking him home."

"Sorry," Dave said, "but—" He paused, looking at the man, who was certainly no tramp. His dark coat was conservatively well cut, his hat—not fur, this time—definitely English. "It's just that I'm around the Cathedral a lot and I haven't seen you before and we do get some pretty peculiar characters wandering through the Close."

"Do you think Cyprian would take up with a peculiar character? Not, of course, that I'm denying that I may be one. You're Josiah Davidson, aren't you?"

"What makes you think so?" Dave asked, anger, suspicion, wariness all mingling in his voice.

"You look very much as you were described to me."

"Why would anybody bother to describe me to you?"

"A mutual friend of ours, Mr. Theotocopoulos."

Dave reacted with rage that equaled Mr. Theo's in passion but revealed itself in the opposite manner: his voice was quiet, coldly courteous. "I don't understand. Some friends of mine happened to describe you to Mr. Theo quite accurately, and he didn't mention knowing you. I think you owe us an explanation."

The man's voice was equally cool. "Whether or not I owe you anything, or what I owe you, is open to debate. And who are these friends of yours and why were they describing me? I think you'd better come into the Deanery and have a cup of tea with me."

Dave realized that he had been almost as indiscreet with the Englishman as had Vicky; he hunched into his jacket and followed up the path to Cathedral House, a grey stone building in the center of the Close. It housed the Cathedral offices and the Dean's living quarters. Cyprian ambled along contentedly, undisturbed by the tension in the air, preferring to sniff and snuff at the bushes to going indoors.

"Cyprian!" the Englishman ordered, and the ferocious-looking beast gave an apologetic sneeze and heeled.

The man had a key to Cathedral House, though he rang the Dean's bell before putting the key in the lock. The Cathedral offices closed at five for the night, and the receptionist's desk was empty, the doors to the Canons' offices shut. He led Dave upstairs. They went into the small library which took the overflow of books from the Dean's much larger study. A fire was laid, and the rather repulsive-looking remains of what had once been a shaggy red rug lay on the hearthstone; Cyprian, wheezing, turned around on it three times, scrabbling it up into an uncomfortable lump onto which he lowered himself with contented gruntings.

The Englishman struck a match and lit the fire. "All right, now, Josiah Davidson, sit down and make yourself at home. I'm Canon Tallis, by the way." He removed his hat and tossed it on a chair by the door on top of the heavy, monklike habit the Dean wore out of doors. It had been given him by a Russian archbishop, and was conspicuous only for its complete simplicity.

Dave stared at the shiny bald pate of the Englishman who seemed so at home in the Dean's apartment. "Sorry, but there doesn't happen to be a Canon here by that name."

"Quite. I'm lately from the diocese of Gibraltar, am now with St. Paul's in London, and am presently visiting Dean de Henares, who should be in at any moment with our tea." He went to the doorway and called, "Juan, put on another cup. We have company."

Juan was the Dean's first name. Dave felt an inexplicable resentment at the bald Englishman's familiarity.

"Do sit down, Dave," Canon Tallis said. "You *are* called Dave, aren't you? By everyone except Mr. Theotocopoulos, that is."

Dave grunted in assent, mumbling something about the indignity of being called Josiah.

"But the first Josiah was a rather great king," the Canon said, looking directly at him, "who remained faithful even when his father and his sons and many of his people turned away and worshipped false gods. Theo is right," he added, as though to himself. "You *do* remind one of the Dean."

Dave took a straight chair between two chintz-draperied windows and sat, unrelaxed, watchful. The room had the pleasant odor of old books, furniture polish, burning applewood from the fire. Over the mantlepiece was a portrait of the Dean when he was much younger than in Dave's remembrance, swarthy and darkly handsome, with a fiery vitality. Dave glared at it, refusing to acknowledge any resemblance.

He rose as the Dean loomed in the doorway, carrying a heavily laden wicker tray. "Hi, Dave," he boomed.

Dave took the load from him, saying, "Hi, Mr. Dean," in return as he put the tray down on a long marble table in front of the fire. The Dean seated himself and lifted an enormous chintz tea cozy from a chipped earthenware teapot, incongruous in the midst of a handsome silver tea service,. There were eggs in china cups, a plate of muffins dripping with butter, and a raisin cake. Dave felt his mouth watering. This would keep him from worrying about dinner when he got home. His father's cooking consisted of stringy and waterless stew, alternating with canned baked beans, and it had not yet occurred to the boy that he himself might vary this menu.

The Dean poured tea, gave Dave an egg and three muffins, and served the Canon, laughing as he gave him only half a muffin. He himself sat back, sipping at a cup of strong tea with neither milk nor sugar. He was a big man and heavy, too heavy, not, Dave knew, because of any desire to overindulge in food, but because he was invited frequently in for meals or 'just a bite of this, Dean, I know it's one of your favorites,' as he walked the crowded streets around the Cathedral. He was a familiar figure in the area in his monklike garb and grizzled hair, and much loved.

"Dave," Canon Tallis said, "with the Dean's permission I would like to ask you some questions."

Dave looked over at the Dean, who nodded, saying in his strongly individual accent, the speech of a highly educated man which still retained traces of Spanish rhythm: "I asked Canon Tallis to come stay with me, Dave, because I need his help. So I would appreciate it if you'd give him your full cooperation."

Dave nodded in silent assent. If there were three people in the world he came close to trusting, they were Mr. Theo; Juan de Henares, the Dean of the Cathedral; and Norbert Fall, the Bishop.

Canon Tallis sat back comfortably, drinking his tea. "How long have you known the Dean, Dave?"

"Since I was about eight, when I started in the Cathedral School."

"How did that happen?"

"My father's on the maintenance staff here. He's a carpenter."

"And a superb craftsman, if sometimes a difficult man," the Dean said. "Dave's mother was seldom around, and she died when he was six. When he was little he used to wander around the grounds and the shop after school. One day Theo heard him singing and grabbed him for the choir. He had one of the loveliest soprano voices we've ever had, though that's hard to realize now, isn't it, Dave? What are you? Bass?"

"Baritone, sir."

"I've come to know Dave better than I do many of the choristers," the Dean said to Canon Tallis, "though there are always a few in each class who are close to me. But Dave's relationship to the Cathedral through his father, his battles with Theo, and his own somewhat obtrusive personality have combined to bring him more than is usual to my attention."

The Canon laughed. "Now, Dave, forgive me if I remind you of something you'd rather forget: about the time your voice was changing, your last year in choir, you began to run with an unsavory group known by the somewhat self-conscious name of the Alphabats."

"Who told you?" Dave demanded, glaring at the Canon, and looking suspiciously at the Dean.

The Dean put two large pieces of cake on Dave's plate. "You remember that I was born in Puerto Rico. I was twelve when we came to New York. We lived on 127th Street, and my gang was called *Los lobos.*"

Dave took a few moments to digest this information. He was surprised and unexpectedly shocked, he who prided himself on his unshockability. The fame, or ill-fame, of the Spanish Wolves was still remembered on the streets of New York. "I don't run with any gang."

"But you did," Canon Tallis said.

"People don't let you forget anything, do they? You do something stupid and it labels you for the rest of your life."

"Has it labeled the Dean?" Canon Tallis asked.

The Dean's spontaneous laugh warmed the room. "A certain monk, Peter by name, said—and I think I quote him accurately; correct me if I'm wrong, Tom—" He grinned at Canon Tallis. " 'The world is passing through troubled times. The young people of today think of nothing but themselves. They have no reverence for parents or old age. They talk as if they knew everything, and what passes as wisdom with us is foolishness with them. As for the girls, they are foolish and immodest in speech, behavior, and dress.' "

"Okay, then." Dave, with his rebellious eyes, did indeed resemble the portrait of the Dean. "That's the way it is, stuff like that. People labeling you. Like when I was at the Cathedral School. It wasn't the other kids, it was the masters. They never let me forget that my father was a drunk who snarled if anybody spoke to him, and they expected me to be a hood."

"Did they, Dave?" the Dean asked. "That is to their shame. I wish I had known."

"Not all of them," Dave said with grudging honesty. "But enough. It was their feeling and talking at me like your Peter the Monk that made me go to the Alphabats. Listen, Mr. Dean, kids aren't any worse today than they ever used to be. So why do people talk about us like that?"

"Peter the Monk wrote that around 1274," the Dean said. "Sorry, Dave. Didn't mean to trap you. Just wanted to make a point."

Dave gave his shrug. He was not amused.

Canon Tallis handed him the plate with the last of the muffins, removed the cozy from the teapot, and poured him fresh tea. "I presented the Dean with this monstrosity. It does serve to keep the tea hot. Where are you in school now, Dave?"

"I'm a senior at trade school."

"And your trade?"

"Electronics."

"Mr. Theo says you also play the English horn."

Dave shrugged.

"And you could, if you wished, have had a scholarship to St. Andrews?"

"It made more sense for me to learn a trade," Dave said.

"But you know a lot of the students at St. Andrews?"

"Some. I read Emily Gregory her lessons. She's a blind kid. Mr. Theo teaches her, and he talked me into it."

"You pick her up after school?"

"If she doesn't come home with the Austins."

"The Austins are the family who live above the Gregorys and look after Emily?"

"Yes. I suppose Mr. Theo told you all this?"

"Most of it."

"Canon Tallis," Dave demanded, "when Suzy and Rob Austin described you at dinner, why didn't Mr. Theo let on he knew you and who you were and everything?"

"Because he wasn't sure," the Canon answered. "I came rather precipitously—"

"As is your wont," the Dean interrupted.

"Whose fault was it this time? I'd only arrived the day that I saw the two young Austins and Emily Gregory with the genie. Very good, Dave, I did learn who they were because Mr. Theo told me. That night after he'd had dinner with you and Emily and

72

the Austins he dropped in to see the Dean on his way home to see if I were really here. I may say that he treated me to one of his more spectacular displays of rage because I hadn't informed him of my presence and he'd learned about it secondhand at the Austin dinner table. I do enjoy his fits of fury. We've been friends, by the way, for years. I knew him in Paris before he came here to the Cathedral, and it was he who introduced me to the Dean. Now, Dave, back to the Alphabats. Are you still in touch with them?"

Dave shrugged again. "Not any more than I can help. I see them around, but I don't have anything to do with them."

"You don't know what they're up to?"

"No. And I don't want to know."

"Or who their leader is?"

"Nope."

"I suppose it's come to your attention that they're more tightly organized than they used to be? And there are more of them?"

"Listen, Canon Tallis," Dave said with fierce control, "I told you I'm through with them. I don't want any more to do with them. I don't want to talk about them."

"I think you'd better," the Dean said. "They may not be through with you. You'd better know that there is a strong leader now, and nobody knows who he is, and we want to know, Dave, it's important that we know. It's no longer the boy called by the letter *A*. It's somebody outside the gang. The leaders within the gang still use the letters of the alphabet, in order of precedence—you were *E* once, weren't you?—but they're being directed by someone on the outside, someone we would guess to be considerably older. Perhaps it would help us if you were to talk with some of them if the opportunity comes your way. How about it?"

"Why?" Dave asked.

"Because they're no longer just a gang, Dave, and I must have more information about them. Will you help?"

Dave gave an angry sigh. "I don't know. Maybe. I'll try."

"You'll have to trust me when I tell you that it's urgent. Will you?"

Dave looked over at the Dean's bulk, emphasized by his black cassock belted loosely around his thick waist. He said somberly, "I only know one thing. You can't trust any human being. Not anyone."

"Factually," Canon Tallis said, "that is a perfectly accurate statement. However, we cannot live without trusting people."

"I can."

"Can you? You can exist, perhaps. And how do we become trustworthy? Only by being trusted. What about your relationship with Emily Gregory? Doesn't the fact that she trusts you make a difference?"

"It's not the same thing."

"You've known her for two years, haven't you?" Canon Tallis asked. "Since shortly after she was blinded. You didn't want the job of being her reader, but you love Mr. Theo— don't deny it—and you couldn't say no to him because you saw his grief over what had happened to the child who was the most brilliant student he had ever had, and who was far more than a student to him, who was the child of his heart. The two of you, you and Emily, are the two people in the world who mean the most to him."

"Dave." The Dean came to him and put a strong hand on his shoulder in a quick gesture of comradeship. "I understand your reluctance to trust people. Trust came hard to me, too. And yours has been betrayed far too often, hasn't it? By us here at the Cathedral as well as everywhere else. Would it help any if I tell you I trust you?"

"Why would you?" Dave asked fiercely. "Hoods aren't trustworthy."

The Dean gave his warm smile. "But, like me, you're an ex-hood. And, Dave, I'd rather you didn't talk about this conversation."

"I don't talk to much of anybody," Dave said, "if I can avoid it."

"What about the Gregorys and the Austins?" Canon Tallis asked. "Don't you talk to them?"

"Emily's different. You said so yourself. She's a musician. I think maybe she's a genius. And the Austins are nuts."

"Nuts how?"

"They're just nuts. Crazy."

"But both you and Mr. Theo are rather fond of this insane family?"

"They're such silly, innocent idiots, and anyhow they're great for Emily, they're the best thing that ever happened to her, they're much better than that hatchet-faced housekeeper, and Mrs. Austin's a super cook."

"Are the Austin parents as innocent idiots as the children?" the Canon prodded.

Dave agreed, saying somewhat crossly, "They keep expecting people to be truthful and good."

75

"Are you sure?"

"They expect me to be." He gave a rasping laugh. "Okay, now: you just met Vicky in the park, didn't you? Look at the way she dumped everything out, telling you about the genie and all, as though she could trust any stranger walking in the park."

"You're not being quite fair to her," Canon Tallis said. "She made rather a point of explaining that it was not her own judgment she was trusting, but her dog's, Mr. Rochester I think his name is—"

"Isn't that nuts, then?" Dave demanded. "And then she comes right home and tells me. And the kids tell their parents things that most kids . . . well, they're babes in the woods, they're sitting ducks, all of them, and I don't know who's going to look after them. So I suppose Mr. Theo's why you knew Vicky's name?"

"Quite. Careless of me, letting that slip."

"But how were you sure it was Vicky? There're lots of kids in the park walking dogs after school."

"There aren't that many Great Danes, nor that many potentially lovely young girls asking strangers if they believe in genies. I realize that the Austins lived in a small village until this autumn, but I should imagine that in the United States generally that's the kind of question the average fifteen- or sixteen-year-old wouldn't be caught dead asking. Right, Juan?"

"Right."

Dave's hazel eyes met and matched the Canon's long, level gaze. "I told you the Austins were nuts. Rob still probably believes in Santa Claus."

"And a high-school girl believes in fairies and genies and pixies and elves and asks strange middle-aged men in the park about them? I still find that rather difficult to believe."

"Okay," Dave said. "She recognized you."

"From where?"

"I don't have to tell you that, do I?"

"Not if you don't want to. However, I can guess."

"Where, then?"

"It's really pretty elementary, Watson. When I came out of the junk shop, Phooka's Antiques or whatever it's called, and the rather spectacular man in smoky green robes was standing by Emily and the two younger Austins, I did enter briefly into the conversation. And if, as you say, the Austins tell each other everything, the incident was probably discussed over the dinner table and I, along with the——uh, genie, described. Didn't you yourself imply this? And I am, you must admit, reasonably easy to describe, even when I am attempting to make myself look as anonymous and inconspicuous as possible."

Dave returned the Canon's smile with a scowl. "No. Not at first glance. It's Rob, the little kid, who has a way of seeing things other people don't notice. Okay, so what about it?"

"About what?"

"The man in green robes?"

"What do you think?" the Canon countered.

"I wasn't there. You were."

"I don't really know any more about him than you do. I went into the junk shop because I thought I saw a rather good icon hidden off in the shadows. Stranger things have happened in places like Phooka's Antiques. But it turned out to be a poorish copy. When I left I could hardly help noticing the unusual group out on the sidewalk: your young friends and a figure out of the Arabian Nights' tales. I admit that curiosity, if nothing else, made me stand and listen for a few moments."

"But you don't think the guy in robes was a genie?"

"I somehow doubt it, though I am always open to the possibility of mystery. How about you?"

"I think there's a rational explanation of everything," Dave said doggedly.

"Everything?"

"Everything."

"Truth is only provable fact?"

"If you like. And certainly there aren't any genies."

The Dean checked that Dave's cup still had tea in it. "It's too bad, isn't it, that we can't be completely open with each other like your friends the Austins?"

Dave shrugged.

"I'd like to meet the Austins, Dave," Canon Tallis said. "Do you think you could arrange it?"

"You've met them, haven't you?"

"Not the parents."

"Can't Mr. Theo arrange it?"

"I'd like it to be a little less formal."

"Is it okay if I ask you why you want to meet them?"

Canon Tallis looked over at the Dean, who said, "When I told you I trusted you, Dave, I meant it. We think there's a connection between Dr. Austin and the leader of the Alphabats."

"I do trust him," the Dean told Canon Tallis. "I've known him since he was a gentle and open child. I'm convinced he was telling the truth when he said he was through with the Alphabats."

The Canon leaned back thoughtfully. "I agree with you that

he wants to be through with them. But you yourself said that they may not be through with him."

The Dean began to pace the small room and Cyprian lumbered up from his lump of a rug and moved back and forth with his master, sighing resignedly. "Over and over again as I walk about the streets I get veiled warnings. The Bats are preparing for something; the city's in danger; the Bats are going to take over. It all sounds absurd, but when one adds the warnings together, and the fact that the people they come from are not known for their naïveté, one has to take them seriously."

"I understand. What you take seriously I am not likely to take lightly," Canon Tallis assured him. "But this isn't all that's on your mind, is it?"

"Go sit down, Cyprian," the Dean said, and the dog thumped back to his rug and flopped down with loud and protesting snortings. "If there's a threat to the Cathedral in all this, and there have been recurring whisperings that there is, then I'm worried about the Bishop. He isn't well, Tom. Ever since his brother's death his frightful headaches have been worse. Something like this could kill him. I'm glad you've come. I was beginning to feel totally alone in a nightmare. You've made me realize that I'm not dreaming, though this is not in itself reassuring. But it's good to know that I'm not alone. Do you think Dave's in any danger?"

"Very likely," Canon Tallis said.

Six

When Dave got to the brownstone building in which he and his father had the front basement room, three leather-jacketed youths were sitting on the crumbling steps, smoking. This was Alphabat territory, and he flicked them a glance of feigned indifference, waved, said, "Hi," and turned to go through the rusty grillwork gate under the brownstone steps. One of the boys ambled down, jerking his head at the other two to follow.

"What're you always running off for, Dave?" he asked. On his sleeve was a small bat with spread wings. "What's the hurry?"

"Long day, A," Dave grunted. "Work to do tonight. Hungry. Pop's waiting."

"Yes," the boy called A said. "But not in there."

Dave looked at him expressionlessly, shrugged, and started in.

"Hold it." A knife appeared in A's hand. Behind him the other two boys produced knives.

"So what's up?" Dave asked impassively, his hand on the rusty latch.

"Message from your pop," *A* said. "He wants to see you."

"He knows where I am."

"Orders are for us to take you to him."

"Who says?"

"Come and find out."

"Not interested." Dave jiggled the latch. The grillwork gate was usually unlocked until he and his father went to bed. He knew the Bats would not let him go in, but if he went with them too easily they would be suspicious.

Dr. Austin connected with the leader of the Alphabats? No! Dave's mind was dark with confusion and unformed anxiety. He had quit the Bats. He wanted them out of his life forever, the past to be past. And now here he was being drawn in again. Did the Dean's past ever backlash at him this way?

"Come on," the first boy said. "You're going with us, so save us all some trouble. *B*, get him. C'mon, *C*."

Dave found himself flanked on either side by *B* and *C*, the points of their knives tickling against his ribs. "Put the knives away. I'll come myself."

"No huggermugger," the first boy said. "Your dad said we was to bring you and we don't want to get rough."

"I told him I didn't want any part of it," Dave said. "I'm through."

"That's what you think. Get moving."

They walked in the direction from which Dave had come. When they reached the always locked back gate of the Cathedral Close Dave was told to get out his key. Silently he unlocked the gate, shook the bunch of keys on his ring so that the back-gate key would be indistinguishable from the other keys. The key ring, a heavy steel one with a small Cathedral emblem, had been given him by the Dean as an act of faith in his reliability. He shoved it back in his pocket, saying, "Dad's left the Cathedral for the night."

"Yeah, we know that," B said.

"You can't get away from us," C said. "Once a Bat—"

"Shut up," A said. "He never took a flight. He don't even know what it's about."

They climbed up to the sleeping buildings of the Cathedral School. On their left, lights shone out of the Dean's rooms in Cathedral House. Ahead of them the Cathedral itself lifted to the sky. As they approached if from the east, where the land sloped sharply down to Morningside Park and Harlem, the Octagon, unlighted now, curved against the wind-racked sky. The boys skirted the heavy curve of a buttress by the south transept; then B and C shoved Dave up a steep flight of steps. Above the door was a number 5.

"Open up," he was ordered.

Dave pulled out his keys again. The Cathedral was locked for the night, and the door opened to a vast plain of darkness. Above the great central altar the Octagon was dark; there was neither moonlight nor starlight to break through. A glimmer of light from the seven hanging lamps in the choir touched the huge cross but did not penetrate the sea of dark. The piers and columns soared upward and were lost in night. The footsteps of the boys were dark, echoing on the marble floor.

A took a flashlight from his pocket, but the beam was thin

and ineffectual in the vast nave. *A,* holding the flashlight, led the way to the ambulatory. They walked around it, passing the seven chapels. During Dave's years in the Cathedral School the choristers had named seven lavatories after the chapels: St. James, St. Ambrose, St. Martin of Tours, St. Saviour, St. Columba, St. Boniface, St. Ansgar. Now they started at St. Ansgar, and walked the half circle, ending up by St. James chapel and the side door which Dave usually used.

Across from St. James chapel was the entrance to the great organ loft, and here again *A* paused. "Open."

"What do you want me to do?" Dave asked. "Play you a lullaby?"

"Don't you touch that organ," *B* said. "It'd give me the creeps in the dark."

"Cut the talk," *A* said. "He's not going up to the organ. His dad says the key to the circular staircase hangs up in there. We're going down into the crypt."

"Burial-alive service?" Dave asked. His lips were cold.

"Get the key."

"I don't have to get the organist's key," Dave said. "I've got one of my own." He took out his key ring. There was no use pretending he couldn't get into the crypt. There were three of the Alphabats and he had already felt the sharp points of their blades. And here, immediately and unexpectedly, was his opportunity to do what the Dean and Canon Tallis had asked him to do. If the Bats were taking him to their new leader he was positive—wasn't he?—that we would not find Dr. Austin there.

With the aid of *A*'s flashlight he opened the gate that led to the smaller organ which was used for St. James chapel. Stone chairs circled up to the organ, pipes, storage chambers, and down to the crypt. The light of the flashbulb wavered as *A* gesticulated with it, and the stairs seemed to sway, to lurch towards the boys. *B* gave un uncomfortable hiccup.

"I'll lead," *A* said. "Dave, put your hand on my shoulder. *B*, your hand on Dave's. *C*, on *B*. Get cracking."

"You been here before?" Dave asked. "You seem to know your way around."

"With your old man."

"How come?"

"Wouldn't you like to know?"

Dave said nothing. He intended to find out. *A* bumped against the wall and the flashlight went out; he swore under his breath. The small light had relieved more of the darkness than seemed possible. He shook the torch and the light came on again, a little yellower, a little dimmer. They circled slowly down the stairs, their feet shuffling from step to step in the shifting shadows, making a sound like sandpaper.

Ahead of Dave, *A* was counting under his breath, evidently the number of steps. The sounds came with soft plosiveness from his lips, like small puffs of smoke. "Okay," he said, and stopped. Ahead of them was a door which opened creakingly when he put his shoulder to it. They came out into a great room that seemed, in the dimming glow of the flashlight, to have no boundaries.

"I thought I told you to put in new batteries," *A* growled.

"I did," *C* protested. "Honest."

A swore again, this time at the low quality and the high price of batteries. In the beam which he swung around the room they could see great white flat slabs of tombstones, some with marble effigies recumbent upon their chill surfaces.

"Who's buried here?" C asked nervously.

"What do you care?" A asked.

"Yeah, but who?"

"Who, Dave?"

"Bad choirboys," Dave said, started to add, "and bums like you who have no business here," instead muttered, "mostly bishops."

A swung the light again, and it moved across an unending clutter of marble saints, kings, angels: angels with folded wings, outspread wings, broken wings. Periodically the crypt was cleaned and emptied; eventually it began again to look like a marble jungle dreamed up by Hieronymus Bosch. The Dean was far more concerned with the problems of the people about him than with what he considered mere details of housekeeping. B and C moved closer to Dave.

A jerked his head. "Come on." He directed the light straight ahead and led them through the jungle of statuary, of unused lecterns, candelabra, pulpits, file cabinets, an old iron range, three refrigerators, a row of dour marble saints. The slight but recognizable odor of fear began to emanate from B and C, and Dave knew that if he were to break loose from them now he could probably get away: he had the keys; he could make a bolt for it, lock A, B, and C in the crypt, and be free.

But would he be free? A was no fool and he very likely carried a gun as well as his switchblade. It would be easy enough to dispose of a dead Dave somewhere in the subcellars of the crypt. And who would know, until he did not appear to read to

Emily the following afternoon? And then, even if Emily and the Austins raised a hue and cry, who would think to look for Dave underground in the Cathedral?

Moreover, added to Dave's respect for *A*'s foxiness, his concern for Emily's need of him, his promise to the Dean and Canon Tallis, was his own personal curiosity. He wanted intensely to know what was up.

They came to a new-looking door, which Dave, again, had to open. He tried several master keys before it gave way. It was a well-oiled door and swung open smoothly into the enormous boiler room, which was clear and uncluttered and in extraordinary contrast to the combination museum and junk room through which they had just made their way. *A* swung his flashlight around the gigantic blue boilers, which breathed quietly now. Even with this mammoth amount of modern heating equipment it was impossible to keep the Cathedral from cold drafts in winter; in this room was perhaps the only section of really warm floor in the entire building.

In one corner of the boiler room was a door which led them into a small, comparatively clear stone storeroom. Cartons, neatly labeled, lined two walls, but the back wall was cold and naked stone. *A* played his beam on it, moving the light in slow circles until he found what seemed to be a particular section of wall, though to Dave the stones here looked no different from the rest, rough, unfinished, dank. *A* began running his hands over a stone that perhaps protruded slightly more than the others, cursing as he scraped himself on a jagged place. But he continued pressing against the stone, muttering under his breath, until a section of wall swiveled slowly under the pressure to make an opening just large enough for them to get through.

Again Dave thought fleetingly of making a run for it—at this point he was quite sure that he could—and lock them in the storeroom until morning. But then what? He would have learned nothing, and he knew that A would not stop at any revenge, and once A was free Dave would not be. In any case his nose still twitched with a combination of curiosity and warning: what was his father up to? Why had the old man sent for him? Where were they going?"

"Come on," A said.

B breathed heavily behind Dave. "We going to get the lamp?" he asked. "I need the lamp."

"Shut up," A said.

C shoved from behind.

They followed A on hands and knees. B, just behind Dave, pushed at him if he slowed down for a moment; the faint light of the torch seemed far ahead of them, the dark of the tunnel deeper than the wider dark of the crypt. The tunnel went on and on, too low for them to walk upright. They seemed to be moving forever into nowhere.

B and C were breathing audibly. "I want to rub the lamp," B mumbled.

"Shut up," A said again.

"Whyn't we go through Phooka's?" C asked. "This way's longer."

"We was told to bring him this way." A crawled steadily on. Dave realized with an odd feeling of relief that now there was no possible turning back.

Then, with a grunt, A raised his light, and the tunnel opened up and they could stand upright. For a moment all they did was stretch their sore muscles. Then Dave began to look around, to try to figure out where the tunnel had led them. He sniffed. To his surprise his nostrils were being assailed not with the damp, fetid smell that had clogged their lungs in the tunnel, but with the unmistakable stench of the New York subway system.

From somewhere above them they could hear the roar of a train, but could see no light other than that given by the dimming flashlight. Darkness still pressed on them, unrelieved. He had no idea how large the place in which they stood might be; Emily's ability to judge sizes and distances by snapping her fingers was always an amazement to him, and he thought of it now, snapping his own fingers; the small sound was useless to his untrained ears.

"Okay," *A* said. "Hands on shoulders. Follow me. Shut up. Not a squawk. Dave——"

"Yeah," Dave said wearily. "I'm here. Where else?"

They shuffled along slowly. They were in what appeared to be a dusty passage, about six feet wide, and high enough for them to walk upright. Over their heads and somewhere to their left came again the sound of a train, and the tunnel seemed to shudder to its reverberations. The air was dense and dead, as though it had lain heavily, unhealthily in the tunnel for countless years.

Dave's usually acute sense of direction had deserted him. When they had started from the crypt of the Cathedral he thought they were heading westward, but the tunnel had taken so many turns that he had completely lost his bearings in the city which he thought he knew like the back of his own hand, his own city which rose higher and delved deeper than any other city in the world, built on a vast, uncharted network of sewers, cable tunnels, abandoned builders' excavations, obsolete electric systems; and here he was, beneath the city, lost somewhere in the extraordinary maze that catacombed in all directions underneath the streets, and which most people knew vaguely was there but seldom remembered. It was the kind of monkey puzzle, Dave knew, which would appeal to his father.

He wondered if the Dean were aware of this particular tunnel: how often did Dean de Henares have reason to go into the crypt?

The tunnel turned sharply and A switched off his torch.

Far below, ahead of them, Dave could see light, brilliant light. They plunged down, A leading them with quickening pace. The tunnel leveled off and they emerged into what Dave realized must be an abandoned subway station. There were a number of them in the New York subway system, he knew, stations no longer needed as the traffic patterns of the great hive shifted and changed. This must have been a station built in the early days of the subway, for the walls were ornately tiled, and the ceiling was brightly patterned mosaic. The design of both wall and ceiling was marred by black flaws where tile had been dislodged, like broken teeth.

In the center of the platform was a chair, magnificently carved and mounted on a red-carpeted dais, so that it gave the effect of a throne. On the throne sat a figure robed in scarlet and gold, cope and mitre and jeweled gloves.

Dave stiffened in shock.

Light fell on the resplendent figure, not from the long-dead and broken ceiling lights, but from floodlights that had been plugged in to a series of cables which lay in snakelike coils on the station floor. The light struck the figure's face—a

89

bishop?—so that he looked extraordinarily like a monkey. Dave swallowed. A trick of light? A primate is . . .

B pushed Dave forward. Just behind the throne, slightly in the shadows, stood a wizened figure in the blue overalls of a Cathedral maintenance man: It was Amon Davidson, Dave's father.

"We're here," *A* remarked unnecesarily.

The figure on the throne raised the scarlet hand. "Yes. I see. Thank you." There was no mistaking the deep, unutterably beautiful voice of the Bishop, Norbert Fall.

Amon Davidson came to his son, took him by the arm, and shoved him in the direction of the throne. "My son: Josiah Davidson."

"Yes, Amon. Thank you."

Dave was too startled to make even the smallest courtesy of greeting. One thing he had shared in common with all the boys in the choir was complete admiration for their bishop, and although he had seldom seen Bishop Fall since his chorister days, the admiration remained. To see the august personage of the primate seated on a throne set up in an abandoned spur of the subway system was so incongruous that he began to think that he was not awake, that this was part of a dream. It was certainly far more incredible than Emily's rubbing a lamp and calling up a genie.

Seven

Bishop Fall moved on his throne so that the shadows no longer distorted his features. He ceased to look simian, like a costumed monkey. The familiar, dignified face was raised to the light; the longish hair, once red, now streaked with white so that it shone with a delicate, rosy aura, gleamed under the golden mitre. The thin, compassionate lips smiled.

"Davidson," he said.

Dave licked cold lips, tried to say, "Sir . . ." but no sound came.

"Are you surprised to see me here, my son?" the Bishop asked.

Dave, still mute, nodded.

"Have you forgotten that the first Christians gathered together in the catacombs? I must meet here with my little band because we are in danger. The whole city is in danger of rebellion and sedition." He turned from Dave to the shadows at the far end of the subway platform, called out, "Hythloday!"

Out of the shadows emerged an emormous figure in flowing dusky green robes and with a pale blue turban. He carried a tarnished and dented lamp which he placed in the Bishop's lap.

If Dave were dreaming, then he was dreaming part of Emily and Rob and Suzy's dream, too. He had rubbed no lamp, but there was no mistaking the genie, or the fact that the lamp, which looked, as Rob had described it, like a gravy boat, lay on the Bishop's brilliant vestments.

"A seat for Davidson, please," the Bishop said, and the genie returned to the shadows and procured a purple velvet stool, which he set down near the throne.

"Sit down, Davidson." The Bishop addressed Dave by his surname as though he were still the young chorister who was leader of Decani, the boys on the Dean's side of the choir, who sang antiphonally with the choristers of Cantoris on the opposite side. The two groups, Decani and Cantoris, played against each other in sports, vied academically, often considered each other mortal enemies, yet were united in the services of the Cathedral. What would they think of seeing their bishop here?

The Bishop continued, "I asked Amon—your father—to have you brought here to me tonight because I want to talk to you."

Still Dave, appalled, outraged, could only nod.

Again came the compassionate smile. "No, my son. You are not dreaming. This is real; it is very real. It is perhaps the only reality, as the catacombs were the repository for truth in the crumbling folly of Rome. You find it strange?"

Now Dave managed a "Yes, sir."

"And yet how much stranger are the things that go on about

us all the time! It is winter, now, and we are living in its chill peace. But have you forgotten the riots and rebellion that tore our streets this past summer, and indeed for many summers past?"

"No, sir," Dave said. "I haven't forgotten." His own last summer with the Alphabats, they had joined the gangs running through the shocked streets, looting and throwing broken bottles. The reasonless violence had revolted Dave and brought him to his senses, and he had spent the remainder of the long, hot weeks alone, sick at stomach and heart, in the almost unbearable closeness of his basement room. It had been his final break with the gang. He was not likely to forget.

"Davidson," the Bishop said, "what is to come, unless we can find means to prevent it, will make the riots of past summers a child's game. We must—I must—see that this does not happen. It is my responsibility, as Bishop, to care for my city." He sighed, deeply. "My son, my son. We live in such a time of tumult and torment that we must find our stability within us, and share it, if need be, deep underground, as we are doing now. There are things which I must do, Davidson, which only I can do, which are perhaps as revolutionary as the revolution I seek to prevent."

This was the voice, the winning, generous voice that Dave had heard from the marble pulpit in the Cathedral when he was a chorister. The choirboys who sang in the Cathedral services also had to listen, or at least appear to listen, to sermons. They knew exactly how long the Bishop would preach, or the Dean, or any member of the Cathedral Chapter. They could accurately, if cruelly, mimic all of them. But could they envision the Bishop here? In an abandoned subway station? No! Dave thought. No! Things aren't so bad that he has to be here; they can't be that bad. I'd have known.

But would he?

The Bishop raised his hand to insure Dave's complete attention. The light flashed against his ring. "Davidson. Do you know why I have sent for you?"

"No, sir."

"Can you imagine the holocaust if there is open rebellion in our city?"

"Yes, Bishop."

The Bishop raised his arms to indicate the area around him. "The church may once more have to go underground. There have been murders in Cathedrals before."

Dave asked, "Sir, does the Dean know about—about all this?"

"Not yet. It would not be safe for him to know. He walks too freely about the city, in and out of tenements where there is always danger that he may be held and questioned. What he does not know he cannot tell, even under torture. If he does not know of this extension of the Cathedral then its future is that much more assured. I love the Dean of my Cathedral, that big-boned peasant with a heart too wide for his own good, and so I must try to protect him as long as possible."

Under the scarlet gloves the Bishop's delicate, narrow wrists were in contrast to the Dean's big hands, usually ungloved; the Bishop's pale, ascetic face in contrast to the Dean's darker skin and joyful smile. They had a reputation for being close friends, the Dean and the Bishop, of working well and easily together. It was, perhaps, an attraction of opposites.

94

"Davidson," the Bishop said, "you are often in the house of the head of classics at Columbia, the house of Mr. Theotocopoulos's blind child prodigy?"

Dave did not, for some reason, like hearing Emily described thus, even by the Bishop. "I read her schoolwork to her."

"Above her lives a family called Austin?"

"Yes, Bishop."

"In the same apartment where once lived two Oriental doctors named Shasti and Shen-shu?"

Here came the interest in Dr. Austin and Shasti and Shen-shu again: why? "Yes, Bishop."

"Davidson, it is perhaps known that when I have a problem which I find difficulty in solving, I turn to a jigsaw puzzle both for relaxation and for help in concentration?"

"Yes, sir."

"Amon, your father, has made me some of my most beautiful and intricate puzzles. But hark, Davidson, to what confronts me now: I have in my hand, as it were, pieces of a puzzle, but I have not as yet been able to arrange them so that they fit together and form a picture. It is my hope that you will be able to help me."

"Me, sir?"

"Yes. Because it has been brought to my attention that you may have access to information I cannot get in any other way. Now, my son, I am going to tell you the pieces of the puzzle that must be assembled to form the picture that will show me what I must do to save the city from the madness that can so easily destroy it. But first: Hythloday!"

The genie came forward from the shadows again, carrying a golden book upon a green velvet cushion.

"Now, Davidson," the Bishop said, "I must swear you to secrecy. You must place your hand on this Bible and give me your solemn vow that you will not tell anyone where you have been tonight, or what you have heard."

Dave looked over his shoulder at the three boys on the subway platform behind him.

"Yes?" the Bishop asked.

Dave had his most stubborn, closed-in expression. "Sir, I don't know where you got them from, but I don't trust them."

The Bishop smiled at him in approval. "And rightly. And you are right to tell me this. Your father brought them to me as errand boys, and I have means to see that they do not talk and that they do not harm you as long as you remain faithful. Hythloday."

The genie held the Bible on its cushion out towards the boy.

Amon Davidson spoke from the shadows. "Put your hand on it. Do as he says."

Dave placed his hand on the book.

"Now," the Bishop said, "say after me: I swear to reveal nothing that I see or hear tonight." Dave hesitated. The Bishop smiled gently. "Do you, perhaps, feel strange or disloyal because you have seen and are about to hear things that I have not yet seen fit to reveal to my Dean? We understand this. But it is his very position of power that makes him vulnerable. You see, Davidson, at this point in your life you are nobody and you wield no power, so you are in no danger. And therefore you can help me as my dearly loved Dean cannot. Swear."

"I swear," Dave said. The genie pressed the Bible against his palm. "I won't tell anything. Not to anyone."

"Thank you," the Bishop said.

The genie returned to darkness.

"The pieces of the puzzle are these: a gang known as the Alphabats— yes, I am aware of the connection of these three boys with this group; I am in control of the situation. As I was saying. the Alphabats; their mysterious leader; the two Oriental doctors now in Liverpool; the country doctor, rather simple, who nevertheless has a touch of genius in the lab; the blind girl; the doctor who heads the lab where Austin works." He paused. "I know where and how some of the pieces fit, but not all. I want you to add, if you can, to my knowledge."

"What I do know," Dave again glanced briefly behind him, "is that the Alphabats are a bad thing. I ran with them. I know."

"But perhaps a bad thing may be changed to a good thing?"

"Not the Bats." Dave was definite.

"And Dr. Austin?"

"He's a good man, sir."

"Why have he and his family taken over Emily Gregory?"

"Taken her over, Bishop? They're the best thing that ever happened to her."

"She's a tender, delicate little thing, is she not?"

"Emily? She's about as delicate as a steel trap."

"And the Austins care for her?"

"Yes, sir. And they love her."

"She loves them?"

"Yes, Bishop."

"And you see them frequently?"

"Well, yes, of course."

"You know, then, something of Dr. Austin's habits?"

"I suppose so. Something. It's Emily I work with. The Austins are very kind to me."

The Bishop leaned forward on his throne. "Tell me. Does Austin do all his work in the hospital lab?"

"Well: no, sir."

"Where, then?"

"At home. In his study."

"Where Shasti and Shen-shu worked?"

"Yes."

"Ah, you see! Or *do* you see, Davidson?"

"No, sir. I'm afraid I don't."

"If they all work at home, instead of at the lab, then perhaps they are hiding something? If so, what? And for what reason?"

Dave shifted his position slightly on the stool. These questions had occurred to him. What had been so important in Dr. Shasti's and Dr. Shen-shu's study in the Gregory house that someone, searching for it, would brutally attack a ten-year-old girl? And why, now, did Dr. Austin come home early from the hospital on so many afternoons and shut himself up in that same study? And why did all of this concern both the Bishop, and the Dean of the Cathedral?

The Bishop's voice was suddenly crisp. "Davidson, Dr. Austin holds the means to control the Alphabats and every other disruptive band in the city."

"Does he control them?" Dave asked. At this point he felt that nothing would surprise him.

"In fact: no. Like many brilliant men of science he is also stupid. He does not know how to apply what he has discovered."

"Sir," Dave said, "the Dean——"

Again the Bishop anticipated him. "Yes. I know that the Dean, too, is carrying on investigations. If he should ever ask you, I know that you will help him in every way that you can, remembering only the things which you may not tell him or anybody else until you are released from your vow. It is with my full permission that he has invited the English canon to help him. Austin holds the key; we both know this." Again the Bishop sighed, deeply, wearily. He spoke in so low a voice that Dave had to lean forward on the stool and strain to hear the words. "The Dean wants to protect me, but he underestimates my strength. There is a misuse of power going on in high places, Davidson. The innocent are drawn into war in heaven because they do not understand what freedom is, nor what will give them happiness." He held out his arms in an all-embracing gesture. "O Jerusalem, Jerusalem, thou that killest the prophets, and stonest them which are sent unto thee, how often would I have gathered thy children together, even as a hen gathereth her chickens under her wings, and ye would not!" His head drooped forward. There was a long silence.

Dave sat at the Bishop's feet, his mind whirling. His brain, which had always, even during the summer of his disenchantment with the Alphabats, seemed a reasonable and adequate instrument, could not cope with this mad confusion of Emily calling up a genie, Dr. Austin being connected in some way with the unknown leader of the Alphabats, the Bishop being forced underground to a throne in an abandoned subway station. Why? Who was threatening him? This was no fit place for a bishop. This was not the way a bishop ought to behave. Nothing made sense. None of the pieces of the jigsaw puzzle went together to make any kind of coherent picture.

On the edge of the platform, broken and rusty subway track behind them, the three boys shifted their weight uneasily. B's gaze was fixed on the pewter lamp in the Bishop's lap. At the edge of the shadows the green-robed figure stood, immobile, imperturbable. Amon Davidson crouched, rodentlike, behind the Bishop. He looked old and wizened and ugly; Dave's dark and fierce good looks had been inherited from the mother who had never paid the scantest attention to him, the mother who was the first person to betray his trust.

The Bishop raised his head. His eyes were dark with compassion and grief. "Amon: take the boy home. Davidson: I will send for you again. If you have need of me or have anything to tell me, I will leave word that I am always ready to receive you."

A, who had been teetering at the edge of the platform, came forward, nervously licking his lips. "Hey, Bishop, what about the lamp?"

The Bishop looked from A to Dave to the tarnished lamp on his lap and back to A again. "Ah, yes. The lamp. But do you think he is ready for the lamp yet? Were you ready the first time? Do you think Davidson is prepared?"

"But I thought—"

"Ah, that is just it, A, my lad. Are you not happier when you let me do the thinking? I said that I would send for Davidson again, did I not? And I think the lamp had better wait. But you three boys may stay. Amon: go."

Amon pulled the shoulder of Dave's jacket. Dave rose

from the low stool, feeling cramped and as though he had been sitting in the same position for hours: was it hours? Time had no meaning in the catacombs.

During the long, uphill journey through the tunnel Amon Davidson spoke only once. "Not a word about this or I'll kill you."

In the darkness behind him Dave raised an unseen eyebrow. "Who'd believe me?"

When Amon Davidson finally led the way through the stone opening he was out of breath. In the furnace room his face was grey and he was panting.

"Wait and catch your breath, Pop," Dave said.

Amon leaned against the wall by the huge blue boilers, pulled a handkerchief out of his pocket, and wiped the sweat from his face. "You vowed," he said.

"I'm not likely to forget." Dave looked at his father. They shared a room, but they had not communicated with each other since Dave was a little boy tagging about the Cathedral after school. Often weeks would go by without their exchanging more than grunts. Now Dave looked at his father and realized that he was an old man and a stranger.

"Pop," he said, "why'd you get involved with the Bats?"

"I'm not," Amon Davidson said. "Bats're involved with me."

"You shouldn't have brought them to the Bishop."

"That's up to me."

"The Bishop doesn't understand things like the Bats. He's a holy man. Not like the Dean: different."

"I'll take care of him."

"Listen, Pop, what's all this tunnel bit?"

"You saw."

"Yeah, but I suppose it was you who found it?'

Amon put the handkerchief back in his pocket, answering with pride, "I do all the Bishop's puzzles."

"How come this?"

"He needed a place no one would know. A place no one would guess."

"So you figured this out? Or did you already know?"

"What I don't know about the Cathedral, no one knows," Amon said. Dave knew this to be true.

"So maybe you just blundered onto this, hanh?"

"In the beginning."

"Why did he have to go underground?"

"He told you."

"No, Pop. There's more than that."

"No one must know."

"Know what?"

"What he's doing."

"What *is* he doing?"

"If he wants you to know he'll tell you."

"You tell me."

Amon shook his head.

"Why not, Pop?"

Amon started out of the boiler room. The big machines purred like enormous prehistoric cats. "You don't trust me. I don't trust you."

Dave followed him. Amon's strong lantern lit the crypt, made weird and dancing shadows. Dave did not like it. "Pop. How much do you know?"

"Enough."

"Enough to what?"

"Keep my mouth closed."

"Pop, who's the leader of the Alphabats?"

But his father's mouth was closed literally as well as figuratively.

Eight

After dinner that same night, while Dave was being taken to the strange and unique setting for a bishop's throne, Vicky sought her father in the study. Dave's anger at her for having talked so rashly to the man with no eyebrows burned in her, particularly because she thought he was probably right and she should have kept her mouth closed. "Are you busy, Daddy?"

Dr. Austin looked up from his desk, controlled impatience. "Yes, but I need a break. Come on in."

"Everybody's mad at me—well, Dave is."

"What have you done now?"

"Talked too much, as usual."

"Who to this time?"

"If I tell you, everybody'll say I've been talking too much again. Do I?"

"We've never been much of a family for hoarding secrets. Some people confuse this with forgetting personal privacy."

"Daddy—"

"What?"

"You've—you've been doing it, haven't you?"

"Doing what?"

"Doing what you just said. Hoarding a secret."

"Why do you say that?"

"Just that—just—oh, it's all so complicated! I love Emily and Dr. Gregory and Mr. Theo and Dave and all, but sometimes I wish we'd never left Thornhill."

"But we have left, Vicky. We're here."

"Everything's different. It's not just moving from the country to the city; it's everything else, too. It's John being off at college and not having him to talk to, or to argue with at the dinner table. Funny: arguing with John is one of the things I miss most. Nothing will ever be the same again, and it scares me. Coming to New York, and knowing Emily, and . . . everything's changing, including me, and I hate it!"

Dr. Austin laughed and took Vicky over to a sagging and extremely comfortable couch, pulling her down beside him. "Now listen to me, Victoria Austin. You've spent a lot of time wanting to be yourself, and to assert your own identity, and all the other typical rebellious adolescent stuff. You've gone on in high and lofty tones at the dinner table about freedom, haven't you?"

"Well, yes," she said, trying to sit up straight on the couch, which was soft and invited relaxation. "I think it's important, people being free."

"So do I, Vicky. But we aren't free to remain static, to refuse to change. That isn't freedom. That's death, death either for the individual person or for the family."

"But *why?*" Vicky demanded.

Her father smiled at her intensity. "You'll find as you grow older that you'll never know *all* your reasons for doing something, no matter how much you've tried to train yourself to be objective. And I've discovered that the better you want your motives to be, the more mixed they are, like mine for moving the family to New York. The primitive, bad emotions, like hatred, or revenge, come closer to purity in us poor human beings than our nobler ones. So, no matter how or why we got here, here we are, Vicky, and our lives and Emily's seem to be woven more tightly together every day. You two are pretty close, aren't you?"

Vicky leaned her head against her father's shoulder in the old familiar way. Her father was a big man, and simply to lean against him, to feel his arm firmly about her, gave her a childlike sense of security, at least momentarily. She did not need to remember how drawn he had looked as she came in and gazed at him across the desk, or that he was older, thinner, part of all the terror of change. *She* could change, but not her father, not her mother . . .

"Yes. Emily's a real friend. We can talk. Or not talk. I forget she's Suzy's age. She seems so much older. And I seem so much younger to myself than I did just a few months ago."

"That, you know," her father said, "is a sign of maturity."

"Is it? Emily is, isn't she? Mature, I mean. She's sort of my first real 'best' friend, though the kids at school would ride me if they knew my best friend was one of the little kids. Oh, Daddy, this year is so different from the way I thought it was going to be! I thought I was going to be grown up and have dates—you know, after what happened with Zachary and Andy on our trip last summer I thought I had it made—but with Andy's family moving to Paris—I haven't even had a letter from either Andy or Zachary since September—I thought I'd outgrown being the ugly duckling but I'm right back in it, and the boys are already making eyes at Suzy. And I get jealous. And—well, I know this sounds awful, but there are times I envy Emily, because she has a talent, a real one, and she knows what she's going to do and who she's going to be—"

"Who is she going to be?"

"Emily Gregory, who is a pianist . . ."

"Can't you be Vicky Austin?"

"That's not enough," Vicky started, then gave her father a shamefaced grin, banged him on the knee, said, "Homework calls. Couldn't you arrange it so's we'd have a few days of peace and quiet? Then maybe I could keep my foot out of my mouth."

Vicky was given, whether by her father's arrangement or no, a week that was almost an ordinary week. The only disruption to the usual noisy routine was that the children argued less than usual. Each was, as it were, sitting on the extraordinary things that had happened, and waiting to see which, if any, were going to hatch. Vicky, who was the only one not to have seen the genie, would have liked to ask about him, but decided it was about time she kept her mouth closed about something. Everywhere she went she looked, instead, not for the man in green robes but for the man with no eyebrows.

Dave, who could have told her who he was and where he was, did not. His mind burned with rage and consternation.

—This is not how a bishop behaves. This is not how a bishop behaves. It's wrong. It's not normal. But things aren't normal. What could have happened to make him sit on a throne in the subway? And why that get-up? He used to dress more like the Dean. What were Bats doing there? What's my father up to? Is it all his fault? No, not Pop, he doesn't care enough about anything. Just his wood carving and his puzzles and doing little things for the Bishop . . .

—And Dr. Austin, Dave thought, reading history to Emily but not listening to his own voice. —No. No. He can't have anything to do with the Alphabats, he . . .

He slammed down the book. "Practice your piano for ten minutes, Emily. I'll be right back."

He ran up the stairs three at a time. In the Austin dining room Vicky and Suzy were at the table doing homework. Dave pulled out a chair, plunked himself down, and sat there silently until Suzy said, "So what's up? Why aren't you down with Emily?"

"She doesn't need me while she's practicing."

"She's supposed to have you read to her first."

"I told her to practice. I want to talk to you."

Vicky looked up from the paper on *Richard II* she was writing for English. "What about?"

"I want to know more about the laser."

"Ask Daddy."

"He'll be too technical for me. How did he get into research on the laser beam, living way off in the country?"

"Oh, it's always been his Thing," Vicky said. "He was always corresponding with people like Dr. Shasti and Dr. Shenshu. And working on formulas and things and using the hospital lab whenever he got a chance. The thing is, he's such a good doctor that he kept having less and less time for research."

"Did he know Hyde before he came here?"

Vicky shrugged. "I don't know. He was always meeting people. Anyhow, when Dr. Hyde offered the job to Daddy, it was exactly the kind of thing he'd always wanted to do."

"How did you kids feel about it?"

"Sort of staggered at first. But then Mother and Daddy took us on a great trip out to California and back last summer, sort of to bridge the gap between the two lives, and by the time we moved here we were used to the idea."

"What do you know about the laser?"

"Not much," Vicky said, turning back to *Richard II*. "Suzy's the scientist."

"Tell me about it, then."

Delighted to show off, Suzy slammed her French notebook. "First of all, it's an acronym."

Dave gave an annoyed grunt. "Okay. What's an acronym."

Suzy gave a pleased and slightly feline grin. Now, at last, Dave would have to realize that she was more than just a pretty little kid with curly blond hair, even if she wasn't a genius like Emily. "An acronym is an acrostic."

Vicky, holding her finger on her place in *Richard II*, her pen over her notebook, said, "An acronym is a word made up of the first letters of something, like NATO," and continued writing.

"Laser," Suzy said, "is from *Light Amplification by Stimulated Emission of Radiation*. LASER."

She was so smug that Dave grinned. "Okay. Now can you tell me what it means?"

He sounded condescending, and she flashed, "Yes, I *can* tell you. But you wouldn't understand."

He apologized quickly. "Sorry, Suze. I didn't mean to hurt your feelings. Try telling me, will you?"

She asked suspiciously, "Why do you want to know all of a sudden?"

"No particular reason. Just never got around to asking before. What *is* a laser?"

"It's a violently intense beam of coherent radiation." She looked at him through limpid violet eyes, was pleased to see that he didn't understand, so she elaborated for him. "It's light, that's all, but it's so—well, sort of extremely *tight* that it's about the most powerful thing going."

"How does it get its power?"

She closed her eyes for a moment, trying to think of terms he could understand. "A water pistol: Daddy said to think of it as the tiniest and most powerful water pistol in the world, one that sends out a fine stream of water under extremely high pressure. Water controlled that way could be as powerful as a bullet, couldn't it?"

"Yeah, I get that. Go on."

"Well, multiply that a million or so times. That's how powerful a laser beam is. If you shoot a laser ray it makes a bullet from a revolver or a machine gun seem as mild as instant whipped cream sprayed from one of those cans. You can cut anything with it, absolutely cleanly and accurately. It's used for eye operations and for brain operations."

—Eye operations, Dave thought. —That's why Suzy got so excited about Emily. But Dr. Austin said it wouldn't work,

110

not for the kind of blindness where the optic nerve's completely gone.

"Anyhow," Suzy continued, "it uses Planck's constant. You take something like a crystal of ruby and you get an electromagnetic wave and then you sort of get stimulated emission of radiation at the frequency f. Is that clear?" She looked at him triumphantly.

"Yeah, sure. Now tell me what it means." As she hesitated Dave said, "Come on. Translate."

Suzy grew pink. "I memorized it," she admitted finally.

"You mean it's just gobbledygook to you, too?"

"Not exactly. Anyhow, you wouldn't understand."

"So what's your father's particular game?"

"Game?"

"What's he do that's so special?"

"Control," Suzy said promptly, relieved not to be asked for further technical explanations she couldn't give. "He makes a controlled Micro-Ray."

"What's that?"

"It's a special sort of instrument that gives the surgeon control over the beam so he can do all kinds of operations quite simply and safely that he couldn't even dream about otherwise."

"Is that what your father does for Dr. Hyde, then? Help him control the beam?"

"Yes," Suzy said proudly.

"I see. Yeah, that's quite something, Suzy." He stood up. "I better get back down to Emily. What're you doing tonight?" He peered over her shoulder at her book.

"French."

"She's okay on French. What else?"

"Math. Set theory."

"Ugh. We're in for a struggle, then. Thanks for the info."

But it didn't really help him very much beyond proving what he had already figured out, that Dr. Austin's work was important.

For the next few days he tried to sort things out, unsuccessfully. Close-mouthed at best, he was, in his confusion, less talkative than ever, so that the children remarked on his taciturnity.

"Can you open your mouth wide enough to read me my history?" Emily asked one afternoon in exasperation.

She, in turn, concentrated so poorly that before the lesson was done she and Dave were at odds with each other.

Finally Dave threw down the book. "We're not getting anything done. Get Vicky to read the rest to you before you go to bed." He got up and stalked to Dr. Austin's study and knocked on the door.

"Come in, Dave, make yourself at home," the Doctor said, trying not to show his surprise. This was the first time Dave had voluntarily come to speak to him about anything. "Sit down for a moment while I finish this bit I'm working on."

Mr. Rochester was lying near the wicker rocker, and Dave sat down and bent over to stroke the dog, fondling his head and ears with a tenderness he was seldom willing to reveal.

But when the Doctor had finished with the problem he was working on and said, "Okay, what's on our mind?" the face Dave raised had lost its softness and was the familiar wary, slightly surly face with which the boy protected himself.

"I want to know about the laser."

"What about it?"

"What do you do with it?"

"I don't really do anything with it myself. What I do is work on a small instrument that will make it a more efficient tool for surgeons like Dr. Hyde."

"What's different about it from the laser beam that's been used up to now?"

"The coherent radiation is more efficiently controlled."

"So that means what?"

"It means that now the ray can penetrate deep into an organ, for instance the brain, without burning any of the tissue except where the surgeon wants it to. And the intensity of the ray can be controlled, too. It can be as light as a feather or as powerful as a hydrogen bomb."

"Is this sort of what Dr. Shen-shu and Dr. Shasti were working on, too? A whatchamacallit?"

"A Micro-Ray. Yes. Did they talk to you about it?"

"No. I didn't know them. Remember, I only came to Emily after they'd gone to Liverpool. How much does Emily know about it? This Micro-Ray, I mean?"

Dr. Austin pulled a pencil out of his little pencil jug; he could always concentrate better with a pencil or pen in his fingers. "The way I tried to explain it to Emily once is that Dr. Shasti and Dr. Shen-shu and I are only the makers of the musical instrument; someone else has to play the instrument before there is music. We try to build the most sensitive piano possible, so that the music can come out as true and pure as the musician can make it."

"Yeah," Dave said. "Okay. I think I see that. You don't use this Micro-Ray gimmick at all yourself, then?"

"No."

"Okay. Thanks, Dr. Austin." Then, totally unaware of his ineptitude as a detective, he asked, "Uh—what do you think about the Bishop?"

Dr. Austin looked a little baffled at this apparent *non sequitur*. "I don't know him, Dave. From what I hear, he's a fine man. But I gather his health is poor. Whenever we've gone to the Cathedral he hasn't been functioning. He's one of Hyde's patients."

"Okay. Thanks," Dave said again. "See you tomorrow." He bent to give Rochester one more caress, got up from the rocker and left, running down the marble stairs and out of the house.

He headed for the nearest phone booth, found a dime in his pockets and called Mr. Theo's number. He had to talk to someone and Mr. Theo would, as always, let him talk without saying any more than he wanted to say, would not ask questions he couldn't answer. He had reached the point where he had to talk to someone, and there was nothing he could tell the Dean or Canon Tallis without breaking his oath to the Bishop.

The old man's studio and home were connected by phone. The bell rang endlessly. No answer. Dave's reaction was inordinate anger that Mr. Theo should not be in either of the predictable places, that he be unavailable when needed.

The boy pushed out of the phone booth, glaring at an innocent old woman waiting to get in, and headed for the Cathedral; it was very possible that Mr. Theo might be there.

He ran up the front steps, pushed against the heavy glass doors that let him into the rear of the nave. Rolling down the Cathedral came the brilliant notes of the organ rising up to the great arched vault in a curving wave of sound. He stopped to listen. Something of Telemann's, he thought. Directly above his head the state trumpets gave forth their golden notes. Who was at the organ? He stood, feeling the music as it swept through the Cathedral, meeting and blending with the light, red, blue, yellow, counterpoint of sound and color.

Yes: Mr. Theo. Nobody else played in quite that way, melody rising into the immeasurable air, becoming part of the glory of the Octagon, of the surrounding sky, embracing the Cathedral and all within it. The music, like the Octagon, gradually rose, strong and beautiful, on a sea of air.

Dave moved through the music down the nave and up the steps to the ambulatory. St. James chapel lay ahead of him, dark now, settling into the shadows for the night. Bishop Potter's great white marble sarcophagus caught a pale glimmer of light; the cross above the altar at the crossing glinted gold. Dave looked along the dim crescent of the ambulatory, past St. James, around towards St. Ambrose, St. Martin of Tours, St. Saviour, St. Columba, St. Boniface, St. Ansgar . . .

Matthew, Mark, Luke, and John guard the bed that I lie on, Rob had sung.

—I wish, Dave thought, that I were like Rob and Mr. Theo, that I believed in guardian angels. We need them now.

But it was Mr. Theo himself who had always been, as it were, Dave's guardian angel. The boy turned away from St. James chapel and tried the door to the organ loft. It was locked, so he took out his keys and let himself in quietly, pulling the door to behind him. He tiptoed up the steps.

The music dropped, sighed to a conclusion.

"Well, Josiah?" asked Mr. Theo.

Dave climbed the last few steps and stood beside the old man. He looked over the side of the organ loft to the choir. From where he stood he could see only the Cantoris side; his own place in Decani was hidden from view. "How did you know who it was?" he asked.

"I've known your step for a good many years," Mr. Theo said mildly. "This isn't the first time you've tried to sneak up and surprise me. Do you remember once, your first year in choir, you tiptoed up and yelled BOO, and I pulled out all the stops and blared out full volume at you and frightened you nearly out of your wits?"

"I wasn't going to say BOO today. I phoned you and you didn't answer, so I came looking for you."

"That," Mr. Theo said, "is a switch."

—I need you, Dave thought loudly. —I want you to know all about the tunnel and the subway and the Bishop and tell me what gives.

But he said, "You'll have to speak to Emily. She's not concentrating on her schoolwork. She's going to flunk a couple of courses if she keeps this up and they won't let her stay at the school and she'll have to go to one of those blind places." He pulled up a small folding chair near the console and sat down. Simply to be here, in the old familiar position, made the burdens of secrecy rest less heavily on his shoulders.

"Why isn't she concentrating?"

"I suppose it has something to do with that idiotic genie."

But the genie was no longer quite so idiotic now that Dave himself had seen him. "Listen, Mr. Theo, the night the kids were talking about the genie at the table you seemed very interested in the Englishman who had no eyebrows."

"It is an interesting phenomenon." Mr. Theo looked not at Dave but at the complicated keyboards and myriad stops of the organ. "Sometimes prolonged danger and exhaustion can cause such a loss of hair. I myself have a friend who withstood torture without breaking and——"

Dave cut him off, "And whose name is Canon Tallis and who's staying with the Dean here at the Cathedral."

Mr. Theo looked fiercely from under his bushy eyebrows. "You know this how?"

"Because I met him last week right after the kids saw the genie, and I had tea with him and the Dean."

"And why have you seen fit to wait so long to tax me with this?"

Dave had, indeed, avoided Mr. Theo when he had come to give Emily her lesson. He sighed. "Because the whole thing's such a mess, and I didn't see much point in blabbermouthing about it and pulling you in until I knew more."

"But if you and Emily are in it, then so am I."

Dave leaned over the organ loft and looked up the length of the nave to the great rose window and the state trumpets beneath it. "Mr. Theo, I thought when I learned that I couldn't trust people that I couldn't ever be surprised again by anything anybody did."

"That was very young of you," Mr. Theo said. "The unpredictability of the predictable keeps life interesting when all else fails. As for me, I find many people trustworthy, but I am no longer surprised when they behave in ways that do not seem in accordance with their characters."

"Some of them have gone too far." He turned back to the old man. "I suppose in spite of everything I've always kept the childish illusion that there's some kind of order in the universe."

"Is it an illusion?"

"There sure isn't any order."

Mr. Theo looked up towards the music open before him on the organ. He played the theme of Emily's fugue with one finger. "I've based my life on order and reason in the universe, Josiah, and a power of love behind that order and reason. I've had many a narrow shave in my day, but I don't believe in the victory of chaos." He switched off the organ. "Come. Let us go over to Cathedral House and see if the Dean and Tom Tallis are there. And tell me, Josiah: how do you happen to have a key to the organ loft in your posession?"

"My father works here, remember? I have keys for the whole place."

"That is not your right," Mr. Theo said.

Dave gave the old man his most stubborn look. "You never know when they'll come in handy."

Mr. Theo did not respond. He put his music away, carefully, turned off the organ light, and led the way down the steep stairs, moving slowly, sidewise, in his slightly arthritic way. He opened the door into the ambulatory, then switched off the loft lights. Dave followed him down the steps outside St. James chapel.

"If you have your keys," Mr. Theo flung over his shoulder as they passed the Dean's Garden, shrouded in darkness and shadow, "you can let us in."

They went through the stone gateposts and Dave took Mr. Theo's arm to help him down the stone steps leading to Cathedral House. He had not touched Mr. Theo for a long time and he was not prepared for the fragility of the old man's arm, or his need of assistance. Even after Mr. Theo had retired, it had never really occurred to Dave or any of the choristers that Mr. Theo could change. One had to retire, because there was a rule about it, but Mr. Theo would always be around, would always be the same . . .

Now, as Dave felt Mr. Theo's bones, brittle as a bird's under his fingers, for the first time it occurred to him that Mr. Theo might not always be in his world. The thought made him violently angry, and he dropped the old man's arm as they reached the bottom of the steps as though it had burned him. He pulled his key ring out of his pocket and jingled the keys until he found the right one.

"More stairs," Mr. Theo said as they went in. "I don't know what they'd do if they had an elderly dean or one with an invalid wife or . . . I get out of breath nowadays. Playing the organ, too. My legs aren't what they once were. I can manage the harpsichord or the piano better. Even in the days of my youth and vigor my legs were always just a shade short for the pedals. This evening they seemed even shorter; I'm afraid this gander's about to be cooked."

The choristers had laughed among themselves at Mr. Theo's legs on the organ pedals, stretched to their full extent, moving with extraordinary rapidity and absolute accuracy. They had laughed, and they had been proud of their organist and teacher, and pride and admiration always outweighed the laughter.

Canon Tallis stood at the open door to the Dean's apartment, silhouetted against the light, a dark figure except for the pallor of the bald head. "Theo!" he said, in pleased greeting, then saw Dave. "Hello, there."

"A fire in the fireplace," Mr. Theo ordered. "My marrow is cold. And tea. Strong tea."

"At your service, Theo," the Canon said. "The fire is already blazing and I can manage the tea in short order."

Mr. Theo went into the library and stood with his back to the fire, rotating himself slightly to the warmth. "It is time that we leveled upon each other," he announced.

"Warm yourself first," Canon Tallis said, "and I'll go make tea. Come with me, Dave."

"Where's Juan?" Mr. Theo called after them.

"In Puerto Rico. He promised last summer to do a few days' lecturing at the Seminary, and he's tooling around the rest of the island preaching. He'll be back Monday night." Canon Tallis went into the large kitchen, took the kettle and splashed water into it. As he set the kettle down on the gas he looked quizzically at Dave.

"How much does Mr. Theo know?" Dave asked.

"Just what he's guessed. I want him out of it. But Theo's no fool." The Canon took a large tray and started laying out the tea things, cups and saucers, spoons, earthenware teapot and homely chintz cozy, plates. He poked around in various cupboards until he produced an assortment of cookies and a slightly stale sponge cake. "Theo knows the Dean sent for me, that I am not here just on a social or preaching visit. Because we're old friends and trust each other he's asked me no questions. And I don't want him involved in danger unless it's absolutely necessary."

"Mr. Theo said if Emily and I are in it, he's in it."

"Quite. That's Theo. Tell me, Dave, why did you go to him this afternoon?"

Dave spoke reluctantly. "Sort of out of habit. He's always been the one person I could go to and not have to tell him what's on my mind. The way you said: he doesn't ask questions. He waits for you to tell him, and if you never do, he still doesn't push you. Even if he has a tantrum I end up feeling better. Canon Tallis, things are getting out of hand."

"Out of hand, how?" The Canon opened the refrigerator door. "No. Let's not bother with eggs today."

"Emily knows something's up, something weird, and Mr. Theo's guessed it from her playing. I think he's right. We've got to level with each other, or put all our cards in one stable, as Mr. Theo would say."

The kettle began to whistle. "What have you learned since last week?"

"Nothing, really." Dave felt the palm of his hand prickle as though it still carried the touch of the golden Bible. He could not break his oath. "I do know that something's troubling Dr. Austin, but I don't know what or why. I'd guess it has something to do with this Micro-Ray gadget he makes. But I don't see how it could possibly have anything to do with the Alphabats. And this genie guy: he's got to be *some*body, doesn't he? But I haven't a glimmer. He's big. So lots of people are big. Dr. Austin's big. The Dean's big. The genie wears smoky green robes, and the Dean wears a smoky black one. It's all so nuts he might as well be the Dean as far as guessing goes."

The Canon poured hot water into the teapot, swished it around thoughtfully, then emptied it into the sink. He took some Earl Gray tea from the cupboard over the stove and spooned it carefully into the pot, then poured boiling water over it. He was whistling softly.

"Canon Tallis, do you think the Bats or some gang are getting ready for a big riot? Things have been hell enough in this city when it's been hot, but if the gangs really tried to take it over——"

"Do you think they could?" Canon Tallis asked.

"I don't know. Maybe. It could make the barbarians taking over Rome look like a Sunday School picnic."

The Canon nodded. "Carry the tray, will you please, Dave?"

When Dave put the tray down on the marble table, Canon Tallis, sitting before it to pour tea, asked, "Theo, what is bothering Emily?"

Mr. Theo had now turned to face the fire, his hands stretched out to the blaze. He gave an annoyed growl. "Sleuthing is your department. If Juan de Henares sends for you so summarily that you have no time to let me know beforehand, I know that you are being called as trouble-shooter, not priest. Tom, you cannot hint that Emily is in danger and drop me like a hot banana."

"Calm down." Canon Tallis was unruffled. "Sit down and I'll pour you some tea." The old man lowered himself into a chair, and the Canon gave Dave a cup to take to him.

"FIVE sugar," Mr. Theo said. "Put it in for me, Josiah. And lemon."

Canon Tallis looked at the pitcher of milk. "I forgot lemon. Dave——"

"NO!" Mr. Theo bellowed. "Forget it. As I am ignored, insulted, inconsulted in every way."

Dave put the cup of tea on the small table beside him.

"Pass him some cake to sweeten him up," Canon Tallis said.

"No cake. I do not eat between meals. I am getting a bulge in my midriffle."

The Canon's lips twitched slightly as he poured for Dave. "You needn't hold back, Dave. Help yourself to the repast, such as it is."

Dave took several pieces of the crumbly cake and a handful of cookies. Thinking of the fragility of Mr. Theo's arm, he would have liked to remark that Mr. Theo could do with something to eat, but one could go so far with Mr. Theo and no further. He sat on a chair between the old man and the Canon and waited.

"All right, Dave," Canon Tallis said. "Suppose you tell Mr. Theo what you know. Everything."

"Chronologically," Mr. Theo ordered. "I do not wish to be confused more than necessary."

"Beginning with when?"

"With the—the genie."

Mr. Theo stirred the sugar in his tea, noisily, while Dave told him what he could. But the visit to the Bishop made an enormous dark hole in his telling.

When the boy stopped, Mr. Theo sipped his tea distastefully. "This tastes like stewed cigarette butts. You have told me everything, Josiah?"

"Yes."

Mr. Theo put his cup down, rose stiffly, and moved to look with his fierce blue eyes into the boy's clouded hazel ones. "No, Josiah. I've known you far too long not to know when you are hiding something from me beyond your usual personal uncommunicativeness."

Dave took a swallow of tea. "Mr. Theo, when the kids were telling you about raising up the genie the other night, wouldn't you have liked to tell us who the bald Englishman was?"

"I did mutter something—"

"But you didn't tell us. And you wanted to, didn't you?"

Mr. Theo acknowledged this by sniffing and going back to his chair.

"I've told you everything I can tell you. I can't tell anything else for the same reason you couldn't tell us who Canon Tallis was."

"A point of honor?" the Canon asked.

"Yes, sir."

"Think about it well, Dave. Some oaths are best kept in their breaking."

Dave sat, looking into his teacup as though seeking an answer in the brown leaves. "I can't break this one, sir."

"Can you tell us who bound you to silence?"

Dave shook his head. "Only that it's somebody both Mr. Theo and I trust."

"Do I?"

"I don't know whether or not you know him, sir, or how well. That's all I can say. Please don't ask me anything else."

Mr. Theo looked under his bushy yellow brows at the Canon. "Pour me some more of your boiled tobacco and listen to me, Tom. If you think Dr. Austin is tangled up in your web you're barking up the wrong hydrant." He took his refilled cup from Dave and leaned back in his chair, stretching out his short legs.

"We all know," Canon Tallis said, "that there is still an unresolved mystery about the day Emily was attacked."

"Nobody is likely to forget. But don't try to drag Austin into it. He wasn't even in New York."

"That's right," Dave agreed. "They were living way out in the country."

"As it happens, Dave, he was in New York for a medical meeting that day. This has been verified."

"But—"

"I know. It proves nothing. And until something is proved he is innocent. However, he did not get in touch with Shasti and Shen-shu that day as he usually did when he was in the city, and, while they were out, someone came to their apartment and took some papers containing vital information, someone who knew what he was looking for."

"Yeah," Dave said, "and Dr. Austin was corresponding with them anyhow; they were sharing everything they knew."

"No one is making an accusation, Dave, but it bears looking into. Whoever stole the papers also took an unfinished Micro-Ray and left Emily blind."

Dave began to curse in a low voice, slowly, methodically.

"That is enough," the Canon said.

"Dr. Austin wouldn't hurt Emily. He wouldn't hurt anybody."

"If the Micro-Ray had been finished and whoever it was

could have controlled it, the flash of light would have given only temporary blindness."

"No!" Dave said. "No. He'd never have used it. Never."

"Why are you so sure?"

Mr. Theo had been gathering breath for a roar. He bellowed in uncontrollable rage, mane flying, "Because we know him! Because we love and trust him!" He turned to Dave, "All right, Josiah, I have not forgotten what I said about never quite knowing what people are going to do. But this I do know."

But could anything anyone did be more strange or unpredictable or wrong than the Bishop in the subway? Dave asked, "Canon Tallis, did you know about the lamp and the genie before the Dean sent for you?"

"No. I became aware of the genie at almost precisely the same moment that the children did. While I was puttering around looking at the icon in the junk shop a remarkable apparition emerged from the bowels of the shop, an enormous man in long robes. I don't put anything past Americans—" (Mr. Theo gave an annoyed snort) "—and I thought at first he was the proprietor of the shop being colorful. He walked to the front of the shop, past the woman of Endor who had been waiting on me—I was the only customer—and stood in the open doorway. When he saw the children outside he nodded in satisfaction, rubbed his hands together as though extremely pleased, and went out to them. As I said, I pricked up my ears and listened."

Mr. Theo put down his cup in disgust. "I thought that we were going to come on a level with each other. I have told you everything, I am as an open paper, and all you do is make wild accusations against an innocent man, while both you and Josiah see fit to continue withholding from me."

"It is not that we see fit," the Canon said gently. "Until I know more of what is going on, it is not safe—not for you or any of us—for me to speak further."

"Think, then, Tom, if you are capable of doing so. What does the genie appearing to the children tell you?"

"Something odd is going on."

"But more. If you want to get at a man, you find his most vulnerable point. What's Austin's? His children. What all this tells me is that someone's after Austin."

"The possibility has occurred to me, Theo."

"Is Emily in danger now? Hasn't she suffered enough?"

"She has. One of the things I hope to do is to see that nothing more happens to her."

Mr. Theo rose. His fingers moved as though feeling for a keyboard. "What was done to her cannot be undone. We have all faced and accepted that. But it has not undone her talent. She will still be the artist I know she can be. This is more than a flash in the dish. She is not only a child prodigy, Tom. The real thing is there, not fully developed yet, but there."

"I know," Canon Tallis said. "You played me her tapes."

"And do not go on at me," Mr. Theo's voice rose again, "about pain and suffering developing talent—"

"I am not going on at you in any way."

Mr. Theo overrode him. "I am aware of the fact. A great many years of life could not fail to make even me become aware of this overobvious truth. I have said it myself: suffering is the finger exercising of the spirit. But Emily has had enough.

127

Too much can kill even a gift like hers. I will not have her hurt again, just as she is making friends, real friends, for the first time in her life, and they are the Austins, mark that, Tom, the Austins whom you so wildly accuse."

"Theo," Canon Tallis said, "whatever we do we must not be ruled by emotion."

"*I* am not a cold, heartless intellect—" Mr. Theo started to roar, then drew himself up. "Sorry, Tom. Sorry. To say that to you, of all people. . . . *I* am the cold, heartless beast—"

"All right, Theo." Canon Tallis poured himself a cup of what by now must be stone-cold tea. Dave saw that his hand was not quite steady. "You must hold your heart, too, in abeyance. And you might pray for Emily, Theo. I don't know what the danger is. If I did, I would not, could not, withhold it from you. All I know is that there is danger."

When Dave shook hands to say good night to Canon Tallis he looked for a long moment into the priest's eyes, and the gaze was returned. Each was questioning, wondering just what it was that the other was not revealing. Had the priest, Dave wondered, also made the trip through the tunnel? Had he, too, sworn silence to the Bishop? Did the Dean know more than the Bishop thought he did?

"Sir," Dave asked abruptly, "how well do you know the Bishop?"

"Moderately. He's not a close personal friend like Mr. Theo, or Juan de Henares."

"What do you think of him?"

The Canon did not inquire why Dave would ask such a

question. "He has a reputation for being a good bishop despite his poor health, a holy man, perhaps not an innovator."

"What do you mean?"

"That his very scrupulousness gives him a resistance to change. When there is talk about the great bishops here, Manning is mentioned, and Donegan, but not Fall because of his rigid concern for the *status quo*."

"Do you think he's apt to—to get more flexible?" Dave asked.

"I don't know, Dave. Do you?"

Was the question loaded? Surely the Bishop's spectacular throne in the subway was innovation of the first order.

Dave remembered suddenly a conversation he had had earlier in the autumn with the chorister who was Head Boy for the year, and who had angered Dave by making uncomplimentary remarks about the Bishop. The boy had been a choir probationer when Dave was leader of Decani, and he defended himself by saying, "He's changed, Dave. He's not the way he used to be. He's different from when you were here. Honest. Everybody says so."

"So what do 'they' say?"

"Sort of that he started to change when his brother died. He sort of aged terribly. Everybody says they were very close and he was all broken up."

"So he's aged, then," Dave had said. "That doesn't mean he's changed, basically. Like, look at Mr. Theo. He's getting old, really old. But he's still Mr. Theo."

"Yeah, but it's more than that."

"More how?"

But the boy, when pinned down, could not put his finger on how the Bishop had changed. All he could say was, "We hardly see him now. He hasn't celebrated Mass in I don't know when. Sometimes he serves. I think it has something to do with his feeling he has to be a servant, or something all symbolic. He does preach regularly, and he's good, Dave, he makes even us listen. I never do homework when the Bishop preaches. But—oh, I don't know, Dave. He's just not the same. All the kids feel it."

"You're just going through your atheist stage," Dave had said, and stalked off.

So the choristers thought the Bishop was changed? What did that do to Canon Tallis's remark about the Bishop's resistance to change? "Look, sir," he said now. "Maybe one thing I can tell you. The Bishop isn't the way he was when I was in choir. He's been different this year. And I'm not the only one who thinks so."

"Right, Dave. Thanks. Keep in close touch, will you?"

"What are you two going on about?" Mr. Theo demanded. "Josiah, you are going to walk me home, no?"

"I am going to walk you home, yes." Dave said.

Nine

On Sunday it rained, a cold, bone-chilling November rain. Everybody came in wet from church. When the children had hung up their outer clothes and changed their shoes, Mrs. Austin suggested, "Let's not go anywhere or do anything this afternoon. Let's just sit around and relax and maybe Daddy and I can actually get through the *Times* for once."

"But we were going to the Cloisters," Suzy protested. "I wanted to see the tapestries. We saw pictures of them in art class last week. And Emily wanted to listen to the concert."

"I am not going to cope with all those soaking navy-blue coats again," Mrs. Austin announced.

"They stink when they're wet." Emily wrinkled her nose. "They're wet enough already from church. I don't mind missing the concert, Mrs. Austin. I'd do just as well to practice. I've skimped on it this week and Mr. Theo'll be furious."

"Yeah, he gets mad at *us*." Suzy was in one of her protesting moods. But she stopped pestering her mother about going to the Cloisters.

After lunch Rob went downstairs to listen to Emily practice. Vicky and Suzy settled themselves at the dining table to finish homework, their weekend assignments having been heavy, and Dr. and Mrs. Austin went into the study with the paper. Mrs. Austin took the theatre and book sections and established herself happily in the wicker rocker; Dr. Shen-shu's yellow paint was a sunshiny bit of color against the dark of the day. She had a basket of mending beside her, but had no intention of touching it. Her husband, leaning back in his creaking desk chair, his feet comfortably up on the desk, began to read methodically through the News of the Week. Comfort and companionableness reigned. Sleet beat against the windows, safely held without. The disciplined and comprehensible sound of finger exercises, cleanly and strongly played, floated up the marble stairs and through the open door.

Mrs. Austin looked up from the drama reviews. "Nobody seems to think much of the new *Coriolanus*. It says here there hasn't been a good performance of *Coriolanus* since Henry Grandcourt, and that was back in the days when I was young and singing a bit and hadn't met you. Let's all have tea downstairs later on, and build a good fire in the fireplace, and get Emily to give us a concert."

"Listen to this," her husband said, and read aloud, "The old gang, the West Side Alphabats, is reported to be recruiting new members in extraordinary numbers, but with a difference. Police have been on the alert as the gang's territory has stretched out into East Harlem, but have been able to see no increase in crime in the areas in which the Alphabats operate. Rather there has been a decrease in the petty thievery and muggings that marked the Bats heretofore, presumably because they needed to procure money for LSD, marijuana, or other illegal narcotics."

"Isn't that Dave's old gang?" Mrs. Austin asked.

Her husband nodded, continuing. "Recruits to the group are coming from an ever widening area. Many of the Bats wear black jackets, but there is no consistent uniform. The leaders, those who call themselves only by the letters of the alphabet, wear an insignia on the right sleeve, so small as to be inconspicuous, of a bat with outspread wings. One ex-junkie, now known to have 'kicked the habit,' told a member of the detective force that he didn't need any more 'snow.' A younger teen-ager, who used to need hospitalization after frequent 'trips,' when questioned said that he no longer needed 'pot' or 'acid,' that the Bats have taught him a new way to 'rub-a-dub' and 'take a flight.' " Dr. Austin broke off.

"What's the matter?" his wife asked, looking at her basketful of darning. She pulled out a navy-blue skirt with half the hem out, murmuring, "I really should make Suzy do this herself," looked at Emily's school blazer with a rip in the elbow from one of her frequent tumbles, and put it on top of the pile. Duty done, she picked up the drama section again. "Go on about the Alphabats."

Her husband continued, "Further investigations are being carried out, but there is no indication that there is anything illegal. Indeed, on the surface at any rate, the new Alphabats seem committed to law and order."

"Well!" Mrs. Austin said. "That's a pleasant switch. Let's ask Dave about it."

"Better not. You know Dave hates being reminded that he ever ran with that pack—or maybe flew with them might be better." He tossed the paper over the desk to his wife, as though he were glad to get rid of it. "Here. Have a look yourself if you like."

Mrs. Austin picked up the paper, looked over it at her husband. "Wallace," she said carefully, "I wish you'd tell me what's bothering you."

"Why should anything be bothering me?"

Her voice trembled slightly. "After all these years you think I can't tell that you've been concerned—to say the least—about something almost ever since we moved to New York?"

He looked down at a pad of scrawled numbers and formulae. "The switch from being a simple country doctor is harder than I'd expected."

"Wally!" his wife cried. "You're shutting me out. Don't! I can't bear it."

But he did not look up from his desk or make any reply.

The evening after Emily's next piano lesson with Mr. Theo, when they were all at the table, with both the old man and Dave part of the close-knit group, Mrs. Austin said, "I keep waiting, don't you?"

Dave asked, with unwonted sharpness, "What for?"

Mrs. Austin looked at him in surprise. "For a word from Emily's father."

"Oh," Dave said. "It's tonight he's due home. I forgot."

"And don't look for a word from him," Emily said. "He

never lets people know about things like arrival times. When he gets home he'll just walk in."

The doorbell rang.

Emily laughed. "At least we know it isn't Papa. He's perfectly capable of having left his keys in the Parthenon but he'd never give an ordinary ring. He always does my fugue."

"But who—" Mrs. Austin asked. "We aren't expecting anybody."

"I'll go see." Rob clattered down from his chair.

Dr. Austin looked silently at Dave, who nodded, rose, and followed the little boy.

"Betcha it's the Fuller Brush man," Suzy said. "He's always after Mother for mothballs."

Mrs. Austin laughed. "This house does look like the perfect sanctuary for homeless moths."

"Papa said there were bats here when he bought it," Emily informed them.

"More potatoes, please," Suzy requested. "The only bats around here are in the belfry." She stopped as footsteps came up the marble stairs. They all listened, more carefully than they would have a week earlier when they would simply have assumed that a doorbell ring would mean something normal and comprehensible.

Dave and Rob returned alone, and Dave brought a slip of paper to Dr. Austin. "It's a cable."

"It'll be from Papa," Emily said calmly.

Dr. Austin tore open the cable, read it swiftly first to himself, then aloud. "STAYING ATHENS EXTRA WEEK STOP CAREFUL OF FALLS STOP LOVE TO EMILY ALL GREGORY."

"I might have known," Emily said. "Once papa gets to Greece he can't bear to leave. Do you mind terribly being stuck with me? He's taking advantage of you, you know."

Dr. Austin put his hand swiftly on hers in a gesture of reassurance. Emily, who usually shied like a wild pony when she was touched, put her head briefly against his shoulder. Dr. Austin let his hand lie on hers.

"You know we love having you with us," Mrs. Austin said.

"Hey!" Suzy called to draw attention to herself. "I'm all over my cold now. If Dr. Gregory's going to be gone a-whole-nother week I do think Emily and Vicky might move up with me. You make me feel like a baby leper."

"With spots?" Rob asked.

"I said *leper,* not *leopard.* And I don't like being treated like a baby. I'm the same age as Emily."

Slowly, thoughtfully, paying no attention to Suzy, Emily removed her hand from under Dr. Austin's. "What did Papa mean by CAREFUL OF FALLS?"

For a moment nobody answered. "You can clear the table now, Rob," Mrs. Austin said. "He probably meant you, Emily."

"Papa knows I fall half a dozen times a day. He doesn't give me warnings. He gets angry."

Mr. Theo, who as usual at the Austins' had been eating as though he had just ended a long fast, growled, "I, for another, would like you to be more careful. You may not be able to see your shins all black and blue. I can, and it gives me no asethetic pleasure whatsoever."

"Speaking of which," Dr. Austin said, "aesthetic pleasure, that is, how's the homework situation tonight? Isn't this the day

136

nobody has very much? How about an hour or so of music after dinner? Mother and I'll do the dishes later on. Dave, your horn is here, isn't it?"

"Yes, downstairs, but——"

"Oh, shut up, Dave." Emily cut him off. "Be nice about it for once, can't you? Nobody's going to tease you to play if you don't feel like it."

Mr. Theo shook back his yellowing mane. "Josiah will play. You and I, Miss Emily, will do the Mozart two-piano sonata. I think you have it pretty well under your sash. And young Rob will sing. What will you sing, Rob?"

Rob stood in the doorway to the kitchen, the empty milk pitcher in one hand, a bowl with a spoonful of leftover lima beans in the other. "We learned a French carol at school. I'll sing that."

Suzy asked suspiciously, "Is it bejeezly?"

"It's about the baby Jesus, if that's what you mean," Rob called back over his shoulder from the kitchen, "but it isn't one of the sky-blue-pink ones. What's for dessert?"

Dessert was deep-dish cherry pie, after which Dr. Austin told the children to forget about the table and go on down to the music room. He himself picked up the cable, read it once more, and took it to his desk in his study before following them.

When he got downstairs Vicky and Mr. Theo were lighting a fire and Dave was cleaning his English horn. It was one that had been bought second-hand for him during his choir days in the Cathedral School, and having survived not only that but four years of rather rough and informal rehearsal at trade school, it looked battered and dented and as though nothing but squawks could come from it.

But when he put it to his lips and blew, the sound was clear and clean and melancholy. He sat in the black leather chair, and the mysterious notes of the horn solo from the prelude to the third act of *Tristan and Isolde* fell darkly into the room. When he put the horn down on his knees the sound seemed to linger. Rob, who was sitting next to his mother on the small gold sofa, shoved closer up against her, and she put her arm around him.

Dr. Austin had taken over the fire-making from Vicky and Mr. Theo, who had not been very successful. Now he sat back on his heels and watched the flames take hold of the kindling and flicker brightly up the chimney. "You can have most of Wagner as far as I'm concerned, but *Tristan* still does something to me. It's going to be a hard choice for you, isn't it, Dave? Electronics or the English horn."

"Electronics," Dave said flatly. He took out his handkerchief and began wiping the horn. All during the dark and ancient notes of the solo he had been remembering the journey through the murky tunnel from the Cathedral crypt to the Bishop sitting on his strange throne in an obsolete subway station.

"The pragmatic choice, eh, Dave?"

"It's a pragmatic world."

Suzy sighed. "Okay, so what does pragmatic mean?"

"Practical," Vicky defined. "What works. Not idealistic. Right?"

"It'll do." Her father left the now blazing fire, shoved his wife and Rob over, and managed to squeeze onto the gold sofa by them. Rob wriggled himself free and got onto his father's lap. Vicky sat opposite Dave, leaning back comfortably in the broken-down wing chair and enjoying the fire. Mr. Theo and Emily were at the two pianos.

"Some scales to warm up with," Mr. Theo said.

Vicky enjoyed even this. The scales under their strong and disciplined fingers had the ease and swiftness of fish leaping upstream in a swiftly flowing river, and she imagined the notes as glistening silver fishes. At a signal from Emily the scales stopped and she and the old man began the Mozart sonata; for Vicky, sitting there with closed eyes, all was flickering light and shadow in a series of shifting patterns. In the country in the summer she liked to go down into the apple orchard and lie under the oldest of the trees, a gnarled tree too ancient to bear apples any more; she would lie against grass and roots and look up at the sky through the moving green leaves, green against blue that went up, up, into a gold infinity. When she would come back into the house Suzy would usually say, "Oh, Vicky's in one of her moods," and the beauty would break up into a squabble. The Mozart had the same effect on Vicky as the light moving through the leaves. She was glad that nothing more had been said about moving in with Suzy. Emily would not mind, or even notice, if Vicky were silent at bedtime. Emily understood silence, that good silence is something that comes from inside, not outside, and that little, unimportant things can break it more easily than the big ones. —I can be silent, properly silent, Vicky thought, —right in the middle of buses and taxi horns and ambulance sirens, so why do I let little things like Suzy dressing entirely in front of the mirror and not letting me have a look in break it up into noise?

The Mozart shifted from the introspective slow movement into a frolic of joy and laughter and swirled Vicky's thoughts along with the soaring melody.

—Well, it'll be all right, she thought, her spirits lifting. — Daddy's here, and he's listening without that closed look, and I wrote a sort of poem today in English and everybody thought it was good and nobody laughed at it, they really liked it, and maybe I should sort of dig out some of the other poem things I've written and go over them . . .

When the Mozart had concluded, leaving its joy lingering on the air, Mr. Theo asked Rob, "What's your French carol, boy?"

" 'Dors, ma colombe'," Rob said, and hummed.

Mr. Theo nodded in recognition, picked up the melody, and played a gentle variation as introduction.

Rob stood up, then reached down to take his mother's hand before singing. Even the structured happiness of the Mozart had not been able to take away for the little boy the incomprehensible sense of darkness, of illimitable void, left by Dave's English horn. Being the baby of his family, he was usually either very young or very old for his age; now, standing close to his mother, unwilling to let go the safety of her hand, he looked small and defenseless. But when he started to sing it was completely unselfconsciously, his treble clear and pure as a mockingbird's.

It was being a good evening, Vicky thought, sighing with relaxation. She stretched her legs out to the warmth of the fire, basking in firelight, in music, in sheer physical comfort and the sense of being with her own people, loved and accepted and safe. The idea of the genie was only something out of a dream world, and so it really held no threat . . .

Mrs. Austin, holding Rob's hand, holding this moment of peace, looked around at her family, at Emily and Mr. Theo, who had come very close to her heart, and thought that almost always when she felt this tangible sense of happiness it was followed by trouble.

Rob, of all the children, was the most fascinated by the Cathedral. Part of this may have been Mr. Theo's recurring suggestion that he leave the safety of going to the same school as his sisters and Emily, and go alone to the Cathedral School, to an unknown world of all boys and men. But part was simply the pull of the building itself. Its very size had an attraction for him. When he looked at it he felt somewhat the same sense of security that he got looking out of the windows of the house in the country and letting his eyes rest on the gentle hills and then on the great purple shoulders of the mountains beyond.

So, the next day after school, when the girls wanted to stop at the drugstore for something to eat, he said, "I don't want anything."

"We'll buy you some ice cream," Suzy offered.

"I'd rather go look at the Cathedral. Okay, Vicky?"

"Okay," Vicky agreed. "We'll come pick you up in a few minutes. Don't hide anywhere."

"I won't."

"Promise?"

"Promise. You know what?"

"What?" Vicky asked.

"If you went by the Cathedral at night you wouldn't see any flying buttresses."

Suzy turned impatiently towards the drugstore. Vicky, who was older, and Emily, who had never had a small brother, were more tolerant. They both asked, "Why?"

"Because they've all gone to bed. They never fly at night." He was not making a joke. He left the laughter of the girls, which he considered rude, and walked with dignity to the Cathedral, seeing in his mind's eye all the buttresses folding their wings like dragons and settling down for sleep.

He trudged up the long front steps. Behind him were two sightseeing buses waiting for their loads of tourists. Before him the building lay. —I will lift up mine eyes, he thought, and tugged at the heavy glass doors to the right of the great bronze doors; these were opened only on special occasions; Rob often stood and studied the scenes depicted on the panels. But now it was cold and he was in a hurry to get into shelter. The wind blew up the steps after him, and he could not, for the moment, get the door to yield against its power.

Behind him a voice said, "Let me help." He opened the outer door and smiled down at the little boy. "Hello. I'm Canon Tallis."

"Hello. I'm Robert Austin."

They stood looking at each other, both half smiling, half questioning, and indeed there was an odd resemblance between them, the little boy and the middle-aged priest, something about the firmness of gaze, the expression of the mouth, ready either to laugh or to steady into seriousness, that had nothing to

142

do with chronological age, that was neither too old for Rob nor too young for the Canon.

Canon Tallis opened the inner door. "Heavy, isn't it? Especially with the wind from this direction. I'm just taking a short cut through the Cathedral to the Deanery. What are you up to?"

"Nothing," Rob said. "I just like to look."

The sun fell lingeringly against the west front of the Cathedral as the Canon and the little boy entered; the long rays of light were refracted by the rose window over the state trumpets, by the crown of windows in the brilliant lantern of the Octagon, so that the stone columns soared upwards in the light, no longer massive supports of granite, but a structure made of color and air, rose, lavender, blue, holding the Cathedral in weightless effort.

The Canon followed Rob's gaze. "Beautiful, isn't it? At this time of day it's easy to see how light is part of the architect's plan, how sunlight itself is part of the skeleton, realized by stone."

Far ahead of them, looking small, so long was the nave, a group of sightseers trooped down the steps of the ambulatory by St. Ansgar's chapel and the baptistry. The guide's voice, sounding like a drone of bored and meaningless gibberish, echoed back to where Rob and Canon Tallis stood.

"Dave said the tour guides don't always tell things right."

The Canon picked up the name, not the information. "Dave?"

"He's a friend of ours. He's almost grown up. But he used to be a chorister here."

143

"That would be Josiah Davidson, then, wouldn't it?"

"Yes. How did you know?" Again Rob fixed the Canon with his piercing look. "You're the man who spoke to Emily when we saw the genie. And then I saw you again the next day by the newsstand and I knew you, and you knew me, and then you went away very quickly. And just now we both knew each other, but we didn't say anything about it."

The Canon looked at Rob thoughtfully. "Young man, how would you like to come over to the Deanery and have tea with me?"

"Can't," Rob said. "The girls are at the drugstore and they said they'd pick me up at the Cathedral. I didn't want any ice cream or anything, and they made me promise not to hide."

"The girls?"

"Vicky and Suzy, my sisters. And Emily."

"The musician."

"Yes. She's my friend."

"Where's Dave?"

"If he doesn't meet us after school he comes to the house around five to read for Emily."

The tourists were coming down the nave now. The guide had finished his spiel and was eager to herd his motley flock out of the Cathedral and into the bus. It was an oddly assorted group, some of the women conventionally dressed with hats and gloves, some casual, some with tissues on their hair ("Tissues are to blow your nose on," Suzy had said ferociously the first time she had seen one used as a head covering), some in slacks, some chewing gum, some already taking cigarettes from pockets or handbags to light as soon as they left the building.

In this conglomerate assortment the three boys in leather jackets did not seem particularly out of place, but the Canon, glimpsing them, abruptly took Rob by the hand and, holding him firmly, pulled him down the side aisle towards the sacristy.

"Hey!" Rob started to protest, loudly.

The Canon put his hand firmly over Rob's mouth, holding the little boy in front of his dark bulk until all the tourists, including the three boys, had gone out the glass doors, which closed slowly, protestingly, pushed by the cold wind which blew an icy draft down the length of the Cathedral. "Rob, you must *not* wander about alone, particularly here."

"Why not?" Rob asked. "What's the matter? You scared me! Let me go!"

"Sorry, old man," the Canon said, releasing him. "Rob, you realize that I've been keeping an eye on you?"

"Yes." Rob rubbed his wrist, which hurt from the priest's grip. "I told you so, didn't I?"

"You did. And did you tell your parents about me?"

"Of course."

"Of course." Canon Tallis echoed him. "Quite. Dave said all you Austins talk too much."

"How would you know what Dave said?"

"He told me when we were having tea together."

"Dave had tea with you!"

"Twice, as a matter of fact."

"But he didn't say anything to us about it—"

"If Dave told me that the Austins talk too much, then perhaps it's not to be wondered at that he himself doesn't?"

Rob thought this one over. "Has anybody else—I mean like Emily or my family—had tea with you?"

"Vicky—that's your elder sister, isn't it?—didn't have tea with me, but we did have a talk. Or at least we started one."

Rob's voice rose in indignation. "Okay, then, if nobody's telling me anything and everybody's treating me like a baby, they keep telling me to grow up but how can I if—well, okay, then, I'll go have tea with you."

"Hold it, Rob. Didn't you make a promise?"

Rob stamped, the rubber sole of his red boot muffling the noise against the marble floor. "Okay. Yes. I promised. I suppose I can't, then."

"And I don't think, Rob, that people are hiding things from you just because you're the youngest."

A fresh blast of cold air whipped about their legs as the glass doors opened again and the three girls came in, their striped red and navy school scarves up about their necks and faces.

"There they are—" Rob waved his hand, still in its scarlet mitten, "—my talkative sisters and Emily. Come and meet them."

Vicky called, "There you are!" to Rob, and her words continued to echo as she saw the man beside him.

"Hello, Vicky. We meet again. I'm Canon Tallis. Emily: hi, we met briefly one afternoon in the rain."

Rob walked deliberately around the bronze medallions set in the floor, not hurrying to meet the girls.

Emily scowled, recognized the voice, pulled off her right glove and stuck out her hand.

Canon Tallis took it in both of his. "Emily. Hello. You've a good hand for the piano."

Vicky was by now prepared to have the Englishman know things: her name; Emily's; that Emily was a pianist. Even to have him with Rob did not seem strange to her, though she could not have said why. As she watched the priest with Emily it seemed to her that he was examining the younger girl's hand only partly out of personal interest, and rather more to give Emily a chance to feel his own hands, to learn him a little, and this pleased Vicky and strengthened her instinctive feeling of confidence in him.

It was Suzy who demanded suspiciously, "Who are you and how do you know Emily's a musician?"

"Hello, Suzy Austin. Canon Tallis. I'm a friend of the Dean's and Mr. Theo's. And I've been making the acquaintance of your friend Josiah Davidson."

Suzy and Emily said simultaneously: "That beast Dave, why didn't he—"

"Why didn't Mr. Theo—he must have known—"

Rob had been standing silently beside the priest. Now he said, "I'm going to go have tea with Canon Tallis."

"Why don't we all—" the Canon started.

Rob's face had the stubborn look that both Vicky and Suzy had reason to know. "No. Just me. You asked me. You didn't ask them."

Canon Tallis understood at once that this was important to Rob, that the little boy wasn't just being disagreeable, that he knew that if the girls came to tea he would be the baby, an afterthought, left on the outskirts of the conversation, so he spoke to him seriously, man to man. "That is true, Rob. But there are things I would like to say to the girls, and questions I'd like to ask that you might not be able to answer. And I would very much like to meet your parents."

"Okay, then," Rob said. "I'll come to tea and then you can come home with me and have dinner with us."

"Rob!" Suzy said. "Grow up."

"It's very kind of you, Rob," Canon Tallis said, "but it might not be convenient for your mother."

"Mother wouldn't mind. Would she, Vicky?"

"I don't think so." Vicky sounded a little confused. "She likes us to bring people home for meals. Dr. Gregory says she runs a boarding house."

Emily surprised them all by saying in her most definite way, "I think it's a good idea and I'm sure Mrs. Austin wouldn't mind. Please come, Canon Tallis."

—Then, Vicky thought, —she must trust him because of the way his hands felt.

The sun had set with winter abruptness, and its rays no longer came through the windows; the brilliance of stained glass was eclipsed by night. The columns were more somber, now, as though the whole Cathedral were settling itself to bear the burden of the dark. Canon Tallis stood in the protection and shadow of one of the pillars and Vicky thought that he looked tired, and somehow sad. But he smiled as he said, "Thank you, Emily. I'll come, though I'll have to leave right after dinner." And to Rob, "Tea, then, old chap, but it'll have to be a quick one. Vicky?" she looked at him questioningly in response. "You the one in charge?"

"Yes."

"Warn your mother, then, please, and if it's not convenient

give me a ring at the Deanery. I have to be at Columbia at 8:30 to give a lecture, so the timing may be difficult for her. Meanwhile I want you three girls to walk home together. You are not to stray from each other for even one moment. You, Vicky, are to see to this. Can I trust you?"

"Yes, Canon Tallis."

"She thinks she's so big," Suzy muttered. "She's always being bossy."

But Canon Tallis heard. "Suzy, you're not in New England now. New York isn't your own safe little village."

"That's what Suzy's always telling *me*," Rob said.

"It's true for you, too, then, Suzy. The streets are full of people who don't love you and who don't even care whether or not you get hurt."

"I know that!" Suzy was indignant. "We've been in New York since September, and I've walked home alone and done errands for Mother and gone places by myself dozens of times. Anyhow, there are gangs in the country where we come from. They broke all the windows at school. It isn't just New York."

"I understand," Canon Tallis said. "But you've seen—we might as well call him a genie   now, and things are different. I don't want to frighten you, but you must stay together. Do you understand?"

"No," Suzy said rebelliously. "I don't believe in genies. I don't like this."

"It's not a question of liking," the priest told her. "Vicky. Emily. Go on home now before its completely dark. The three of you stay together. Come along, Rob. You and I will go this way." But he waited while the three girls went out the glass

149

doors together, Suzy hanging back a little but not quite daring to pull away, especially as Emily was holding her arm.

When the girls were out of sight the priest led Rob down the nave, slowing his pace to Rob's, waiting as the little boy carefully walked around each medallion, not stepping on the polished bronze. They went past the altar, and up the steps to the ambulatory, where the priest turned right and crossed the west entrance to St. James chapel. They went out through a side door which Rob had not used before and descended a flight of steps and walked through the Dean's Garden. The shadows of rhododendron bushes and chrysanthemums looked like draggled birds in the November evening. Beyond the garden, lights were on in the choir buildings, the Bishop's house, Cathedral House. The Cathedral offices were closing for the night, and two pretty young secretaries came out, called good night cheerily to Canon Tallis as though he were a particular favorite of theirs, and hurried down the path, talking and laughing. Rob followed Canon Tallis into the building, looking around in open curiosity.

"Never been here before?"

Rob shook his head, mouth slightly open, then remembered his manners. "No, sir."

"Not very exciting, is it? Mostly offices downstairs. Upstairs there's a nice dining room and meeting hall you might like to see sometime, and the Dean's study, which is a room I dearly love. We could have our tea in there, but I think there's a fire in the library in the Deanery, and this is Martha's day to clean for the Dean, so she'll have tea ready, and she sets out a splendid spread and knows all the things I like best. We'll need the fire there, too. I've kept the thermostat all the way down while the Dean's been away, but he'll push it right back up when he gets home from Puerto Rico tonight. He likes all your central heating. I don't."

"You'll be comfortable in our house, then." Rob followed the Canon into the library. "It isn't very centrally heated. It's supposed to be, but the furnace is elderly. But we have fireplaces there, too, and anyhow we're used to houses not being warm in winter. Our own real house in Thornhill was sort of cold, especially if there was a west wind, and Mother always fussed about our being frozen around the edges until the middle of April at least." He stood in the center of the library, looking around as he chatted. His gaze was arrested at the portrait. "Who's that?"

"Dean de Henares."

Rob shook his head. "The Dean has grey hair and he isn't thin like that and he's old."

"He was younger when that portrait was painted. Does it remind you of anybody?"

"Dave."

Canon Tallis smiled. "The Dean wasn't at all unlike Dave when they were the same age. If anyone had told Juan Alcalá de Henares that he was going to be a priest, much less the dean of a great Cathedral, he'd probably have bonged him."

Rob continued to regard the portrait with his small boy's gravity. "My grandfather said that Dave would end up a bishop, and Dave almost bonged him. You'd like my grandfather. If you're here for Christmas—he's coming to stay with us again for a couple of weeks then."

"I'm expected back in England by Christmas," the Canon said, "but who knows?" He gave Rob tea and crumpets, and poured himself a cup, stirring his sugar absent-mindedly, thinking that during this trip to New York he was spending more time drinking tea and coffee than solving the problem which had brought him across the ocean.

Rob's eyes had strayed to a slip of white paper lying on a silver salver on the table between the windows. "Is that a cable?"

The Canon picked up the slip. "What do you know about cables, young man?"

"Daddy got one from Dr. Gregory."

"Did he? Telling him that Emily's father was staying away another week?"

"How did you know?" It had become almost a refrain.

"My cable's from one of Gregory's friends." Canon Tallis handed Rob the white slip. "Here. You may read it."

Rob took the paper and read aloud, slowly and carefully, but not stumbling: "GREGORY STAYING EXTRA WEEK STOP CAREFUL OF FALLS. That's funny. That's what Dr. Gregory said to Daddy. CAREFUL OF FALLS. What do you suppose it means?" He held the cable close, then looked at the signature. "SHASTI. Do you know Dr. Shasti?"

"He's a friend of mine."

"But he's in Liverpool."

"So is Dr. Gregory."

"No," Rob contradicted. "He's in Athens."

"He went to Athens," Canon Tallis corrected, "but he flew from there to Liverpool. That's where he is now."

Rob shook his head. "But Daddy's cable said Dr. Gregory was staying another week in Athens."

"Are you sure?"

Rob replied with dignity, "I know the difference between Athens and Liverpool. I'm not that young. This is most peculiar."

"Peculiar indeed," Canon Tallis said.

Ten

Rob and Canon Tallis walked back to the Gregorys' house in a strangely companionable silence. Halfway home Rob reached out for the Canon's hand. The priest's grip was strong and steady and he did not let the little boy's hand go, nor tell him that he was too old for this kind of thing. As Emily learned through touch, so the Canon and Rob learned about each other walking wordlessly along the crowded streets and holding hands. Neither of them was aware of the boys in black jackets following half a block behind them.

At dinner Canon Tallis sat on Mrs. Austin's right. Rob was on his other side, and the little boy unexpectedly moved and touched him by saying, "We have to sing the Tallis canon for grace." He turned gravely to the priest. "In your honor, you know."

The family held hands, singing the simple melody as a round.

Be present at this table, Lord,
Be here and everywhere adored.

These mercies bless, and grant that we
May feast in Paradise with thee."

Tallis, listening, looking at Dr. Austin's kindly, guileless face, at the family holding hands around the table, understood Mr. Theo's indignant defense of the doctor.

But if suspicion were lifted here, then it fell on even stranger and more unlikely shoulders. He had to be sure.

For a while the conversation was general, easy, mostly about and including the children. They talked about the transition from the quiet village and the regional school to the great city and St. Andrew's. Emily spoke of the change the coming of the Austins had made in her life. Rob talked of his friends, the newspaper vendor, an Irish policeman, people walking their dogs in the park, Rabbi Levy.

—He will need his friends, the Canon thought.

"And you, Mrs. Austin?" he asked. "What has the change meant to you?"

She laughed, looking with affection at her family seated around her. "Not as much as I'd expected. I shop in different markets and cook on a gas stove instead of an electric one, but I still seem to spend most of my time in the kitchen. And this is fine. I'm really happiest in a domestic setting. And I'm no slave. The children all share in the chores. But I'll admit that I had visions of dressing glamorously and going to the theatre every week." She indicated her neat but not particularly stylish tweed skirt, her practical drip-dry blouse. Her face was devoid of make-up, and this emphasized rather than detracted from the fineness of her bone structure.

Dr. Austin apologized. "It's my fault we don't go to the

155

theatre more often. I'm up early and I bring home a great deal of work from the lab. But I really should take Victoria"—he looked warmly across the table at his wife—"to more plays. It's one of the things she was looking forward to in this move to New York."

"Mother used to be in the theatre," Vicky said, with pride.

Mrs. Austin moved her hands disparagingly, as though brushing off Vicky's words. "No, Vicky, don't exaggerate."

Suzy said, "She's not, for once. You *were* in the theatre, Mother. We have that album of records you made to prove it, so there!"

"In my extreme youth—" Mrs. Austin started.

"And pulchritude," her husband added.

"I sometimes sang in hospital wards, just folk songs and simple things."

"And a *night* club," Suzy said. "She sang in a *night* club."

Vicky looked at her mother cutting up meat for Emily. It was quite impossible to imagine this familiar figure in the setting of a New York night club. And yet there were, as Suzy had reminded them, the records to prove it.

Mrs. Austin flushed. "Just for a brief season. It makes me sound a lot wilder and more glamorous than I was."

"That's just the point," her husband said. "It was precisely because you were *not* wild and glamorous, because you were completely unselfconsciously your own self that you were irresistible."

—Like Rob? Vicky wondered. —The way he sings? Could be. She looked at her mother's familiar face, the greying ash-brown hair pulled tidily back. Suzy came honestly by her beauty, but Vicky was not yet objective enough to recognize her mother's classic features.

Dr. Austin gave a sudden, very boyish grin. "I wandered into a hospital ward one day, wondering where the singing and laughter were coming from, and there she was." His wife got up from the table and brought the salad over from the sideboard. "And look at her now, the picture of domestic bliss. *Sic transit gloria mundi*."

"No, it's Tuesday," Rob said, and couldn't understand why everybody laughed.

"But they don't make record albums of just *anybody*," Suzy persisted.

"Don't they?" her mother asked. "When I listen to some of the stuff you kids play, it seems to me that they do."

"We have eclectic tastes," Vicky said. "You wouldn't want us to be one-sided, would you?"

"It's amazing." Emily spoke in her clear and authoritative way, her brow clearing. "I suppose I'm glad Mrs. Austin stopped singing and married Dr. Austin and had all you kids, but she could have become famous, Canon Tallis."

"And rich," Suzy added.

Mrs. Austin shook her head. She was both embarrassed and annoyed. "Nonsense. I couldn't have been famous and I have no desire to be rich. I'm not like you, Emily. I didn't have any vocation to be an artist. Not everybody needs to, you know."

"The only actor I ever knew, even slightly," the Canon said, "suffered from that desire to be rich and famous, and when it started to slip from his grasp he became bitter and more bitter, until he finally dropped out of sight completely and died almost forgotten. Henry Grandcourt: he was a fine actor in his time."

"Henry Grandcourt!" Mrs. Austin said. "What was it I saw him in? Oh, I remember. *Coriolanus*. He was superb. I wondered what had become of him. So he died?"

"A resentful old man."

"He was a friend of yours?"

"In a way. He was brother to an acquaintance of mine. Someone you all know. Bishop Norbert Fall."

"That's who he reminds me of, then," Mrs. Austin said. "The Bishop, I mean. I knew there was somebody—so I suppose Henry Grandcourt was a stage name, then?"

"Yes. The Bishop supported him during his last years. He has a small place in Maine, and Grandcourt stayed there much of the time, a recluse, dreaming of a comeback. The Bishop was with him in Maine when he died, and I've always been grateful for both their sakes that poor old Henry didn't die alone."

Suzy and Rob began to clear the table and Vicky went out to the kitchen to bring on dessert and to refill the milk pitcher. When she returned, the conversation had shifted from the theatre to Dr. Austin's work on the Micro-Ray. He looked gravely at Emily as he explained how the laser was being used for cataract operations, so simply that the patient would not even need to be hospitalized once the technique had been perfected. Retinal detachments could also be taken care of with ease and very little danger or discomfort.

"And brain surgery?" the Canon asked.

"Yes. Here especially the Micro-Ray can be useful, because it can get at tumors that were inoperable before because they couldn't be removed without damage to the surrounding tissue."

"I read somewhere," Suzy said, "that grey matter—that's what we think with, it's what the brain's made of—well, the brain's the only place in our body we have grey matter except the tips of our fingers. Do you think that's so, Daddy? Emily thinks with her fingertips, doesn't she?"

Emily touched her fingers together with an interested expression. "I do. Much more than I used to, at any rate. Sometimes it's almost scary how much I can see with them."

"You'd have to ask a neuro-surgeon about that, Suzy," Dr. Austin said.

"If I ever see Dr. Hyde I'll ask him, then. But he scares me."

"Scares you why?" Her father looked at her keenly.

"I don't know. Maybe it's because he's so brilliant it makes me wonder if I have to be that brilliant if I want to be a surgeon."

"You want to be a doctor?" the priest asked.

"Some kind. Maybe I'll go back to being a vet the way I used to want to be. Animals are okay. They never talk back. Or maybe I'll just marry, like Mother, and have kids, and lots of dogs and cats and horses. You don't have to *be* something."

Dr. Austin smiled. "Hey, there. Don't you think Mother *is* something, Suzy?"

"Well, she's just Mother. She decided she didn't want to be something, didn't she?"

Mrs. Austin laughed. "It's not a choice of to be or not to be. It's a choice of what you want to be, or need to be. And I'm not sure we really have any choice. If I'd been meant to be a singer I couldn't have given it all up as happily as I did. How much choice do you think Emily has about her music? It chooses Emily as much as she chooses it, doesn't it?"

"I'm going to do my own choosing and make up my own mind," Suzy said stubbornly. "I think it'd be more fun to be a surgeon and perform great operations and cure people, than work on formulas the way Daddy's doing this year."

Canon Tallis picked this up. "Just what is your work, Doctor?"

"I design and make a small surgical instrument known as the Micro-Ray."

"This is on the principle of the laser?"

"Yes." Dr. Austin quite obviously did not want to expand the subject. "It's quite a change for me, who've spent so much of my life as a country doctor. In Thornhill we still weren't too far from the horse and buggy days, and we got very close to our patients."

"And here?"

"I work only in the lab."

"But you know something about the patients on whom your Micro-Ray is used."

"Yes. It's important for me to follow their case histories as closely as possible."

"How many patients are there, on an average?"

"It varies. There are three at present in the hospital, one a kidney graft, one a corneal transplant, and one a benign brain tumor which would have presented all kinds of complications a few years ago because of its inaccessibility. The surgeon couldn't have removed the tumor without destroying part of the brain, so calling it benign would have been rather foolish."

"How about the possible misuse of the Micro-Ray?" the Canon asked.

Dr. Austin finished his dessert, leaned back in his chair. "Anything can be misused."

"True. But the Micro-Ray's a powerful tool, isn't it?"

"Yes. And you're quite right. This makes it even more liable to misuse. But primitive man couldn't refuse to use fire, could he, because its misuse would burn down forests and homes?"

The Canon sighed. "We do love to oversimplify, don't we? Of course you're right. How about using the Micro-Ray for mental illness?"

"Certainly, where the illness is caused by tumor, or brain damage from a difficult birth, or accident, it may prove very useful."

"How about psychiatric use?"

"I don't advocate it." Sharpness came into the Doctor's voice.

"Is it being used at all in that way?"

"Not that I know of."

"How about using it either to stimulate or to sedate certain centers of the brain?"

"I would feel against it as strongly as I did against frontal lobotomies."

The children did not understand the conversation, but they felt the tension between the two men.

Dr. Austin asked, "You've worked with Dr. Calvin O'Keefe, haven't you, in his experiments with starfish?"

161

Canon Tallis rejected this idea much as Mrs. Austin had rejected Vicky's announcement that her mother had been in the theatre. "Not in the actual laboratory work. I'd be a bull in a china shop helping in the lab. Theology is of very little use in grafting nerve rings onto the central disc of a starfish."

"Wouldn't you say that O'Keefe's experiments with regeneration in the starfish were at least as dangerous and open to misuse as mine with the Micro-Ray?"

The Canon's face was cold. "Possibly." He looked at his watch. "Mrs. Austin, I must ask you to excuse me. I would much rather stay and continue talking than go on up to Columbia and lecture an ecumenical gathering. But Cardinal Forrester has the flu and I promised I'd pinch hit. Dr. Austin, if it wouldn't bore you, perhaps you'd come with me, and we could have a cup of coffee afterwards and continue our conversation."

There was a challenge in Tallis's voice, and the Doctor accepted it. "Yes. I'll come."

After the men had left, Mrs. Austin asked Vicky to walk Mr. Rochester. She or the Doctor usually took the dog on his evening walk, but an unformed anxiety made her loath to leave the children alone in the house without the protection of dog or parent. She knew that she didn't have to worry about Vicky as long as Mr. Rochester was with her.

Dr. Austin and Canon Tallis walked up Broadway towards the University. "Don't stop walking and don't turn around," the priest said, "but there are two boys in leather jackets following us."

"Following us in particular?"

"I rather think so."

There was only the slightest hesitation in Dr. Austin's step. "Why?"

"I noticed them when we left the house. They were standing in the shadows; they let us get about halfway up the block and then they followed."

"Why?" Dr. Austin asked again.

"I was hoping that you could tell me," the priest said.

They crossed 110th Street and continued uptown. Dr. Austin sighed. "I suppose they're Alphabats. It's a rather bad gang which Dave, the boy who reads for Emily, used to belong to. I hoped I was wrong but maybe I'm not. For the past week, about, there've been one or two walking behind me or just across the street when I've gone to take the subway to the hospital in the morning. In the afternoon when I've come home I've seen them near my subway stop."

"Do you know why they would be following you?"

"I wish I did." Dr. Austin looked about him at the busy street which had become familiar through daily association but which was, like Dave, still an unknown quantity to him. They moved through the conglomerate crowd of passers-by, students, old people shuffling along with canes, dog walkers, mothers with babies, light, dark, Oriental. "I'm a simple man, Canon Tallis. I'm not used to living in a melting pot. I have no idea why they're following me. This winter has in almost every way been more than I'd bargained for." He and the priest had gone beyond the shops now, many of them still open in the evening, florists, fruit stands, drugstores, paper stores, psychedelic cafés, and reached the conservative buildings of the University campus.

Canon Tallis led the way into the big open quadrangle and up the granite steps of the massive edifice that still bore the name of King's College. "How well do you know Josiah Davidson?"

"We see a good deal of him because of Emily. But I'm not sure anybody knows Dave very well."

"What do you think of him?"

Dr. Austin was slow in answering. He had to admit to himself finally that he was being followed as he went to and from work. He knew, too, that the English priest was trying to pump him, but there seemed no reason not to answer this question. "There's tremendous potential in Dave. But he's a confused kid, and still full of resentment."

"Does he ever talk about this gang he belonged to?"

"No. He quite naturally dislikes being reminded of that part of his past."

"You're sure that it is past?"

"I'm convinced of it."

An elderly, professorial type bore down on them, swept them in through the doors. "Canon Tallis? . . . *So* good of you to come. We're anticipating your talk with the deepest interest . . ." They were taken upstairs in an elevator and led to a lecture hall.

Walking with Rochester in the park, Vicky was feeling moody, not like her favorite, Emily Brontë, this time, or seeing herself as a character in a story, objective, happy, aware, playing her proper role. Instead she was turned in, confused, brooding anxiously about her parents, the genie, the English priest. She was unable to find a part for herself to play in the events of the past days. Whatever was happening, she seemed to be on the outside of the drama, while everybody she loved was being drawn in.

—And yet, she thought, —it's as though I were on the edge of the whirlpool, too.

—Slowly, inexorably, she thought, savoring the words, her imagination as usual helping to lift her gloom, —the young girl was being surrounded by dark forces beyond her comprehension . . .

But this was too close to fact to give her a pleasurable thrill. She shivered.

Rochester growled and pressed closer to her side.

She looked up. She had walked, in her reverie, into the midst of a group of leather-jacketed boys. She did not like the way the boys were staring at her, deliberately, insolently, from head to toe. One said something in Spanish, gave a mocking laugh. Another answered in coarse English, "Naw, leave her alone."

"Rochester, let's go!" she said sharply. She turned; the dog growled, and the boys parted to let her by. One of them turned his transistor radio on, full blast, right in her ear as she passed, and laughed noisily when she jumped.

She hurried home, more angry than frightened at her own stupidity in blundering into them. She had told Emily and Dave about her encounter with Canon Tallis but she would not, she knew, tell them about this. She wasn't going to have Dave make

165

her feel like a hick again. Anyhow, what was there to tell? She hadn't been paying attention to where she was going and she had walked into a group of boys. What was so sinister about that?

—But they *were* sinister, she thought, trying to concentrate on her studies. —It's not just my imagination. They were like the boys I met with Canon Tallis. He didn't want them to see him, and he told me to go home.

Her mother, hearing her sigh, asked, "Anything wrong, Vic?"

"Just life," Vicky said, "and a stinky old Latin translation I should have done last night."

She began to work diligently.

Dr. Austin enjoyed Canon Tallis's lecture. It was a concise and brilliant analysis of mob psychology throughout the ages in different countries and cultures. Babel and Babylon, Sodom and Gomorrah, Tiberius and Hitler; illustrations and examples were clear and pointed. The audience was silent, attentive, appreciative with applause. There was a reception afterwards. The Doctor drank punch that tasted like melted Jell-O and looked around him at the groups of people all wanting to talk to the priest. There were a good many other clergymen of various denominations, and a number of rabbis. He recognized Rabbi Levy from the synagogue down the street. There was a smattering of students, and most of the audience was masculine. They were not eager to let the Canon go, and Dr. Austin got into a long discussion with a psychology professor who was also a Baptist minister, while Canon Tallis had a conversation with Rabbi Levy, who was shaking his beard and waving his hands with enthusiasm.

It was after eleven when the gathering broke up, and Canon Tallis and Dr. Austin sat side by side at a counter drinking black coffee that helped take away the sickly sweet taste of the punch.

Picking up where they had left off, the Canon asked, "Why do you think Dave is through with the Alphabats?"

"Because of Emily." The doctor took a handful of paper napkins from the container and mopped up the coffee the counter girl had sloshed in his saucer.

"Why?"

"Because he loves her."

The Canon accepted this. "Tell me about Emily."

"Emily's quite a girl. We're all very fond of her. My kids can learn a lot from her."

"Such as?"

"Her acceptance of discipline, for one thing."

Two bearded students who had been at the lecture pushed through the door, their arms full of books, and spoke to the Canon, and were followed by two nuns, who entered into the conversation. When they had all gone on to find empty seats farther down the counter, Tallis said, "The discipline of music. And now the added discipline of blindness. That's quite a load for a child."

"Yes. But all Emily thinks of is how best to carry it, not how heavy it is."

"And you think Dave has learned something from this?"

"I hope we all have."

"What, in particular?"

Dr. Austin looked around at the assortment of people in the food shop, at the white-capped cook turning hamburgers, at the tired waitress mopping the counter. "In spite of it all Emily has remained completely herself, and untamed and free. I don't suppose she's old enough to realize that she's an extraordinary example of the fact that structure can liberate as well as imprison."

"Do you think Dave knows this? Not about Emily, but about himself?"

"Not yet."

"But you think he may?"

Dr. Austin half listened as the waitress called, "Two eggs, eyes open." He smiled slightly. "You said in your talk tonight that we often forget that freedom doesn't necessarily mean disobedience. It can also mean freedom to obey. This is something Emily knows instinctively. It's something I hope Dave will learn from her."

"One hamburger, with," the waitress called.

Dr. Austin continued, "He can't help seeing this kind of freedom in action every day when he works with Emily. He can't help hearing it when she plays Bach. He can't help noticing that when pride, or temper, or plain fatigue makes her disobedient, she comes to grief."

"So you think his feelings for Emily, even if they're largely unconscious, would preclude his running with a gang of young thugs?"

"I do. I have a lot of faith in Dave."

"What do you know about the Alphabats?"

168

"Nothing, really. I suppose they're an excellent illustration of what you were talking about tonight."

"Kids, nice normal kids," the Canon said, "turning into violent, destructive mobs." He looked at a group of teen-agers sharing banana splits and laughing. "Right here. Or in Russia, or China, or England. Everywhere. It's worse now than it's been in years."

"Why?"

"Why was the Black Death worse in the ninth century than in the nineteenth?"

"You think it's a disease, Canon Tallis?"

"Yes. That's the most frightening part. These kids who band together to do violence all show the classic symptoms of psychosis. The normal adolescent endures his confusions and resentments, as you and I did in our day, and grows up over them. The psychotic acts them out in violence and crime. This isn't original thinking on my part, by the way. I came across it in reading Robert Lindner. But it's prophetically true."

"An epidemic of psychosis, eh?" The Doctor closed his eyes, pressed his fingertips together, an expression of pain on his gentle, too vulnerable face. "Near Thornhill, where we lived in what seems the distant past, a gang of boys with no provocation took stones and broke every window in our excellent regional high school. Just a warning that the peace and quiet in which we lived was a precarious illusion. One girl who was hit and cut by a rock kept crying, 'But they were our friends! They were all kids we knew! Who can you trust?' I must admit that this episode was one of a number of things that made it easier for me to take my family away from our home and bring them here to the city."

Canon Tallis pushed his empty coffee cup across the counter. "How many people can you trust here in New York?"

Dr. Austin looked about him at the unknown people seated at the counter, at the little tables crowded along the wall. "I believe that people become trustworthy only by being trusted."

The priest gave a startled smile at hearing his own words come back at him from this gentle doctor so completely different from himself.

Dr. Austin continued, "I know that I'm infinitely more trustworthy because of my wife's faith in me. I know that there are all kinds of things I'll never do or say because she trusts me, and so do my children. But how sure am I of myself, really? Haven't you ever spoken when you should have kept your mouth shut, or not spoken when you should have stood up to be counted?"

The Canon looked somberly into the dark dregs remaining in his cup. "I am constantly being reminded by my own behavior that I am a fallen human being in a fallen world."

The Doctor smiled. "You sound like my father-in-law, who is not far from being a saint—"

"I am," the Canon put in.

"He would add that when we fall, as we always do, we pick ourselves up and start again. And when our trust is betrayed the only response that is not destructive is to trust again. Not stupidly, you understand, but fully aware of the facts, we still have to trust." He turned on his stool to look at the priest. "You're not sure you trust me."

Canon Tallis returned the look. "Nor you me." Then he asked, sharply, "Do you know your children are in danger?"

Dr. Austin put his coffee cup down with a jolt. "Danger? What do you mean?"

"Doctor, you aren't the only one in your family being watched. Why would someone be interested in your children or be in any way threatening them?"

"Does it—could it have something to do with their experience with the Aladdin's lamp and the so-called genie?"

"I think it must. Don't you?"

"Canon Tallis, the children saw you at the same time that they saw the genie."

"True," the Canon said, "and you are quite logically thinking that I may be a threat, too, and the fact that I wear my collar backwards doesn't automatically guarantee my reliability. I do often get into the predicament of seeming to be allied with the powers of darkness rather than the powers of light. If you care to get in touch with Dean de Henares at the Cathedral, he will vouch for me."

"I told you that I tend to trust people," Dr. Austin said, wearily. "I don't think you'd have accepted my hospitality this evening if you'd meant any harm to me or my family."

Tallis smiled. "Don't be misled by the old saw of honor among thieves. I've known people who would happily slit your throat as they left your table. Doctor, you do know that your own work may be endangering your children?"

Dr. Austin's face looked old and lined with anxiety. "But what am I to do?"

The Canon picked up their check, got down from his stool, and went to the cashier. When they stood out on the street again in the acrid November night, he said, "I've seen trust betrayed more times than I can count. I've also seen it kept when all odds were against it. The only thing I can tell you at the moment is to watch your children if you love them. See to it that they are never out on the streets alone. Do not, under any circumstances, go out in the evening with your wife, leaving them alone in the house, certainly not before Dr. Gregory gets back. I'm very glad you have the dog; they're all right when they're with him."

"Yes. Mr. Rochester's better than a private police force. But it's going to be difficult to restrict them without frightening them," the Doctor said. "You see, we know that we *can* trust them, and as a result of this we've given them a good deal of independence."

"Then you'll have to frighten them if necessary." Canon Tallis pulled a white slip of paper out of his pocket and handed it to Dr. Austin as they stood in a pocket of light by a flower shop. "This came to me from Dr. Shasti. Does it mean anything to you? It was sent yesterday from Liverpool."

Later that night after the Dean had returned, Tallis said to him as they sat in the library, "Austin knows something is going on, Juan, but he has no idea what. He's a naïve idealist in a situation that is beyond his comprehension. He's like a good child who lacks the sophistication to catch the scent of evil even when it's in front of his nose. I'm sure now of one thing: he's not the man you're looking for."

"Who is, then?" the Dean asked.

"I know what you're afraid of," Tallis said. "It's what I fear, too. But let's not put our suspicion into words until we're surer. Madness isn't easy to diagnose."

172

"Remember in Revelation," the Dean asked, "who the beast was?"

"Hush." Tallis put a firm hand on his shoulder. "What we must do now is keep an eye on Austin's children. They're in far graver danger than their father knows."

Eleven

In the morning at breakfast Dr. Austin looked up from his cup of coffee. "Everybody listen carefully."

There was something in his voice that made the children put down knives and forks with a small clatter. Rob choked over a bit of French toast.

"Emily, this is Dave's day to pick you and Rob up at school, isn't it?"

"Yes. Vicky and Suzy have art."

"You and Rob wait inside the building until you're sure Dave is there." He turned to his daughters. "Girls, your mother will come for you."

Suzy was not pleased. "Nobody gets called for except the really little kids. It's bad enough when you make me walk home with Vicky—"

"Just because I try to make you behave—"

"I do behave," Suzy protested. "I can't help it if the boys

fight over who's going to carry my books. I've got dozens of kids who'd walk home with me."

"Be quiet, both of you," their father said. "You will walk home with your mother because I tell you to, and there is to be no more discussion of the subject. I want all of you to understand that you are not to go out of doors alone unless you are with Mr. Rochester, and even then not without our knowledge. I realize that you are undoubtedly safer with Mr. Rochester than you are with your mother or me, but we want to know where you are at all times."

"Can I go to the corner now with Rochester and get your paper?" Rob asked.

This was Rob's regular morning job. "Yes, Rob, but if anybody approaches you or tries to speak to you, let me know. And you are not to talk to anybody."

"But I talk to lots of people! Every morning! If I don't say hello they'll think I'm very rude."

Dr. Austin thought that Rob, with all his friends along the street, was probably the safest of the children. If anybody tried to accost Rob, one of his many acquaintances would be sure to see and come to the rescue. "All right, Rob. Go get the paper. Here's the money. But I don't want you to dawdle this morning."

When Rob had gone, Emily asked, "Dr. Austin, what's wrong?"

"You rubbed a lamp, Emily, and you called up a genie, and since that day the city has been a dangerous place for us."

"Why?"

"It's dangerous at the best of times," Dr. Austin said. "These are just precautions, but I want you to observe them. You are

175

not to go out alone, and that goes for all of you. Dave or Mother will meet you at school in the afternoons, and with permission you may go out with Rochester. Understand?"

No. They did not understand. They only knew that this was not the time to ask any more questions.

French toast was a special treat, but not one of them was able to finish.

The Doctor walked them up to school. Mrs. Austin looked at the unappetizing mess of French toast and syrup that the children had scraped off their plates into Mr. Rochester's bowl, put most of it in the garbage, got out the vacuum cleaner and set about cleaning house.

In the late afternoon Mrs. Austin came in to the music room, where Dave was reading English literature to Emily. She dangled Mr. Rochester's leash in her hand. "Dave, Rob and I are going up to school to walk the girls home. You'll stay with Emily till I get back, won't you?"

"I am perfectly capable of staying by myself," Emily flared. "I'm not totally incompetent! In my own house I can see just as well as you can."

Mrs. Austin cut her off. "Calm down, Emily, and remember what you were told at breakfast. Dave——"

"I wouldn't leave her," Dave said. "She won't have her work done by the time you get back, anyhow."

Mrs. Austin and Rob walked Rochester up through the park. Evening had fallen, and the street lamps glowed. But the park had lost its beauty for her. It seemed dark and comfortless and full of unknown terrors. She held Rob's hand, forgetting that she had been trying to make him independent of her, to make him walk in the park and on the street without needing the security of the hand of parent or sister.

A group of small boys in navy-blue pea jackets came tumbling out of the school, banging each other with their book bags, galloping up the street, and shouting. Three young mothers, looking tired, followed slowly, discussing their jobs and what they were going to have for dinner. There didn't seem to be anything about the evening that was different from any other evening, and Mrs. Austin felt comforted. She said to Rob, "Stay right with Rochester, Rob. I'll get the girls. I won't be long."

Rob nodded acquiescence. He did not feel the same sense of comfort at the ordinariness of the school building and the noisy children as did his mother. His parents had never before showed fear in his presence, and only the Great Dane standing solidly beside him was unchanged, a symbol of security.

He almost fell flat as Mr. Rochester jerked unexpectedly to the end of his leash, barking ferociously. Rob, regaining his balance, looked around and saw two boys in leather jackets standing close by him. One of them said, "Hi, kid."

Rob eyed the boys warily, for Mr. Rochester had now pressed close up against him and was growling, ears flattened, tail rigid. One of the boys stepped back.

The other, holding his ground, asked, "Aren't you a friend of Dave Davidson's?"

Rob opened his mouth just enough to say, "Yes." He held Rochester on a short, tight leash. He knew that he was completely safe with the dog, and he also knew that Mr. Rochester never snarled in this way, lips drawn back, teeth bared, without reason.

"We're friends of his," the boy said. "We're his oldest pals.

He sent us to tell you he wants you to meet him in the Cathedral. Come along. We'll take you there."

Mr. Rochester moved slowly away from Rob and towards the boy, flattening himself as though he were about to spring. The boy took a step backwards. "Call your dog off."

Rob's voice was thin and small. "Go away, or I'll let Rochester at you."

The second boy called, "Let's go, *N*."

Mr. Rochester took another slow, deliberate step. The boy turned and ran. The one called *N*, falling back, gave a sickly grin. "Not very friendly, are you?"

"Go away," Rob repeated. "Rochester—"

The ferocious growl deepened, and the boy wheeled and ran down the street. Mr. Rochester gave a last warning bark, then moved back to Rob, his tail still pressed tightly against his body. Rob put his hand on Rochester's head, and the great dog turned to lick him.

The two boys had not in any way been menacing; the first one had said that he was a friend of Dave's. But why would Dave send someone with a message? Wasn't he still at the house with Emily?

Mrs. Austin came out with the girls, who were busily talking about art class. Rob turned from them to bend over Rochester and pat his head lovingly, in case any fright still showed in his face. Because everybody else seemed to be keeping secrets, for the first time in his life he held back and did not blurt out what had just happened.

On the way home they passed, as usual, the synagogue. The Rabbi lived above, and Rob looked up at his windows and saw that they were lit.

"I want to speak to Rabbi Levy," he said suddenly. "Is it all right if Rochester and I go up?"

His mother, too, looked up at the lighted windows. "Are you sure you don't bother him?"

"I asked him to tell me if I got in his hair, and he promised he would."

Suzy giggled. "Well, he's got more hair for you to get into than most people."

"More than Canon Tallis at any rate," Vicky said.

"You may go for fifteen minutes," Mrs. Austin told Rob, "but not a longer visit this time."

She waited until the Rabbi's buzzer released the latch and Rob and Rochester were safely through the door.

The little boy and the dog climbed the stairs.

If he could stay for only fifteen minutes there would not be time to tell everything, and this was what Rob really wanted to do, as he would have told his grandfather. He could trust his grandfather implicitly; he knew that he could also trust the Rabbi; and he knew that he could trust Canon Tallis: he *knew*.

The Rabbi was waiting at the top of the stairs. Rochester's tail was waving in delighted greeting: the wildly wagging tail was not an unmixed blessing; it had more than once been known to knock china or glass shatteringly off tabletops, including the Rabbi's, so the old man and the little boy waited for the first excitement of greeting to die down before going into the Rabbi's study. Rob loved the strange, mysterious books and was beginning to learn the Hebrew letters, but this afternoon instead of going directly to the book on the reading stand, as he would usually have done, he said, "Rabbi Levy, you're my friend, aren't you?"

179

"Of course, Rob. And you are mine, I hope?"

"Forever," Rob said seriously. "And if friends are in danger, they come to each other's rescue, don't they?"

"If they possibly can."

Rob reached into his pocket and drew out a roller-skate key; several pieces of string; three dog biscuits, one of which he gave to Rochester, who had to sit up and beg for it; an old pen of John's that no longer held ink; a tongue depresser; a rusty Brownie knife inherited from Suzy; a scrap of a poem of Vicky's which he had rescued from the wastepaper basket; an extra Braille stylus for Emily just in case she needed one; and finally several broken pieces of chalk. "If I ever need to be rescued," he said, "I'll try to write an *R* with this chalk where you can see it on the synagogue. I'd be much obliged," he said formally, "if you'd kind of keep a look out for my *R* every day, just in case."

The Rabbi did not laugh. "Very well, Rob. But do you have any particular reason to feel that you are going to need rescuing?"

"I'm not quite sure. I'd like to tell you all about it, but Mother said I could only stay fifteen minutes, and Rochester took up five of them, so there isn't time. It would just make me feel lots better to know you were feeling ready to rescue me if necessary."

The old man regarded the child who was standing, looking white and small, on the dark Oriental rug of the study. "I will be ready to rescue you, Rob. Do your parents know about this—whatever it is?"

"I'm not quite sure," Rob said. "That's why it's all so very peculiar. There's another thing I'd like to ask you, please."

"What's that?" The light from the colored glass of a Tiffany lampshade flowed over the Rabbi's long hair and beard, and

180

brightened his deep, dark eyes. In the warmth of this strange, rather foreign room, with its heavy dark hangings and massive furniture, Rob felt warmed and safe, and no longer small and cold and afraid as he had been out on the street with the strange boys. "Daddy keeps saying it's a small world in spite of the population explosion. Do you maybe know someone called Canon Tallis?"

The Rabbi looked sharply at Rob. "Why, yes. I met him only last night. He was the speaker at an ecumenical meeting I attended. I thought him brilliant but questioned a few points, and we got into a long and amiable argument afterwards, a good argument, the kind of sparking dialogue one is seldom privileged to have."

"He's all right, then, isn't he?" Rob asked.

"How do you mean, all right?"

"Would my grandfather think he was all right?"

The old man pondered for a moment. "He and your grandfather represent very different disciplines, as your grandfather and I do, and as Canon Tallis and I do. And yet we are very close, very close. Yes. Your grandfather would think he was all right. I presume you mean theologically?"

Rob hesitated. "I'm not quite sure what that means."

"The word about God," the Rabbi said.

"Oh. Yes. Well, if he's all right about that, then he's all right, isn't he? I mean, he has to be, doesn't he?"

"If he's really all right, Rob, yes. But no human being can ever be wholly all right. If we could—you're too young to have heard of Hitler, aren't you? And I don't suppose you've studied the Crusades—"

"Vicky has."

"If we were really all right, then we wouldn't be having race riots, or wars. We'd treat each other as human beings."

"But he does, doesn't he? Canon Tallis? Treat people as human beings?"

"Yes. I think he does."

"And you do."

"I try," the Rabbi said, rather heavily.

"And Mother and Daddy do. So that's a start, isn't it?"

"It is at least a start," the Rabbi said.

"I think my fifteen minutes must be up. You will remember about the chalk, won't you?"

"I will remember."

As Rob went to shake hands goodbye, he said once more, anxiously, "Please don't forget."

The Rabbi held the little boy's hand. "This is more than a game, or something in your imagination, isn't it, Rob?"

"Yes."

"Will you come tell me about it tomorrow after school?"

"Yes. I'll ask Mother. Goodbye."

Rabbi Levy stood at the head of the stairs and watched after the little boy and the dog as they descended to the dim front hall, then went into his study and to his window and watched as they turned up the street, both of them running to get home. He felt distinctly uneasy about Rob, as though he ought to have made the child stay long enough to spill out whatever was on his mind. A phone call to Mrs. Austin would have taken care of the time restriction, would have reassured her that Rob wasn't being a nuisance.

He looked at the open volume of Hebrew on which he had

been working when Rob rang the bell and to which he was eager to return. It was his life's work, the study of the demand for obedience given by God to his people.

He had tried to explain this demand once to Rob and Dave when the two boys, so utterly different in type and temperament as well as age, had been visiting him: at Rob's instigation, he knew; every gesture and movement of Dave's bespoke unwillingness.

"In a life in which there is no demand," he had told Dave, "there is no meaning."

"That's nuts," Dave had snarled rudely, then apologized. "Sorry, Rabbi, but demands are the whole trouble."

The Rabbi had stroked his shapeless beard, looking over his steel-rimmed reading glasses at the surly boy, who did not appeal to him at all. "If no demand is put on you, then you are in a sense excluded."

"From what?"

"Life itself. To be demanded of gives us dignity."

Rob, obviously not understanding, was nevertheless listening. He stood on tiptoe by the reading stand and looked over it at the Rabbi. Dave shrugged.

Rabbi Levy spoke severely. "If someone expects, demands something of you, it means he takes you seriously."

The angle of Dave's shoulder said quite plainly that he couldn't care less.

The Rabbi found that he had the stale taste of anger in his mouth. "Don't you see?" he asked, knowing that he was failing to make sense of any kind to Dave, "that the demand is that you take part in the huge cosmic struggle that is going on? Apathy is the gravest of sins." He turned from Dave to the fair little boy he had come to love. "Even the tiniest creature can shake the universe . . ."

He did not want Rob to be caught up and hurt in the battle.

He stood, now, at the window, watching Rob and Mr. Rochester turn the corner of Broadway and head towards the river. When they were out of sight he went to his books and papers. "Only obedience," he said aloud to the room, as though to convince himself, "is perfect freedom."

But obedience to what?

Was he, at this moment, in letting Rob go when the child was obviously in distress, disobeying the command that gave meaning to his life?

The Hebrew letters blurred and jiggled before his eyes. He took off his spectacles and wiped them on his beard.

He could not work.

He went out to the kitchen to make himself some supper.

On the crowded subway on the way home from the hospital, Dr. Austin looked again at Dr. Gregory's cable. He had examined it the moment he got home the evening before, and he had seen then what no one had noticed: the cable said that Dr. Gregory was staying in Athens, but it had been sent from Liverpool. Had Dr. Gregory expected Dr. Austin to notice this? Was it supposed to be some kind of warning like CAREFUL OF FALLS, assuming that meant anything? And why had Emily's father gone to Athens, and then, evidently, to Dr. Shasti and Dr. Shen-shu in Liverpool?

Twelve

After Mrs. Austin had left with Rob and Rochester to pick up the girls at school, Dave had found himself unusually restless, unable to concentrate on the book he was reading to Emily. He read her the words but his mind strayed far from the adventures of Achilles.

"Mind what you're reading," Emily said. "The *Iliad*'s confusing enough as it is."

"Just pay attention and shut up." He envied inchoately Emily's singleness of purpose with her music. When he finished trade school in the spring he could, he knew, get a job, either with his English horn (but I will not be a starving musician) or in electronics. But he saw no reason for a job; he had no aim, except a vague desire to make a great deal of money, to get even with "them." But he did not know who "they" were. Were "they" the Cathedral, who had opened doors for him and then left him on his own, to go through the doors or not as he chose? Or were

185

"they" the Austins, who were so secure in each other that they could open the doors of their family wide for Emily, for Dave?

Emily had walked in.

Dave was afraid of open doors.

—What's in it for me? he thought. —If I go in, if I start loving them, I lose my freedom. Emily, okay. I accept Emily. She's blind and her father lives in a world that's been dead twenty-three hundred years, and Mr. Theo doesn't see anything but music. Emily's needed me. She couldn't have managed without me. But she doesn't really need me any more. She's got the Austins . . .

So when Mrs. Austin returned with the girls he put Emily's book down, demanding gruffly, "Where're Rochester and Rob?"

"Visiting the Rabbi."

"I'll be off, then."

Suzy asked wistfully, "Aren't you staying for dinner?" She gave him her most winning look.

"Not tonight." Dave did not add thanks. He pushed into his jacket and out into the November wind.

N and *P* were waiting for him on the corner of 110th and Amsterdam. "Bishop wants you," *P* said.

"What for?"

N glowered. "That damn dog. He couldn't expect us to get by that damn dog."

P stuck his hands in his pocket. "They locked Phooka's and I want the lamp. It wasn't our fault. That dog could of kilt us."

"He wants the little kid," *N* said. "But the dog—"

186

"Shut up." *P* jerked his head towards Synod House. "C'mon."

"Too many damned dogs around this place anyhow," *N* muttered.

And as they turned towards the iron gates of the Cathedral Close they came face to face with Canon Tallis and Cyprian.

If Rochester, when angered, could look fierce, Cyprian could look ferocious simply by being friendly. But Cyprian was not looking particularly friendly. He gave an asthmatic snort. Before it could turn into a menacing growl the two Alphabats had evaporated around the corner.

"Friends of yours?" Canon Tallis asked Dave.

"I don't go in for friends," Dave answered sullenly.

"Going some place?"

"What's it to you?"

Canon Tallis looked thoughtfully at the boy. If Dave had not been wholly cooperative during their previous meetings, at least he had not been discourteous. "Got the wind up about something?"

"I don't know what you're talking about."

"Something on your mind?"

"Plenty."

"Cyprian and I weren't going anywhere in particular. How about another cup of tea?" —Tea again. Oh, well, all part of the drill . . .

"Nix," Dave said, then mumbled, "Sorry," and "Thanks." He glanced towards Synod House. "Bishop still in his office?"

"Yes, I believe he is."

"I think he wants to see me."

"What makes you think that?"

"I think he sent me a message."

Canon Tallis looked at his watch, then turned towards Synod House. "Let's go along and see, then."

They walked down the path in silence. It was past five o'clock and the entrance to the offices was closed. Canon Tallis took out a bunch of keys and opened the door. Dave did not tell the priest that he himself had a passkey. Why did he, who was so afraid of open doors, always carry keys?

The secretaries had all left, and the entry was only dimly lit. Canon Tallis left Cyprian by the door, telling him sternly to sit and wait, and led Dave through the empty reception room and knocked on the inner door.

"Yes?" Even in the monosyllable, the Bishop's superb voice was unmistakable.

The priest opened the door. "My Lord," he said, addressing the Bishop in the English manner, "young Josiah Davidson here has reason to believe that you wish to see him."

"Yes. Send him in, please." The Bishop looked at the ormolu clock that ticked steadily in one corner. "Is six-thirty convenient for you, Canon?"

"Fine, my Lord."

"My house, then."

Canon Tallis nodded in agreement, then nodded to Dave, who went into the office.

Bishop Fall sat in a chair of carved wood and cerise velvet, pushed slightly back from his fruitwood desk. He wore a deceptively simple dark suit; above his clerical collar his face was serene, framed with his extraordinary hair that was more an apricot color than a mixture of red and grey. There was nothing in the least simian about his looks as he sat there, and Dave wondered at the trick of light in the subway station that had made the Bishop's skull look like a monkey's. The whole memory of the scene in the subway station still had for Dave the unreal quality of a nightmare. He could not have told anyone with assurance that it positively had happened.

At the far end of the room stood Amon Davidson, fitting an ebony wall bracket for a superb small marble of David and Goliath. He looked up at the sound of the door, saw that it was his son, and continued his work without the slightest expression of recognition or greeting.

To the right of the Bishop, overpowering the delicate gilt chair on which he sat, was the huge bulk of Dr. Hyde. He looked up and smiled in greeting, but did not extend his hand. "Emily coming along all right with her schoolwork?" he asked Dave.

"Reasonably well, sir."

"Theotocopoulos not pushing her too hard?"

"You can't push Emily too hard as far as music's concerned."

"Everything else progressing satisfactorily?" Dr. Hyde directed his next words to the Bishop. "Emily has been so quick to learn that it has been a particular satisfaction to me to have arranged for her training since her accident, lessons in Braille, techniques of using the cane—she's a remarkably acute child."

"Sit down, Davidson, my boy," the Bishop said. "Dr. Hyde, here, has been a support to me as well as to our young friend,

189

Emily. Without his ministrations my health would never have allowed me to carry out my work as I have. He is not only my physician, but also my friend. I've called him here this afternoon because I can depend on his advice and suggestions, and because of his connection with the Austins and the Gregorys. Also, as a brain surgeon, he is well trained in putting together the pieces of a puzzle. How about you, my son? Have you begun to see the picture?"

"No, Bishop," Dave said. "There just seem to be more pieces and more of a mess. I know a little more about Dr. Austin's work, but that's something Dr. Hyde can tell you about far better than I."

"The sad truth of the matter," Dr. Hyde said, "is that I cannot."

"Sir?"

"You say you know something of Austin's work, Davidson?"

"Just a very little."

"But you understand of what importance it is?"

"I can guess."

"Do you think a colleague should withhold important information from his superior?"

"I don't know much about it, Dr. Hyde."

"Davidson," the Bishop said. "I have known Dr. Hyde for many years. When he tells me that Dr. Austin is withholding from him certain formulae and equations which are essential to him for his work, I do not doubt his word."

"I don't understand, Bishop. Why would Dr. Austin keep anything from Dr. Hyde?"

"We were hoping that you might be able to help us answer that question."

"No, sir. I can't."

"I am correct, am I not, Davidson, in thinking that you have observed Dr. Austin a little more carefully than usual this past week?"

"Yes, Bishop."

"And you've seen nothing?"

"Everybody's been edgy and jumpy. Dr. Austin's looked tired and worried. But there hasn't been anything definite."

"Mail," Dr. Hyde said to the Bishop.

"Tell me, Davidson, has Dr. Austin had a letter from Dr. Shasti or Dr. Shen-shu lately? Or has he written to them?"

"Not that I know of, sir."

"Did you know Dr. Shasti or Dr. Shen-shu?"

"No, sir. They had already gone to Liverpool when I came to read for Emily."

"Do you know why they left New York after Emily was blinded?"

"Well, I think that they were only here on a two-year grant."

"You imply that they would have had to leave the United States in any case? That they had nothing to do with Emily's— accident?"

"Well, Bishop, from what Emily says the only thing they had to do with it was that she was in their apartment when she was attacked."

"Davidson." Dr. Hyde stood up; the gold and damask chair, relieved of his weight, made a small, cracking noise. He and Dave stood face to face, the boy's thinness emphasized as it was when he stood near the Dean. "What you must understand is that Dr. Shasti and Dr. Shen-shu were working against me. When they fled to England they took with them the results of work they had done in my lab. Their formulae are now in the hands of a foreign power. Although since they themselves are foreigners they may not realize the difference. The problem with which the Bishop and I are concerned is that they seem to have managed to get Dr. Austin to carry on where they left off."

"Why are you telling me this?" Dave asked. "I don't want to know." He knew that Dr. Austin sometimes did get letters from Liverpool. It had never seemed sinister before. He was drawn to Dr. Austin as much as to any adult. He did not care for Dr. Hyde despite his kindness to Emily. "Bishop, I can tell you one thing. I don't know anything about Dr. Austin working with Dr. Shasti and Dr. Shen-shu, but I do know that he doesn't have anything to do with the Alphabats."

The Bishop and Dr. Hyde exchanged glances. "How do you know, Davidson?" the Bishop asked. "Perhaps I know more than you do. Perhaps I even have some of the Alphabats—or ex-Alphabats—working for me. Is this any more strange than that I should be driven underground, that I should have had to use members of your old gang to bring you to me?"

"I thought that was my father's doing."

Amon Davidson turned for a fraction of a moment from his work.

"Your father has been most helpful in putting me in touch with sources of information which otherwise would have been inaccessible to a mere bishop." He smiled, then instantly sobered. "Davidson. You love Emily Gregory, don't you?"

"Yes."

"Do you want to know who attacked Emily on the afternoon that she went, in her childish innocence, up to what is now Dr. Austin's apartment? Would you like to know who was responsible for her blindness?"

Dr. Hyde looked briefly at Amon Davidson, then said, "I think we'd all like the answer to that question, Bishop."

"That justice may be done," the Bishop said. "We're close to an answer, Davidson. But I need your help."

"How can I possibly help?"

"I want you to bring the little Austin boy to me," the bishop said. "I want to talk to him."

"Rob? Whatever for?—sir."

"Out of the mouths of babes . . ." the Bishop said.

"I don't get it." Dave stared at the Bishop.

"I don't ask you to get it, Davidson. I simply ask you to trust me. I ask you to trust me without question, even if what I request seems strange or unreasonable. I'm close to solving this most difficult of puzzles. There are only a few small pieces to put into place, but if I do not get them, everything will fall apart again. I know that you are not concerned for your own safety, but Emily is being threatened again, and the little boy is in grave danger. If you will bring him to me this evening, as I ask you to do, I will be able to protect him. Otherwise . . ." The Bishop lowered his voice: "If I canot keep these streets from running with blood—and I have not given up hope that I can prevent a holocaust—I can at least take the little boy where he will be safe. This is all I can tell you now, my son, and it should serve to show my trust in you. Will you do as I ask?"

"Here?" The Bishop had asked Canon Tallis to come to his house, Dave thought. If Canon Tallis were in on this, then it might be all right. . . . Confusion and uncertainty swarmed about him like a dark cloud of insects.

"No. He will not be safe here. Bring him to St. James chapel. We will meet there at seven-thirty."

"Sir," Dave said. "If I bring him—just me, understand, please. I don't want any of the Alphabats around."

"Davidson, Davidson, what can you think of me? They are errand runners, and it gives purpose to lives that otherwise would have none, does it not? Where do you think those boys would be if I didn't find small jobs to keep them occupied?"

"I don't know," Dave said. "I don't see them any more than I have to. I don't like the company they keep."

"And the company you kept?"

"Not any more."

"Not any more for them, either, Davidson. They are redeemed. No more holdups for money for 'pot' or 'acid.' No more running as an angry and rebellious gang. They have something to work for now, to give their lives to."

"What?"

"The redemption of this city. And that is what I want you to help me with, Davidson. The Church is often accused of turning its back on the very people who justify its existence, the poor, the dregs, the addicts, the bums, the prostitutes and pimps, the discriminated against. We are afraid of them, we comfortable people, so we ignore them instead of giving our lives for them."

"You promise Rob will be all right?"

Dr. Hyde said, "Don't blame the boy, Bishop. It's no wonder that he's confused."

"Of course I don't blame him."

"How long will it take?" Dave asked. "I'll have to tell his parents when we'll be back—if I can think up an excuse to take him out."

"Only a few minutes."

"I'll try," Dave said. "I don't know if I can manage it."

"I have more faith in you than that." The Bishop indicated that the interview was at an end. Dr. Hyde let Dave out of the office.

The boy stood on the steps of Synod House and sniffed the cold winter air. Above the bare trees the stars were clear. The light still shone through the beauty of the slender lancet windows of the Octagon. Canon Tallis and Cyprian were nowhere to be seen. If he had bumped into them now he might almost have broken his vow to the Bishop and told Canon Tallis everything. But the Close was deserted.

He went back to the Gregory house to get Rob.

Thirteen

At six-thirty promptly Canon Tallis presented himself at the Bishop's house and was admitted by the butler. The Bishop's rather impressive staff of servants was new since the Canon's last visit to the Cathedral, and in marked contrast to the efficient but plain couple who had run the house and the Bishop for many years.

This was one of the things Tallis had questioned the Dean about.

"The old pair did get rather elderly for the work, Tom. But the Bishop has seemed to get unexpectedly elegant in his tastes in the past year. Everything was always rightly and properly done before; you know Fall; he can't stand anything slipshod or shoddy, to the point of scrupulosity, and that includes his domestic life. But I have been disturbed lately by a tendency to—well, Tom, there isn't any word but ostentation. And it doesn't go with his humility in other areas. But that, too, is becoming exaggerated. And his fear of unworthiness—Tom, he assists at Mass.

He serves, but he never celebrates. It's another of the strange contradictions which mounted up until they grew to a reason to ask you to come. Something's wrong, and I don't know what. I've admired and trusted my bishop for a great many years. I can't be objective about this. You know I wouldn't have sent for you if it weren't necessary."

Now Bishop Fall kept Canon Tallis cooling his heels for several minutes. The small reception room in which he waited was noteworthy only because of the fact that one wall was devoted to a photographic history of the Bishop's brother's career. Tallis amused himself, as no doubt he was intended to do, by looking at the Bishop's brother as Coriolanus, as the Player King in *Hamlet,* as Montecelso in Webster's *The White Devil.* Coriolanus was undoubtedly the actor's most important role. There was a superb photograph of Grandcourt as the lamplighter in *Cyrano de Bergerac* but, as Tallis remembered the play, the lamplighter had only one small, peripheral scene. There was a splendid picture of Grandcourt as Cardinal Wolsey, though the Canon did not know from what play, in which the actor bore a striking resemblance to his brother the Bishop, though Grandcourt's hair was dark, indeed almost black, in contrast to the Bishop's pale red.

In the doorway the butler cleared his throat to get Tallis's attention.

The Bishop and Dr. Hyde awaited the Canon in a large and formal drawing room furnished in ivory brocades and brown velvets. As he entered the room Tallis noted a Rouault Christ on one wall, a Miró on another, a portrait of Grandcourt as Wolsey over the mantelpiece: it was in all ways a beautiful room, a costly room.

"Tallis? He's all mind." The Canon heard the Bishop's clear

and beautiful voice, the voice that could carry through the great Cathedral without amplification. "He's the coldest human being I've ever run across. I think he positively enjoys watching people suffer just to see what they'll do next when he could so easily help them. He has no idea what love is about. Perhaps it's his work. He's so busy being a sleuth he's forgotten he's a priest."

—No, Tallis thought, —that is something I never forget.

But would the words have hurt so, had there not been a grain of truth in them?

Had his own fear of showing how deeply he cared (and therefore how deeply he could be hurt) kept him from giving the word of reassurance, the touch of tenderness the moment's need demanded? Dr. Hyde had gone to great pains to help Emily and yet given nothing of himself. Why is it so difficult to reach out and take a hand, to say, 'Yes, I love you. I care. You matter to me'?

In the doorway the butler cleared his throat again to get the Bishop's attention. Then he announced the Canon.

The Bishop said, "Dr. Hyde is my personal physician and is in my complete confidence. You may speak freely before him. I asked him to be here this evening precisely because I thought he might be of some use to you in your investigation."

Canon Tallis skipped preamble. "Dr. Hyde, do you have similar confidence in Dr. Austin?"

Dr. Hyde had his pale hands, already scrubbed-looking, as though for an operation, spread out on his knees. He looked down at them and stretched his fingers apart. "No. I can't in honesty say that I do."

"Why not?"

Dr. Hyde continued to contemplate his hands as though they held the answer to the question. "When Shasti and Shen-shu left I thought we could carry on with a reduced staff, and I managed to do so for two years. But the pressures on me were beginning to be intolerable. I simply could not continue alone. Therefore I offered the post to Dr. Austin since he was the only other pioneer in the field of the Micro-Ray."

"But Dr. Austin is not a surgeon."

"Precisely. Therefore he could relieve me of the research and other practical laboratory problems so that I could spend more time in the operating theatre."

The Bishop leaned back in a champagne-colored damask arm chair which set off his apricot hair, and closed his eyes. Lamplight fell on the pectoral cross, set with rubies and emeralds, which lay on his purple rabat. Canon Tallis remembered that the last time he had seen the Bishop the cross had been simpler, and hung on a considerably less ornate chain.

"Is Dr. Austin," the Canon asked, "making the same kind of relatively inexpensive and simple Micro-Ray that doctors Shasti and Shen-shu were working on?"

"Yes, although his has been carried several steps further."

"How simple is this instrument?"

Dr. Hyde gave a thin, pale smile. "If I had the formula I could take one of the stones from the Bishop's cross, dismantle a ball-point pen, buy a few things from any supply house, and have at my disposal the kind of instrument I need only for the most delicate operations."

"*If* you had the formula."

"Shasti and Shen-shu made the Micro-Rays for me, as

Austin does now. Shasti is Indian, Shen-shu Chinese; one expects Orientals to be devious. I have, during my career, worked with a number of highly respected Eastern men of science, and I have learned that their intellects are second to none, but they lack loyalty and honor."

Tallis said, "The instrument is simple, but the formula is not?"

"You might put it that way." The Doctor sounded irritated.

"As I understand it, the instrument, unless it is absolutely accurately made, can burn and destroy instead of producing a cool light that heals?"

"More or less. You wouldn't understand it, I'm afraid, if I explained it more technically."

"No, I'm sure I wouldn't. I can see that you might not be pleased not to have the formula at your own fingertips, but a Micro-Ray takes a considerable time to assemble, doesn't it?"

"Yes."

"And surely isn't the main thing to conserve your valuable time and to have the instrument at your disposal?"

"Surely you can see," Dr. Hyde said, "that it is more complicated than this?"

"But is the formula really being deliberately withheld?"

"It is."

"And yet, Dr. Austin continues to provide you with the instruments you need for your operations?"

"Thus far."

"What is the life of one of the Micro-Rays?"

"About twenty-four hours."

"And then it's finished? Useless?"

"Yes. Of course that's one of the things being worked on, greater stability and durability."

"Has Dr. Austin—or did Shasti or Shen-shu—provide any other hospital with their instruments?"

"Not as far as I know. Remember, Reverend" (the Canon shuddered), "that the use of the laser is now general. But the Micro-Ray as refined by the Orientals and Austin is completely unique, infinitely superior as well as infinitely simpler, than any other device being constructed today."

Canon Tallis turned towards the Bishop, who sat with his eyes still closed but an alert and listening expression on his serene face. "My Lord, I think I can understand Dr. Hyde's annoyance, but not why you have used the word *sinister* in describing Dr. Austin."

"Ah, Canon, that is the question, is it not? I had hoped that you would have been able to answer it for yourself by now. Whoever controls that gun can control the mind. Think of that, Tallis. Think, Tallis, think of this city. Think of the rottenness with which this Cathedral is surrounded. Think of the stench of corruption that rises from the streets. Think of the sin and evil, the crime and murder that—" interrupting the flow of his own words, the Bishop held up his hand for silence. "Listen, my children, listen."

Around them they could hear the uneasy breathing of the city. An ambulance wailed. There was a sound that might have been gunfire, or a car's muffler backfiring. Horns honked. Brakes screeched. Tires screamed. There was the distant wail of a child. "The sound of terror, Canon," the Bishop said, "Listen. It has become the same in every city in the world. All our churches, all our police force, firemen, ambulances, relief agencies, are waging a losing battle against the plague of violence that has stricken our cities. But now: imagine that someone has a Micro-Ray. He can take the most hardened criminal; he can then touch his brain with controlled light in such a way that the man can become a lunatic, even worse than he already is, or docile as a little child."

"But that's monstrous," the Canon said.

"It can be. Misused, it is. Or misunderstood, as Austin fails to understand it. But now think. Think of the possibilities. Think of taking a vicious degenerate, someone whose willful descent into evil has made him subhuman in every way. A brief and painless touch by the Micro-Ray can turn him into a happy law-abiding citizen. What do you think of that?"

For a long moment Tallis did not answer. Then he said, "My Lord, I think that is monstrous, too."

"Why?"

"Because it would be to take away man's freedom, my Lord. Because to take away a man's freedom of choice, even his freedom to make the wrong choice, is to manipulate him as though he were a puppet and not a person."

"You persist in extolling this freedom even when it is abused? And even when this abuse can be corrected?"

"I have spent my life trying to correct the abuse, my Lord."

"And yet you balk now at the means to correct it?"

"Surely you are not serious, my Lord."

"I have never been more serious."

Tallis answered, heavily. He looked infinitely sad. "I don't believe in the value of instant virtue, my Lord. I don't believe in instant goodness."

"You reject instant goodness for constant badness?"

"A young man I cared about very much," Tallis said, "was murdered last summer in Lisbon because of the kind of constant badness, of evil, that you so rightly say is spreading like a plague in our cities. And yet: to save him by a beam of light shifting and changing the brain patterns of his enemies: my Lord, isn't that as much murder as firing the gun which ended his life?"

Dr. Hyde rose, angrily. "You would, I assume, have been against vaccination at the time smallpox was endemic? Or against the pasteurization of milk? Or—"

Canon Tallis cut him off. "Hardly, Doctor. The deliberate changing of personality, of taking away someone's identity, of destroying his integrity, is not the same thing as inoculation against disease. I agree that the violence in our streets is a disease, but this is neither the proper preventive nor the cure."

The Bishop rose. "You have not seen these regenerated people, Tallis. I have. I hardly think it murder. But we are straying from the point. We are talking not about the use but about the misuse of the Micro-Ray. Or the refusal to use. We are talking about Dr. Austin. The Dean and I brought you here from England to investigate Dr. Austin. I gather your investigations thus far have yielded little fruit. I wished to leave you alone as long as possible, to give you that freedom which you value so highly but understand so little. I feel that the time has now come when I must tell you that I personally believe Austin to be a dangerous man. I want you to watch him more carefully, and to investigate him further. I gather you learned little or nothing the other night when you were at Gregory's mansion for dinner. Yes, Tallis, I know you were there." He paused, waited until silence lay coiled like a snake in the room. "Is Austin my enemy, Tallis? Or are you? Or are both of you?"

When Dr. Austin got home from the hospital, tired from long standing in the subway (he was old-fashioned enough to have given his seat to an elderly woman and modern enough to have made sure that it was she and not somebody else who got it), he asked his wife for the mail.

"You have an airmail letter from Dr. Shen-shu," she said. "It cost him a fortune in stamps."

He glanced cursorily at the rest of the mail, pushed it aside, and took the letter from England. "I'm going to the study. Bring me a cup of coffee." So might he have spoken to a nurse during an operation, or to a lab assistant during a critical experiment, his mind wholly preoccupied with what he was doing. He was not in the habit of giving his wife orders in this peremptory manner, and he did not even notice her startled reaction.

She went out to the kitchen to make the coffee. Suzy was there before her, interestedly inspecting the roast in the oven, the saucepans on the stove. Suzy could (and did) eat an incredible amount of food, and her weight was always just what it ought to be, her complexion unblemished peaches and cream.

"New York's an island city, isn't it?" she asked her mother, wrinkling her nose in distaste at the spinach in the steamer.

"Put the lid back on the steamer," Mrs. Austin ordered automatically, measured water and coffee, plugged in the percolator. She was trying to concentrate solely on counting out cups of water, spoons of coffee, in order to keep from feeling panic and hurt at her husband's words. Why was it suddenly so important for him to get a letter from Dr. Shen-shu when the two men had been corresponding for years? She had a sensation of being completely shut out from her husband's life, and since whatever it was that he was hiding concerned her children, her cubs, she stood, her body tense as a lioness', ready to spring.

"But it doesn't seem like an island, Mother, with all the bridges and tunnels and subways and buses connecting it to every place. We seemed to be much more on an island up on our hill in Thornhill."

The coffee was bubbling up in the percolator. Mrs. Austin sat down at the kitchen table. "Thornhill probably was more of an island, at that."

"Today I had a free period in the library, and I'd finished my lessons and I was poking about looking for a book to do a report on, and I came across this old book—"

"Which old book?" Mrs. Austin corrected, but she was not really listening to her child. Her ears were cocked for any sound that might come from the study.

"An old book by this old writer," Suzy answered, "I mean *an* old writer, Ernest Hemingway, and in the beginning of the book there was this quotation—*a* quotation by—oh, who is it Grandfather loves so much?"

"Einstein?"

"No, no, not anybody like—"

"Lancelot Andrewes? St. Chrysostom?"

"No, no. Oh—"

"Lewis Carroll?"

"No, Mother, oh do please keep quiet while I think! The quotation was about how no man is an island—"

"John Donne."

"Yes! And it's all about what Grandfather's always saying, how we can't love each other if we separate ourselves from anybody, anybody at all, and how anything that happens to anybody in the world really happens to everybody. And Grandfather says that you sort of understand this especially in a family——"

Still half listening, Mrs. Austin murmured, "That's very true."

"Well, then, Mother, something seems to be happening to *us,* our family, ever since we found the lamp and Emily called up the genie. And everybody's trying to be islands about it, and John Donne and Grandfather both say it doesn't work, and I think they're right!" She realized that she did not have her mother's full attention and she stamped to try to get it.

"You're too old for stamping, Suzy," her mother said.

"You're not listening!"

"Sorry——"

"You and Daddy are having secrets from us. You're being islands, and I suppose that's not so peculiar. Grown-ups never think children can understand anything. But you and Daddy are being islands with each other, and that *is* peculiar."

"Why do you say that?" Had it become that apparent? Mrs. Austin opened her mouth as though to say something, but at that moment the percolator made the loud gurgling noise that indicated that the coffee was ready. "Daddy's waiting," she said. "And it's almost time for dinner. Is the table set?"

She went into the study, where her husband sat at his desk, the pages of Dr. Shen-shu's letter spread out in front of him. She never asked him what was in his professional mail; usually he told her; over the years she had come to have a working knowledge of his research and he liked talking things over with her.

She put the coffeepot down on Dr. Shasti's brass table, poured her husband a cup of coffee and set it down on the desk in front of him, looking at him questioningly.

He picked up the cup, gesturing to her that he didn't need or want anything more, as though she were the lowest of scrub nurses.

She left the study and went into the dining room, where the children were setting the table, and on through into the kitchen. Was there time to make some cookies or a cake before dinner? If she could occupy herself with something familiar like baking, perhaps she would not cry.

Dave walked swiftly along Broadway. Occasionally he glanced carefully behind or around him. When he was quite certain that he was not being followed he began to think about how he would get Rob to the Bishop.

Fourteen

The family was seated around the dining table when Dave arrived. At Mrs. Austin's suggestion he pulled up a chair to join them for dessert. He had eaten little during the day, but he was singularly unhungry. When Rob started to clear the plates, Dave, his dessert hardly touched, rose to help him and followed him out to the kitchen.

"I wanted to talk to you," Rob said, putting the plates in the sink, "and you went rushing off."

"That's funny," Dave answered. "I want to talk to you, too. That's what I've come back for."

"But why did you go off, then? I only stayed at the Rabbi's fifteen minutes. Dave, I want to talk to you alone. It's important."

Dave had not expected it to be this easy. He put his pile of dishes down. "Why don't we take Rochester for a walk after dinner, then?"

"Okay."

"Do you mind if I take you to see someone?"

"Who?"

"The Bishop."

Rob looked at Dave. "What for? I don't think I need to see the Bishop about anything. It's you I want to talk to."

"The Bishop wants to see you. But you must promise not to say anything about it."

"Not to Mother and Daddy?"

"Definitely not."

"Why not?"

"Do you have to tell your parents everything?"

"Why shouldn't I? The only time I don't tell them is when I'm ashamed to tell them something. And then I always feel so awful that I end up telling them anyhow. Is there anything wrong about the Bishop?"

"How could there be anything wrong about the Bishop, idiot? I'm just going to take you to St. James chapel to talk with him. Shh. I'll explain later. Not a word." He grabbed the little boy's arm so roughly that Rob let out a small cry of pain.

"Dave! You hurt!"

"Shut up," Dave said, roughly.

Rob, open-mouthed, was on the brink of tears. Dave was often moody, sometimes rude, but he had always been gentle; he had never been like this.

Dave's grip relaxed, but he did not let Rob's arm go. "Don't say anything. Not anything. Promise."

"I won't say anything."

"Not to your mother or father. Not until I say you can. Okay?

"Okay, Dave."

Dave let him go and turned to go back into the dining room, met Emily coming into the kitchen with the milk pitcher and almost bumped in to her. "Listen where you're going!" he said.

Emily flashed back, "You *look* where you're going, you big lug!"

Rob returned to the table. He was no longer hungry, even though there was leftover chocolate mousse.

"Are you all right, Rob?" his mother asked as he refused it.

"I just don't think I'm very hungry. Could I eat it at bed-time, maybe?"

Mrs. Austin looked at him, thinking that he seemed pale, and not himself.

"Rob and I'll take Rochester out for a walk," Dave said.

Dr. Austin paused, on his way to his study. "Okay, Dave, thanks. But not a long walk, please. I'd like Rob to get to bed on time for once. Keep it down to fifteen minutes."

"Okay," Dave mumbled. If Rob were in danger, then getting him to the Bishop, to safety, was what counted. The one thing that seemed clear to Dave in this mud of confusion was the un-doubted presence of danger.

"It's always fifteen minutes," Rob said. "Whenever I want to do anything." But he did not argue with his father.

As soon as the table was cleared the two boys set off, leaving Vicky and Suzy washing up, with Emily drying.

"Okay, Rob," Dave said as the front door slammed behind them. "What'd you want to talk to me about?"

"Do you know two boys in leather jackets?"

"I know dozens of boys in leather jackets. Practically every kid in my school has a leather jacket."

"These guys had things on their sleeves that looked sort of like bats. And they said they knew you."

"When?"

"This afternoon, right outside school. They came up and said you wanted to see me, and Rochester didn't like them and growled at them and they ran away."

"Listen, Rob," Dave said fiercely, "any time you see someone with a bat on his sleeve, stick close to Rochester. And tell me right away."

"Well, I *am* telling you. If you'd been here when I got home I'd have told you then. Why? What did they want?"

"I don't know. But no good."

They were going by the synagogue. "Wait a minute." Rob began to feel in his pockets.

"Come on, Rob. You heard your father. We don't have much time."

"I know. Why did you tell Daddy we'd be back in fifteen minutes? You know we can't walk to the Cathedral and back in fifteen minutes." He had succeeded in finding what he was looking for, a stub of chalk. Carefully he wrote a large *R* against the wall of the synagogue.

"What're you doing!" Dave expostulated. "Rub it off. You're defacing private property."

"It's all right, Dave." Rob gave Rochester a shove so that the dog strode up Broadway, pulling Dave along with him. "The Rabbi knows about it." He hurried along, half running, half walking to keep up with Dave and Rochester. He felt that he had stumbled out of the real world and into a nightmare. If he could only wake up he could go running across the hall and into his parents' bedroom, and his mother would hear him, and wake immediately, and roll over in bed, and open her arms to him and everything would be safe and all right and in the known world, and she would walk him back to his own bed, and it would be his bed in Thornhill, not his bed in New York . . .

But then there would be no Emily . . .

Would he want to wake up and have Emily be only a character in a dream?

There would be no Emily, no Dave, no Rabbi . . .

The large yellow *R* on the synogogue was his link with reality, with a world in which there were people who could be trusted. If he was moving through a nightmare now, it was a real nightmare; the chalked *R* was his hope, his belief in love. He knew that the Rabbi loved him. He had thought that Dave loved him because he, himself, loved Dave. For the first time in his short life it occurred to him that this did not necessarily follow.

He looked at Dave, at the older boy's dark face set in grim and determined lines, and the thought that Dave might not love him, might not, indeed, love any of the family, surged coldly across him like the unexpected breaking of a wave.

Dave loved Emily: Rob was sure that Dave loved Emily. Perhaps he put up with the rest of them only for Emily's sake.

They crossed Amsterdam Avenue. The south gate to the

Close was locked for the night and Dave said, "Hold Rochester," thrust the leash into Rob's hand and opened the gate. They walked across the Close and Dave led the way up the steps which Rob had gone down only the day before with Canon Tallis. Rochester's claws clicked against the granite. Rob looked around, wildly hoping to see Canon Tallis, but the Close appeared deserted.

Dave unlocked the door which opened near the back entrance to St. James chapel. There were a few lights on in the chapel, but shadows lurked in the corners. On Rob's right the tomb and effigy of Bishop Potter jutted whitely out of darkness.

"Rob." A form emerged from the shadows behind the tomb.

Dave jumped. But it was not Bishop Potter sitting up and leaving the sarcophagus; it was Bishop Fall, walking around the tomb and holding out his hand to Rob.

Rob took the Bishop's hand, shook it, not bowing, but looking up through the shadows into the Bishop's face.

The Bishop looked past Rob, spoke to Dave. "What is that dog doing here?"

"It's the Austins' dog."

"I didn't ask whose dog it was. I wished to know what it is doing here."

"Walking the dog was my reason for bringing Rob, Bishop."

"The dog can't come with us. He'll have to go back." The Bishop snapped his fingers and three leather-jacketed youths stepped out from the darkness of the choir stalls. "Take the dog back."

The three boys backed away.

"Bishop, I said no Bats——" Dave started.

Rob spoke clearly. "Mr. Rochester won't go with them." He looked at the Bishop. "Anyhow, Rochester won't go anywhere without me. And I'm not going anywhere except home. Daddy said we were only to stay out fifteen minutes and it's more than that already."

"Robert," the Bishop said gently, holding his beautiful hands out to Rob as though coaxing a puppy or an unbroken pony. "Why are you afraid of me?"

"Mr. Rochester and I don't like those boys," Rob said.

"Bishop——" Dave started, but the Bishop snapped his fingers again.

The boy called N stepped forward. "It wasn't our fault. We didn't do nothing, and the dog was ready to eat us."

As N stepped forward, Rochester began to growl, very softly, deep in his throat.

"See?" N said, and stepped back again.

"Robert," the Bishop said. "Do you know who I am?"

"The Bishop. Bishop Fall."

"And you are afraid of me?"

"I don't know much about bishops," Rob said, "but I think maybe you ought to be a little bit afraid of a bishop, oughtn't you?"

"What you ought to be, most of all, is open and truthful, and obedient. I want to ask you some questions, and I want you to answer them, truthfully. But we are not safe here. Therefore I would like to take you to a place I know about where we won't be interrupted. Will you come with me?"

"I can't now," Rob said. "Daddy said we had to come right home."

"I will send Davidson home with your dog—he will go with Davidson, won't he?—and Davidson can tell your father that you are with me, and then he won't be worried about you. Certainly if he knows that you are with the Bishop he won't be concerned for your safety. Davidson, take the dog back to the Austins, please. *Now,* my son."

"Bishop—" Dave started.

The Bishop's voice was low, urgent. "You *must* trust me now. For the little boy. For Emily. Davidson."

Dave took Mr. Rochester's leash. Mr. Rochester simply moved closer to Rob, placing his four feet firmly on the marble floor, and stood stiffly, unbudging.

"Robert," the Bishop said, "will you tell your dog to go with Davidson, please?" He looked down at the little boy's pale, confused face. "For Emily's sake, Robert? If I tell you it is for Emily's sake? If you do not do as I ask you to do, Emily will be in great danger. Do you remember what happened to Emily in the house in which you now live? If Mr. Rochester had been there to protect Emily she might not be blind today. Emily needs Mr. Rochester now."

"Rochester," Rob said. "Go with Dave. Go, boy. Go with Dave."

Tail down, ears flat, Rochester stumped heavily, unwillingly after Dave. Rob heard the outer door shut, heard their steps on the stairs. The Bishop snapped his fingers again, and the three boys reemerged from the shadows. The Bishop nodded at them, and they walked swiftly, silently down the aisle. The outer door closed again, softly, this time. Rob could not hear their muffled feet on the stairs as they went after Dave.

"Now, Robert," the Bishop said. "Come."

When the dishes were washed and dried and everything was cleaned up, more quickly than usual because Suzy was the only one of the three girls who was at all talkative, Emily pulled at Vicky's sleeve. "Please take me downstairs for a minute, Vicky, and help me find something."

This was the kind of help Emily never asked, but Suzy, called into the living room by her mother, did not stop to question it, or to say, "You're just trying to get rid of me."

Emily led the way downstairs and into her room. "Vicky," she said, "we have to go to the Cathedral right now."

Vicky had paused as usual at the window seat and was looking out over the drive and the river. "The Cathedral? At this time of night? Don't be silly."

"Listen, Vicky," Emily said, "and I mean *listen*. *I* do. Listening is something I've learned. I hear lots of things nobody else does. I came out into the kitchen while Rob and Dave were clearing the table and I heard Dave tell Rob that the Bishop wants to see him tonight at the Cathedral."

"That's nuts," Vicky said. "You couldn't have heard right."

"I did. I don't make mistakes about what I hear."

"But it's absolutely nuts. The Bishop wouldn't want to see Rob. Why didn't you ask Dave about it?"

"Because Dave didn't want anybody to hear. When he knew I was there he shut up like a clam."

"It doesn't make any sense," Vicky said flatly. "Anyhow, Rob and Dave should be back any minute. Daddy said they weren't to stay out more than a quarter of an hour. They wouldn't have had time to go to the Cathedral."

"They've been gone almost half an hour now," Emily said. "Is all this any more peculiar than my rubbing an old lamp and calling up a genie? Vicky, listen to me and don't just say no. You've got to take me to the Cathedral."

"All right. We'll go after school tomorrow."

Emily raised her voice angrily. "Don't be reasonable, Vicky! Things passed the point of reason a long time ago. We have to go to the Cathedral *now*."

"Mother and Daddy would never let us go."

"I know that. We have to slip out. Right now. What I hope is that we'll meet Canon Tallis. He knows more than anybody else about what's going on, whatever it is. Listen, Vicky, that cable Papa sent. The CAREFUL OF FALLS. Does it mean anything to you?"

"No," Vicky said irritably.—I want to go to bed, she thought, pressing her cheek against the cold glass of the window. Her breath steamed up the pane so that it was as though she were looking at the bare trees through fog.—I'm scared.

"The Bishop's name is Fall."

"I know that."

"Do you suppose Papa was giving us a warning about the Bishop?"

"I don't suppose anything. I don't think it has anything to do with it. Let's tell Mother and Daddy about it."

"No," Emily said. "It would take time. And we're wasting time already. Are you going to go with me or are you going to let me go alone?"

"You can't go alone," Vicky said. "Anyhow it's dark now. You wouldn't be allowed even if you—"

"It's not dark for me," Emily snapped.

"But it is for truck drivers and—"

"If you don't come with me, I'm going." Emily was cold
with fury. "Someone would help me. Someone would take me
there." She walked rapidly out of the room, started down the
stairs.

Vicky hurried after her.

Fifteen

Suzy sat at the dining table doing homework. She was furious with Vicky and Emily for going off and leaving her. She kept looking up from her work, towards her father's study. Her mother had gone in to the study and shut the door, and this meant that the Austin parents did not want to be interrupted except for an emergency. It wouldn't be an emergency for her to go blundering in and say that Vicky and Emily had abandoned her, that they had gone down to Emily's room and Vicky hadn't done her homework . . .

It wasn't an emergency to go rushing in and say that Dave and Rob ought to have come back with Rochester at least twenty minutes ago and weren't back yet . . .

She got up, leaving her papers and books spread out on the table and went into the living room, to look out the front windows down on to the Drive; she might see them coming home.

There was a teen-aged couple walking along arm in arm,

singing; there was a girl with a transistor radio, on too loud, so that the raucous music came blaring up, louder than the Mozart which Mrs. Austin had on the phonograph. There was a very old man with his very old schnauzer, both of whom were friends of Rob's; there was a group of boys coming from the direction of the Buddhist temple and talking rapidly in Japanese; they carried small satchels and probably had been practicing judo; there was a boy in a black leather jacket, a cigarette dangling from his lips, a tiny glow waxing and waning in the dark.

And no sight of Rob or Dave or Rochester. Sighing, she went back to the dining room. If her mother came out of the study she'd tell her, all right, about Vicky and Emily, about Dave and Rob, about . . .

She stood in front of the mirror over the sideboard, looking at her reflection. To see herself usually gave her pleasure and a sense of confidence; this was a combination of naïve vanity and legitimate enjoyment of the fact that she was extremely pleasing to look at.

—I'm prettier than Vicky, she said to herself. —I'm ever so much prettier than Vicky.

But she was not comforted.

—I wish Mother'd come out. What're the girls doing downstairs without me? Where are Rob and Dave? What're Mother and Daddy talking about? I don't want to learn French verbs . . . What's happening? Please, what's happening?

Mrs. Austin sat in the study after dinner, her fingers around the bowl of her coffee cup as though to warm them. The Doctor was at his desk. He had again in his hands Rob's chunky paperweight. His coffee stood, untouched and cooling, on a stack of papers.

"Rob and Dave've been gone well over half an hour," Mrs. Austin said.

"They should be back any minute."

Mrs. Austin leaned back in the yellow wicker rocker, jumped at the loudness of its squeak. "Suzy—Suzy of all people was quoting *no man is an island* to me before dinner."

"Justified, wasn't she?" he asked. "I've tried to keep the island of safety. I've thought I could keep you and the children separated from the mainland. I should have known that it can't be done. And we're all paying now for my folly."

"But what's happening?"

"I don't know. But perhaps whatever it is, we've got it coming to us. We're paying for our insulation."

"You mean justice? Retribution?" She shivered.

"No. I don't mean that. I'm not naïve enough to believe in a balance of justice, right for wrong, good for evil, in this world. But you and I have been in ways as immature as our children. . . . Have I told you about Gregory's cable?"

"We all read it."

"No, not that. It wasn't sent from Athens. It was sent from Liverpool."

"Liverpool—"

"Canon Tallis had a cable from Shasti. Gregory's with Shasti and Shen-shu in Liverpool. Both cables said CAREFUL OF FALLS."

"But what " she started.

There was a knock on the door.

Suzy poked her head in.

"Is it an emergency?" her mother asked automatically.

"Yes."

The second automatic question followed. "Would *I* think it an emergency?"

"Yes," Suzy said breathlessly. "I went down to Emily's room and Emily and Vicky aren't there. I looked all over for them and they aren't anywhere."

"That's nonsense, Suzy," Dr. Austin said. "Why were you looking for them anyhow?"

"They went off together, having secrets from me, and then I got worried because Dave and Rob were gone so long, and I didn't want to interrupt you unless it was a real emergency and I didn't know how long a real emergency would be, so I went to ask Vicky and Emily and they weren't there. Their coats are gone."

Downstairs they heard Rochester's bark, loud, demanding.

"They're back. Thank heavens," Mrs. Austin said.

Dr. Austin had risen from his desk and was running down the stairs. His wife and Suzy followed him.

Outside the front door Mr. Rochester was barking. Dr. Austin flung it open and there was Rochester, alone, leash trailing, his bark rising to a high, almost hysterical pitch. Dr. Austin looked up and down the street. No one was in sight.

"Rochester," Dr. Austin took the leash. "Which way? Tell me."

Rochester started up the street, pulling the doctor after him.

"Get your coat—" Mrs. Austin started. Then she and Suzy, not pausing, coatless, followed the Doctor and the dog.

At the corner they met the Rabbi, his beard blowing in the wind. When he saw Dr. Austin and the dog, he called, "Is Rob all right?"

Rochester stopped when he saw the Rabbi, and whined.

Mrs. Austin held her arms about herself, against the cold. "Suzy, your coat . . ."

"Let's go back to the house." Dr. Austin looked swiftly up and down Broadway but saw neither his children nor Emily nor Dave.

They hurried, without talking, down the street to the Drive. Dr. Austin unlocked the door and they went in. Dr. Austin stopped in the front hall, turning to the Rabbi. "Why do you ask about Rob?"

The old man was panting, his beard disheveled from the wind. "Yesterday he paid me one of his visits. He had something on his mind, but you had told him to stay with me only fifteen minutes, so he said he didn't have time to tell me about it. But he asked me if ever he left a chalked letter *R* where I could see it, to come rescue him, that he would need rescuing. I just now saw a yellow chalk *R* on the synagogue wall."

Dr. Austin leaned against the closed front door. Mrs. Austin sat on the marble stairs as though her legs would not hold her up. Suzy said, "Oh, Rabbi Levy, Rob and Dave went out with Rochester about an hour ago, and Rochester just came home alone. And Vicky and Emily have disappeared and their coats are gone." She burst into a spasm of tears.

Now Mrs. Austin was able to get up from the stairs, to go to her child, to hold her, say, "Hush," quiet her.

Dr. Austin asked the Rabbi, "Did Rob tell you about the Aladdin's lamp and the genie?"

"Yes. Last week."

"What did you think?"

"I thought it was one of his fairy tales. I was busy that day, and I wasn't listening with all my ears. It was not a fairy tale?"

Dr. Austin shook his head. "But what it was, what it means, we don't know. Rabbi Levy, will you do me the kindness of staying here with my wife and little girl? I'm afraid to leave them alone."

"Where are you going?" Mrs. Austin, her arm still around Suzy, held her voice under control with difficulty.

"I'm going to look for the children." He did not say where or how.

"Take Rochester with you."

"I want Rochester here with you."

"Please, Wallace—"

"No," he said. "Rochester is to stay here with the three of you. I'll be as quick as I can. If I find out anything and I'm near a phone I'll call you. I can't tell you not to open the front door, in case it might be one of the children. But don't open it unless you have Rochester right beside you. I think you'd better stay downstairs. If I call I'll use Gregory's number." Without waiting for a response he opened the front door and shut it quickly behind him.

Sixteen

Vicky and Emily walked rapidly up Broadway. Every once in a while Vicky would open her mouth as though to expostulate with the other girl, then close it again without speaking. She could see that Emily was concentrating on counting the blocks to 110th Street. Once Emily panted, "I wish we had Rochester with us . . ."

A long block away, on Amsterdam Avenue, Mr. Rochester and Dave were passing them, unseen, like ships in the night. Behind them the three Alphabats stalked. When the boy and the dog turned west towards the river, they sprang. Dave felt his arms grabbed, pinioned, himself pulled backwards. The side of a hand came down sharply against his wrist so that he let go the dog's leash.

"Home, Rochester! Home, boy!" he shouted.

The three youths did not seem inclined to go after the dog,

who was galloping down the street, leash trailing. They shook Dave until his teeth hurt.

"None of your funny business."

"Don't drop your gourds."

"C'mon. Bishop wants you."

He was propelled up Amsterdam. "Leave me be," he snarled. "I'll come."

"Let him loose, but watch him."

"He's never rubbed the lamp."

"Shut up. C'mon."

Dave walked angrily between two of the boys. The third walked ahead, setting the pace, occasionally glancing over his shoulder to see that the others were following properly, that Dave did not try to get away.

—Who does he think he is? Dave asked silently. —*N*? He might as well be *A,* or *F,* or *R.* They're all faceless. They're letters without names. Did I ever want that? "What's this about a lamp?"

N looked back. "Shut up. Never mind."

"He'll see, won't he, *N*?"

"C'mon."

—Mr. Rochester'll go back to the house, Dave thought. — They'll see him and know something's wrong. What is the Bishop doing? What have I done?

Mr. Rochester was his only hope.

—I'm responsible for Rob, he thought. —Emily'll never forgive me if anything happens to Rob.

And then he thought: —It's not because of Emily that I care about Rob. It's me. I care.

• • •

When Vicky and Emily reached the Cathedral Close, the lower gate was locked, so they walked past Diocesan House to the gate at 111th Street, which was left open for cars until midnight. Just uptown of the gate was the great slumbering body of the Cathedral.

—But is it asleep? Vicky wondered. She thought of Rob's flying buttresses, wings folded for the night.

"St. James chapel," Emily said, fingers tight on Vicky's arm. "Take me there."

"The Cathedral's locked for the night. You know that."

Emily's fingers dug through Vicky's heavy navy school coat. "Of course I know it, you nit. But if the Bishop wants Rob to meet him in St. James chapel there must be some way in. It wouldn't be any of the big doors. But there are doors that go into the nave from the side. Let's walk along and you look."

When Emily was walking an unfamiliar route her steps became slow, tentative, shuffling. Usually this infuriated her. She loathed walking like a blind person. Only Mr. Theo or Dave could snap back at her: "Which is what you are."

Now it was Vicky who was annoyed at Emily's dragging steps, at being slowed down. Finally she exploded, "This is nuts! I don't believe you heard Dave right."

"Shush." Emily snapped her fingers, listened. "Aren't we near a door?"

On their left were steps. There was a door at the top with a light above it, showing a number 5. "Wait. I'll go see if it's unlocked." Vicky placed Emily's hand on the cold iron stair rail.

This door was about two thirds along the length of the nave,

Emily thought. She listened to Vicky running up the steps, tugging unsuccessfully at the door. "Okay," she said as Vicky descended. "There're more doors. I know there are. There's that one off St. James chapel; I've gone in that door with Dave when we've come to listen to Mr. Theo play. Come on."

"Just one more door," Vicky said stubbornly. "Just one, and that's all. And if that's locked I'm taking you home," she went on as they walked slowly along by the side of the Cathedral. "I never should have come with you. Mother and Daddy'll be furious with me and for once I don't blame them. I'm three years older than you are and I never should have let you drag me here."

"Oh, *hush*," Emily said. "How can I listen to anything?"

"You hush. There's a door here. Wait a minute." Vicky darted across the path to the door. Again it was closed tight. When she came back, saying, "Locked," Emily was trembling with rage.

"Don't ever go off and leave me that way again!"

But Vicky was too agitated to feel the contrition that normally would have filled her had she left Emily in the midst of unidentified and unfathomable darkness. "Okay! The South Transept steps are right here."

"No! The Transept'll be locked. I want to try the door by St. James. Come on, Vicky. Please. It's right around through the gates and by the Dean's Garden. I *know* it is."

Emily was right.

Vicky steered her past the sacristies, through the stone gate posts and into the Dean's Garden. She did not say that a stone statue by a marble bench looked, in the shadows, like someone crouched, waiting to pounce on them; that the rhododendron bushes, huddled against the wall, might be witches.

Emily said, "Vicky, I want to go up the stairs with you this time. Even if the door's locked I want to listen. *I* can hear if something's going on better than you can."

This was true. But it was, at this moment, the smallest part of it. Emily was terrified at being left alone again where she had no idea where she was, where she was totally lost and unable to help herself. The feeling of the ship of the Cathedral, solid and strong in the waters of darkness, became a menacing threat instead of a symbol of security. She had a sensation that the great pile of stone instead of floating magnificently on the bones of the city island was lowering over her, would fall on her and crush her. Without realizing what she was doing she began to rub at her eyes as she had done in the early days of her blindness, as though by doing so she could open them to light again.

Vicky did not argue. The two girls went up the steps together.

"Shush!" Emily said. "Don't clatter so. The guard'll hear us."

"He's over by Diocesan House. I saw him. He can't possibly hear us." But Vicky wished that he could. If the guard heard them, caught them, then all he could do was to return them safely to their parents, and then everybody would know if Rob hadn't returned with Dave and Mr. Rochester as he was supposed to . . .

The door she now tried was, like the others, locked.

Emily put her ear against the cold wood of the door and listened, listened. But she could hear nothing beyond what might be the normal night noises of a vast and empty building.

"Let's go ask the guard——" Vicky suggested tentatively.

"Ask him what?" Emily snapped. "If Dave and Rob are with the Bishop?"

This wasn't, Vicky thought, such a bad idea. "Why not?"

"No. I want to talk to Canon Tallis. He's the only one who knows anything about what's going on. Take me over to Cathedral House and, whatever you do, don't let the guard see us."

They traversed the route to Cathedral House without mishap. In the small vestibule Vicky rang the bell marked DEAN'S GUESTS. Rang and rang. She could see through the iron and glass doors to the empty reception hall, where a lamp was lit on the magazine table. There was a nighttime feeling of desertion about the place which added to her anxiety.

"We'll have to go home," she said. "There isn't anybody here."

Emily's shoulders sagged in defeat. "Okay. Let's talk to your parents."

"That's what we should have done in the first place."

"There wasn't time."

"Look at all the time we've wasted this way! And if Mother and Daddy've found out we're gone, they'll——" she broke off, pulling Emily back into the shadows of the vestibule.

"What's the matter?"

"Shh!" Vicky could hear Emily breathing quickly, nervously beside her, could sense the other girl's frustration at not being able to see what was going on. She whispered, "It's Dave! There're three kids with him, like the ones I saw in the park with Canon Tallis and—Rob isn't with them."

"What're we waiting for!" Emily cried. "Come on!"

"*Hush*," Vicky said again. "Em, I think they've hi-jacked Dave or something, the way he's walking, the way they're looking at him——"

"Okay," Emily whispered, "we've got to follow them. Which way are they going?"

"Towards the Cathedral. They must have come in to the Close by the 110th Street gate."

"How?"

"Dave has keys."

"Come on," Emily said. "We can't let them see us but we mustn't let them out of sight."

"Emily." Vicky tried to sound calm, reasonable. "I can manage better without you."

"No—"

"You'll be all right here in the vestibule."

But panic rose in Emily's throat. "No—"

In the light from the reception hall Vicky could see Emily's face, tight with terror. "Okay, then," she said, putting Emily's hand on her arm. "But we'll have to move quickly. You mustn't shuffle, Emily. You'll have to trust me."

Usually when Emily walked with Vicky her hand rested lightly on the older girl's arm; she was able to feel through her sensitive fingertips before Vicky told her that they had come to a turn or a curb. But now fear made her hold on to Vicky with all the strength of her pianist's fingers. She moved through a darkness where all shapes, unseen but felt, were menacing, all echoes a confusion of chaos instead of a pattern of sound ordering her night.

"Step up," Vicky ordered in a hissing whisper. "Up. Up. Up. One more. Turn right."

"Where are we?" Emily asked, though she should have known that the choir buildings now lay ahead of them, that they were going back in the direction of the Dean's Garden.

She stepped out into nothingness, trying not to shuffle, trying to keep up with Vicky; the ground seemed to rise up and hit her outstretched foot too soon, so that her whole body was jolted and her teeth were set on edge. "Where are they?"

"Shh," Vicky said. "I'm trying to see. I think they're going towards St. James chapel." She hurried along the path. "Turn left."

Emily, following, stumbled and almost fell. Vicky jerked her upright. She realized that Emily was incapable now of using the acute senses that usually gave her an astonishing amount of independence.—What I'll do, Vicky thought, —is try to see where they're taking Dave and then I'll take Emily home . . .

She halted, suddenly, at the entrance to the Dean's Garden. She could see the boys at the top of the steps. Dave was evidently having trouble opening the door, and the boys were looking at him, at the door, otherwise they would surely have seen the two girls.

Vicky pulled Emily into the protection of one of the stone gateposts. She put her lips to Emily's ear. "They're there, at the top of the steps. Dave can't get in. Please try to listen."

They crouched against the wall. Vicky could feel her heart pounding, thought she could hear Emily's. The boys were muttering. She strained her untrained ears.

"Hurry."

"Get that door open."

"Quit stalling."

Dave's voice: "The key's jammed."

"He did it on purpose."

"Let me try."

"Lay off."

A sound of scuffling. Then: "Here it goes."

"Can't get the key out."

"Leave it."

"C'mon. Bishop's waiting."

Silence.

Vicky peered around the gatepost. "They've gone in."

Emily had moved through the wild ocean of her terror into a cold sea of calm. "Come on, Vicky. You heard what they said about the lock."

"No," Vicky said. "We're going home. We'll tell Mother and Daddy."

"Vicky! We've got to find Rob."

Rob. Oh, Rob.

Go home without Rob? Without knowing what had happened to him? When maybe—

No. They couldn't go home. Not now.

"Okay."

They moved through the Dean's Garden, up the steps. Emily was walking normally again. She had followed this path before, been up these steps. The feel of the route was caught firmly in her body's memory.

Mr. Theo would play a few measures for her on the piano and her ear would hear and memorize the notes; then, once the correct fingering had been worked out, her hands would always remember; it was the kinesthetic memory she had talked about to Vicky; it guided her movements in the house and on the streets as well as her fingers in music. It guided her now.

At the top of the steps her hands moved over the door, found the lock with Dave's key still stuck in it.

Had he jammed it on purpose? She was sure he had.

"Let me open it," Vicky whispered. "We mustn't be seen." Carefully she put her fingers on the wooden lip of the door, pulled it open a crack.

Emily asked, "Is there any light?"

"No. It's pitch dark."

"Let me go first, then. I think I can remember it."

They slipped in. Vicky could see nothing. She was in Emily's world of night.

"Don't hold me!" Emily whispered fiercely.

Vicky let go; stopped; listened. She could hear Emily's feet moving carefully, surely, on the marble floor of the ambulatory.

Then Emily was caught in the beam of a flashlight.

Vicky pressed back into the shadows. She heard Dave's angry voice.

"Emily!"

"Dave!"

Vicky, hidden by the corner of St. James chapel, could not see what was happening, could hear only the noise of feet, a voice saying, "Take the girl, too. C'mon." Evidently Dave was being silenced. If the boys did not know that Emily was blind they wouldn't realize that she couldn't possibly have got there alone. For Vicky to come out and declare her presence would only be for them all to be captured.

She waited.

Listened.

There was the crash of a gate clanging. A sound of feet: where were they going? She thought it was feet descending. She could not tell how many footsteps there were. Emily would have been able to count them. Vicky thought it was the three leather-jacketed boys, plus Dave and Emily: all of them. But she could not be sure. One of the boys might possibly be lying in wait. If she stayed still long enough, if she listened as Emily would listen, then if one of them were still there he would be bound to give himself away, especially since he did not know that Vicky was there, that anybody was listening . . .

She waited, straining her ears. It seemed as though she were listening with her entire body. Her skin tingled with effort.

—I'll count to a hundred, she thought. —No, that's not enough. I'll count to a thousand.

Darkness.

Silence.

Counting to a thousand seemed to stretch into hours, not minutes.

Nine hundred ninety-eight. Nine hundred ninety-nine. One thousand.

Slowly she moved her cramped body. She had heard nothing. She felt that she could be quite certain that nobody had been left behind.

Holding on to the wall, she tiptoed into the ambulatory. If only Canon Tallis were at the Cathedral instead of off somewhere just when he was needed. . . . If only she could see something. . . . Then she remembered that she had had a double period in chemistry lab that day, that she had used matches to light the Bunsen burner. With fumbling fingers she unbuttoned her navy-blue overcoat, felt in her blazer pocket. Yes. The matches were there, almost a full packet. She lighted one, and its small light flickered feebly, revealing nothing but darkness.

Nevertheless, when its tiny flame was gone (she blew it out only when it started to burn her fingers) she was reassured that she was indeed alone. If one of the boys had remained behind then she would have been seen, would have been caught and taken prisoner.

A wild idea came to her. She would leave a signal before she left. If Canon Tallis or the Dean returned to the Close and saw light in the Cathedral they would come at once to investigate. She struck another match and went into St. James chapel. Another match took her to the altar, and there she was in luck, because not only were there two great candlesticks on the altar, there was also a taper. Her fingers were trembling so that it took her half a dozen matches to light the taper. Then she lighted the candles. But could anybody from outside see their light? She doubted it.

Now she could think of nothing except that Canon Tallis must see her signal. Shielding the taper, she went from chapel to chapel, St. James, St. Ambrose, St. Martin of Tours, St. Saviour, St. Columba, St. Boniface, St. Ansgar . . .

Now all the candles on the chapel altars were lit. Her signal was a half circle of light which Canon Tallis could not fail to see.

The only thing left for her to do was to go home to her parents as fast as she could possibly run.

Seventeen

Canon Tallis was, at the moment that Vicky was lighting the candles, that Dr. Austin was fruitlessly walking the streets, that Mrs. Austin, Suzy, and the Rabbi were waiting in the music room and Mr. Theo was dialing the Gregory number, standing with the Dean in the smelly hallway of a Harlem tenement house where they had dined well, if more heavily than either of them liked.

A rat scuttled around a clutter of garbage cans. Despite the clean new high-rise housing developments there were rats in the houses and streets as well as the park walls. Tallis looked at this one broodingly. "But listen, Juan: when evil declares itself in its absolute form, it declares itself as an angel of light. Don't look for it in places like this. It can come coped and mitred and offering salvation."

"No," the Dean said. "No, Tom."

But Tallis continued, quiet, stern. "We underestimate the

powers of darkness if we assume that any rank of the created order, even the Apostolic college itself, is safely sealed from them. We totally miss the point of the Fall."

"Fall," the Dean said. "The Fall. Dear God, Thomas, I can't bear it."

"You can. If you have to, you will. But I'm not at all convinced that you'll have to."

"What do you mean?"

"It's so fantastic I can't speak about it until I'm surer. But I have an idea that His Darkness is doing a strange impersonation indeed."

"You're really on to something?"

"I think so. Let's go."

They moved past the garbage cans, out the door, and down three steps to the street. Cyprian, on a loose leash, gave a snort of relief and moved from his master's side to investigate the gutter. The Dean let him sniff for a moment, then jerked on the lead and started walking briskly, his long legs moving loosely and comfortably under his heavy, monklike habit. A wet wind cut across his cheeks, blew through his short-cropped, tightly curling and grizzled hair. Beside him the Canon strode, muffled in his dark coat and fur hat, his face gleaming pale in contrast to the Dean's swarthiness.

During these nocturnal walks the Dean had made enemies as well as friends. He had been shot at more than once: he was aware, now, that they were being stalked. He could not see *A,* sliding along in the shadows behind them, but he could feel that someone was there. He said nothing about this; he was certain that Tallis also knew that they were being followed; therefore neither of them needed to mention it.

The Dean had won general respect, if not admiration, in the crowded streets around the Cathedral, because he was strong and a fighter and walked casually through danger. As people had come to trust him they had come to the Cathedral; the great place was filled now for most of the services. Some who could not bring themselves to enter the Cathedral itself came to the Cathedral offices for money, for food, for help with a greedy landlord or extortioner, or simply for a word of kindness or encouragement. Sometimes they came to the Dean quite literally to be held in his strong, comforting bear hug.

So he went to them in return, accepting invitations to countless cluttered kitchens for meals, and the luxury of a solitary dinner in the Deanery was something he seldom allowed himself.

They walked in silence, glad of the exercise after the heavy meal, until the Dean asked, "Tom, what about Hyde?"

"I don't like him."

The Dean laughed. "And that's that? No, Tom. It won't do. It's not enough. You know that." He paused to speak to a group of teen-agers outside a drugstore, slipping into the staccato Spanish in which he would always be more at home than in English.

Tallis's classical Spanish was not up to the affectionately insulting idioms that flew back and forth, but he thought he caught the hint of a warning, for which the Dean seemed to be saying thank you, then gave his spontaneous, infectious laugh, waved goodbye, and walked on, Cyprian snuffling close behind him. The hideous dog had submitted graciously to assorted caresses from the boys, but now his ears were flattened, his ungainly body tense.

"I've learned over the years," Tallis continued, "to trust my instincts, especially when they're this strong. It's almost as though one could tell something basic about people by their smell. What were those kids warning you about, Juan? Other than that we're being followed?"

"That unlikely plot to take over the city."

"Aren't most things unlikely? Isn't the Micro-Ray? Something smells very bad about Hyde, Juan. Of that I'm sure."

"He's given a lot to the Cathedral. The Bishop says he's deeply religious."

The Canon gave a short laugh. "It isn't the people who think they're atheists who worry me. It's those who think they're religious."

"Hyde's a brilliant neurologist. That's an incontestable fact."

"I don't contest it. Nevertheless he's dangerous. He's power-mad, Juan. He let that much out this afternoon."

"And Austin? How does *he* smell to you?"

"I've told you: like a good bright child. Dave sees this. He put his finger on the man's naïveté, his innocence. They're a good family. Perhaps they've been a little too self-sufficient up to this year, but their relationships are essentially healthy. One can tell a great deal around a dinner table. The parents aren't devourers. They don't manipulate. I think the closest we ever come in this naughty world to realizing unity in diversity is around a family table. I felt it at their table, the wholeness of the family unit, freely able to expand to include friends, to include me even through Austin's and my suspicions of each other, and yet each person in that unit complete, individual, unique, valued. But Austin has no right to be so innocent, you know. It's a bad flaw. It may be as dangerous as Hyde's viciousness."

"Viciousness?"

"Yes. It's there in him. I'm positive. But Austin's a good man. In the lab he's obviously got a touch of genius."

The Dean cut in, "As Hyde has in the operating theatre."

The Canon sighed. "Granted. One of the mysteries of this world is that a man's genius and his moral perception are sometimes in inverse proportions. Why can't the great men be good, and the bad devoid of gifts? But it just isn't the way human nature works. I have a suspicion that Hyde's a very bad man indeed, brilliance or no. And Austin's a good man and a fine scientist. But I'm not sure he's very bright."

"Can't that sometimes be a strength?" the Dean wondered. "I console myself that it may be. I've been called a fool often enough for cutting official functions to wander about the city this way. The Bishop has visions of Utopia, Tom, and it is always a heresy, no matter how nobly conceived. He's straying further and further from reality. And something very strange——"

"What?"

"For almost a year he hasn't done one single ordination or confirmation."

"Why not?"

"His health. Those ghastly headaches always seem to knock him down whenever there's a major Cathedral function."

"So one of the Suffragans takes over?"

"Yes, but——" He broke off as a voice behind them called, "Hey, Dean! Is that you?"

The two men and the dog turned to see a boy hurrying along the street to catch up with them. Cyprian pressed against the Dean, teeth bared, ready to spring. The boy wore the familiar leather jacket with the bat on the sleeve. He took the butt of a cigarette from his lips, threw it to the sidewalk, and ground it out with his heel. "Listen, Dean," he said, panting, "listen to me!"

"I'm listening," the Dean said quietly. "Take your time. Catch your breath." This, he knew, was not their stalker, who still lurked somewhere in the shadows near them.

"There isn't time," the boy said. "I'm Q, and I'm never going to rub the lamp again. He's kidnapped the little kid."

A gunshot rang through the tense air.

Cyprian sprang.

"Dean!" Q cried. "Are you hurt?"

Eighteen

Mrs. Austin continued, after her husband had left to try to find the children, to sit on the marble stairs. She poured out to the Rabbi all that she knew of the events of the past days, and she realized that she knew very little, certainly not enough to explain Dave and Rob's disappearance and Mr. Rochester's return alone; or Vicky and Emily's going off into the night by themselves without a word. She felt isolated, an unwilling island torn from the mainland, cut off from her husband and children. The family unit which had been so warm and close seemed now to have exploded into separate, unknown fragments.

"Are you keeping anything from me, Suzy?" she asked.

"No."

"If you know anything, you *must* tell me."

"I don't know anything, Mother, honestly."

"Everybody else seems to," Mrs. Austin said bitterly. She turned to the Rabbi. "My husband does. I've known all autumn that he was keeping something from me, something that was troubling him."

"Mrs. Austin," the Rabbi said gently, "I think we should go into the music room, where we can sit more comfortably and where we will be by the phone if it rings."

Mrs. Austin managed to get up off the stairs. Her legs felt like water. She knew that she was not hiding her panic from Suzy. She went to the desk chair and sat, reaching one hand out towards the telephone, then dropping it helplessly onto her lap. Suzy sat directly in the center of the small gold sofa and looked at her mother. Mr. Rochester paced, back and forth, up and down.

The Rabbi had seated himself on Emily's piano bench. "I should have realized that something was wrong before Rob had to mark his *R* . . ."

Suzy, looking from her mother to the Rabbi, thought of Mr. Theo's remark about "parlous" times. "What does *parlous* mean?"

"Perilous," the Rabbi told her. He rose from the piano and began to pace slowly, as though in imitation of Mr. Rochester, his head bowed, his beard moving slightly against his caftan. Mr. Rochester went out into the hall and sat in front of the door.

The phone rang.

Mrs. Austin picked up the receiver. "Hello? Hello? . . . No. . . . No, it's not." She hung up. "It was a wrong number."

There was a long, empty silence.

The phone rang again. This time Mrs. Austin did not fling herself at the receiver. "It's probably the same wrong number, someone wanting Gladys again. . . . Hello? . . . Mr. Theo! . . .

Oh, Mr. Theo, I'm glad you called! . . . No, everything isn't all right. . . . We don't know where Rob and Dave are, or Vicky and Emily, they've all disappeared. Mr. Rochester came home alone and my husband went off to try . . . I'm here with Suzy and Rabbi Levy. . . . Oh, yes, please do come . . ."

Her mother was talking to Mr. Theo, Suzy felt, as though the old man were her father, and the realization hit Suzy for the first time that indeed Mrs. Austin and Mr. Theo were a generation apart, that her mother would seem a child to the old man, that all grown-ups are not an indistinguishable chronological lump.

As Mrs. Austin put down the receiver, there was a pounding on the door and Mr. Rochester began to bark.

Rob was not quite certain how frightened he really was during the trip down the winding marble stairs and through the Cathedral crypt. His journey was different from Dave's the week before because now all the lights were on, and the Bishop turned them off behind him, so that as they moved into light they left a wake of darkness. The clutter of marble statuary, tombs, discarded wrought-iron lecterns, broken carved wooden thrones, all the paraphernalia of the crypt was even more fascinating to Rob than the clutter in the familiar attic in the country, and he felt the edges of his fear receding as the Bishop turned to him with a gentle smile. "Wouldn't this be a wonderful place for a game of hide-and-seek, Robert?"

Rob agreed. "Or for plays. We used to put on lots of plays in the attic in Thornhill. We had a big trunk full of costumes, and Vicky wrote plays for us."

"Interested in the theatre, are you?"

"I don't know that much about it, except for our attic plays. Dr. Gregory said it was very classical of us. My mother knows about the theatre, though, and she pasted lots of pictures of actors and actresses up on the attic walls."

"Who, for instance?"

"Somebody from olden days called Duse, I think, is one I remember, because I liked her face. And then there was a picture I liked of a man in a Roman toga, Henry something or other."

"Grandcourt?"

"Yes, I think so," Rob said absently, inspecting a broken stone gargoyle, an imp with an expression half-threatening, half-charming, made lopsided by the absence of one of the horns curving from its forehead, and a large chip off one ear.

"Grandcourt, eh?" the Bishop asked with a pleased purr. "So you like that little gargoyle, Robert? There used to be stone masons here at the Cathedral who would do that kind of work, but Amon Davidson's the only one left, and he works only when he feels like it. But not for long, Robert. The Bishop has plans. For Amon, for the Cathedral, for the city. We have now what we have never had before, the vision of Bishop Fall and the help of the lamp."

Rob looked up from inspecting a broken angel's wing. "The lamp? And the genie?"

"Ah, the genie, Robert! You would like to see the genie again, would you not?"

Rob straightened up. There was something about the pleasure rumbling deep in the Bishop's throat he did not like. It was on the surface similar to Emily's deep, purring chuckle, but it had no mirth in it. Now Rob knew that he was afraid.

One ought to be a little afraid of a bishop, he had said. But not afraid this way.

"Come." The Bishop's hand closed over Rob's. Emily had made all the Austin children very conscious of the touch of a hand. This was not in the least like holding hands with one of his family. It was not in the least like holding hands with Canon Tallis.

Then Rob remembered how, in *The Princess and Curdie,* Curdie was given the great gift of being able to tell, when holding someone's hand, what he was really like inside. The paw of an animal might be the trusting hand of a child; the hand of a man might turn to the slithering cold of a snake. What was the Bishop's hand? It was thin, delicate, bones and veins marked in an intricate pattern, and it held Rob's warm fingers in a cold, hawklike talon.

The bishop urged him into the enormous boiler room. "To the lamp. To the genie." With his free hand he picked up a powerful batteried lantern from the floor by one of the great blue boilers. "Come, Robert. We're going through a lovely long dark tunnel to my palace, where everything will be brilliant and beautiful. Won't that be fun?"

"No!" Rob cried. "Let me go! You hurt! I want to go home!"

But the talon clamped more tightly around the little boy's wrist.

"It's only a scratch," the Dean said. "Stop fussing."

He pulled away from Tallis and pressed with the fingers of

his right hand against his left upper arm. Cyprian came bounding back. Their attacker was nowhere to be seen, but Cyprian carried a scrap of leather in his powerful jaws. "Good boy," the Dean said. "Good boy, Cyprian." His voice was muffled through teeth clenched against pain. "Come. Back to the Cathedral. Q, tell us what you know while you walk."

They headed towards Morningside Park, Q panting out a tale of an unused subway station discovered by Amon Davidson, of a bishop's throne, secret meetings, the lamp, the genie.

"What you do, see," Q said, as he hurried up the steep hill of the park with the Dean and the Canon, "is you rub the lamp. And then this guy in green robes comes out. He's called a genie, see, and you have to go along with all this zug if you want to fly."

"How do you fly?" Tallis asked. Beside him he could hear Q breathing heavily.

"You lie down on this couch, like, and this genie guy points this sort of pencil thing at you, and you take a flight."

"What do you mean?"

"Like you feel good. All over, everywhere, see? All you do is feel. You could sing and dance, it's so good. Sometimes if it lasts long enough you scream."

"Because it's so good?"

"Yeah. It's so good you'll do anything to rub the lamp again."

—The pleasure center of the brain, the Canon realized. — He's using the Micro-Ray to stimulate the pleasure center, to—

"Hey, what's—" Q started, for the Dean had stopped so

abruptly that he bumped into Tallis and the boy, and Cyprian sat heavily on his haunches.

"Look."

They looked uphill to the Cathedral. High on the roof the archangel Gabriel with his trumpet was silhouetted against the wintry sky. Below him was the semicircle of chapels, St. James, St. Ambrose, St. Martin of Tours, St. Saviour, St. Columba, St. Boniface, St. Ansgar, all showing a flickering of light.

"Fire!" Q cried.

The Dean was already running up the hill, Cyprian bounding clumsily beside him. Tallis followed as best he could. Q evaporated downhill into the darkness.

Nineteen

D r. Austin came in the front door of the Gregory mansion, Rochester rushing to greet him, stopping, tail down in disappointment as he saw that his master was alone. Suzy realized that the pounding, though hurried, had been in the rhythm of Emily's fugue, to let them know who was at the door.

Mrs. Austin rushed to the front hall.

"No," her husband said. "Nothing. Anything happen here?" He took her arm and led her back to the music room.

"A wrong number. I think it was legitimate because it sounded like our usual wrong numbers, and it was someone wanting Gladys, and we've had her before. And Mr. Theo called. He's on his way over. He says he's been worried about the children all day . . ." She looked at her husband. "Oh, Wallace. Wallace, I'm so glad you're back. . . . I don't believe that any of this has happened. What I really believe is that Dave and Rob will come in with Rochester, that Vicky and Emily are off somewhere

250

having secrets from Suzy . . ." She pressed her knuckles against her lips to control her mounting hysteria.

"It's not a time for secrets," Suzy said. "Daddy! Daddy!"

Rabbi Levy said, "Your daughter is right. I think that you must tell us, Dr. Austin, everything that you know. You must tell us what it is that has been worrying you, what it is that you have been trying to spare your wife. And you must not exclude your daughter. No matter what this is about, your whole family is involved, the children perhaps even more than the adults."

Dr. Austin nodded in agreement but did not speak. He went over to the fireplace, put his hands on the marble mantelpiece, and looked searchingly at the cold ashes in the grate.

His wife asked, "What was in your letter from Dr. Shen-shu? Why is Dr. Gregory in Liverpool?"

"The letter first." Dr. Austin looked slowly round the room, at his wife, his child, at the old man. "They're on their way here, Shasti, Shen-shu, and Gregory. Tallis sent for them."

"Why?" Mrs. Austin asked.

Dr. Austin stared into the cold grate. "When Shasti and Shen-shu left here they knew that something was wrong, not only about Emily's accident, but with the whole set-up at the lab."

The Rabbi struck one note softly three times on the piano. "Did they tell you that?"

"Not before I came. It was all in the letter my wife referred to that came today. They didn't tell me before because their suspicions were so incredible that, as scientists, they could only doubt the evidence that seemed to be piling up. They wanted to see if I, too, found something rotten in the state of Denmark."

"Denmark!" Suzy exclaimed.

"It's from *Hamlet,*" her mother explained quickly. "Did you?"

"Yes. I did. I began to smell something I didn't like at all."

"What?"

"And when?" Rabbi Levy closed the piano keyboard to keep himself from hitting the keys; the nervous sound might help him but could only distract the others.

"After we'd been here about a month. After I'd learned that Emily had been attacked in my office. After I began to dislike my superior."

"Dr. Hyde?" Suzy asked.

"Yes."

"But I thought you thought he was so wonderful, Daddy, the way he arranged for Emily's lessons and was such a brilliant surgeon and all."

"All that is true, Suzy, and I was certainly both impressed and blinded by it at first."

"But the good doctor is too good, perhaps?" The Rabbi asked.

"Yes. I began to get tired of his moral platitudes. All autumn he has become more fulsome, more eloquent, with his talk of the redemption of the city. And then, not long ago, he came to me with a wild story that it is going around that I am the one responsible for Emily's blindness."

"You!" his wife exclaimed. "But we weren't even here! We were in Thornhill."

"As it happens," the Doctor said, "I was in New York that day for a medical meeting. But it was a quick trip. I had a very ill patient in the hospital and so I didn't stay overnight. I didn't even take time for a phone call to Shasti and Shen-shu. But the story is

252

that I came here, that I went through their desk, that Emily came in, that I grabbed a Micro-Ray that was not yet controlled, and directed it at her, intending only to have the flash blind her temporarily so that she wouldn't see who it was, but——"

"Daddy!" Suzy rushed at him and flung her arms around him.

He held her. "It's close enough to the truth to be frightening, Suzy. That's evidently what did happen. Someone, not I, but someone, must have blinded Emily just that way."

"I hate Dr. Hyde!" Suzy shouted. "I hate him!"

"Hush, Suzy. That won't help." He disengaged her gently, turned to the old man. "Remember, Rabbi Levy, I am a doctor. I must often make decisions not only for myself and my family, but for my patients."

"Medical decisions?"

"What is one? To make an isolated medical decision isn't as easy as all that, except perhaps in the operating theatre, where one has to decide, for instance, if indeed an organ is diseased enough to warrant its radical removal. This is the surgeon's problem. The patient, and the patient's family, lack the training that would give them the ability to make the choice. But otherwise? It's a fine line. Human beings don't divide into three separate and isolated entities, body, mind, and spirit."

"I don't understand. You sound like Grandfather," Suzy said.

"Your grandfather has taught me a great deal."

"What's this got to do with that terrible Hyde?" Mrs. Austin asked.

"Hyde pays no attention to the fine line between guiding his patients towards wholeness, and manipulating. As you know, I cannot stand a wishy-washy doctor. But I don't accept fascism, and Hyde is a fascist."

"But things have gone beyond mere theory, haven't they?" the Rabbi probed.

"There have been more brain operations than necessary. Hyde's playing with the Micro-Ray the way Suzy used to operate on her dolls when she was little."

"This is a grave accusation. Are you sure?" The Rabbi stood looking at the heavy piles of Braille music on the piano.

"A young boy about Dave's age came into the hospital for an appendectomy. Dr. Hyde also happened, luckily, to find a tumor in the brain, which he removed with the Micro-Ray. I accepted this the first time, even the second and the third. But this kind of thing is happening too often."

"So," the Rabbi suggested, "you wrote to Shasti and Shen-shu?"

"Right. And went over all our old correspondence while I was waiting for an answer. And now that I was looking, it seemed to me that I could see veiled warnings, that they had been giving me hints all along which I had blindly ignored."

"Daddy," Suzy asked, "what's this about Dr. Gregory going to Liverpool?" She had pulled herself together perhaps better than the adults. "I thought he went to Athens for somebody's birthday party."

"He did. That was his legitimate excuse. But right after the party he flew to Liverpool. He's not as lost in the past as he sometimes seems, and he cares very much about his ewe lamb, though he has odd ways of showing it."

"But what did he go to Liverpool *for*?"

"To see Shasti and Shen-shu. He'd begun to get his own suspicions, not of me, thank God. At first he was too upset over what had happened to Emily, and too grateful to Dr. Hyde for taking care of all the practical things which he knew himself to be too vague and uninformed to handle, to be able to see anything else. But before Shasti and Shen-shu left, they had a talk with him. They took upon their own shoulders a great deal of the responsibility for Emily's blindness. They told him that they would not rest until they found out who had gone through their desk, and who had attacked Emily. From that moment on, Dr. Gregory made this his business, too. But he works slowly, methodically. He doesn't go off half-cocked."

"Daddy, what's he going to do when he comes home to-night and finds Emily gone?"

Dr. Austin looked at his watch. He did not answer.

"And what about Canon Tallis? Where does he come in?"

"He's an old friend of the Dean of the Cathedral's, and he knew Shasti and Shen-shu years ago when they were working together in India. And evidently Tallis has a reputation for being able to solve problems of international skullduggery. I know he broke up some kind of a power ring centered in Portugal. So he was asked to come over here and find out what's going on."

"Why now?" the Rabbi asked. "Why at this particular mo-ment in time?"

"Because everybody seemed to feel that things were con-verging, coming to a climax, that there was going to be some kind of crisis."

The doorbell rang, sharply, Emily's fugue. Then they heard a key in the lock.

The Bishop sat on his subterranean throne.

His golden mitre was brilliant in the floodlight. The

255

tarnished lamp which Rob had said looked like a gravy boat lay in his lap. Behind him the ornate tile of the old subway station reflected a distortion of the throne, the red-carpeted steps. He was flanked on either side by a group of leather-jacketed youths, some with the Bat emblem on their sleeves. They had been assembling for the past hour, while the Bishop sat with Rob beside him on the throne and recited to him:

> *"In Xanadu did Kubla Khan*
> *A stately pleasure-dome decree;*
> *Where Alph, the sacred river, ran*
> *Through caverns measureless to man,*
> *Down to a sunless sea . . .*

"You must stop being afraid, Robert. You must stop being afraid of me."

Rob's voice came thin and high. "I want to get down."

The Bishop's vulture's talon held the rigid little body. "Now listen to me, little hostage. I will recite to you from *Doctor Faustus.*"

Rob stiffened, tried to jerk away. The Bishop did not loosen his grasp.

"I will recite to you from *Coriolanus.*"

"No. I don't want to hear. I want to go home."

One of the leather-jacketed boys called, "Let him have a piece of sermon, Bishop. Talk to him about freedom. Give him that bit."

The Bishop dropped his voice from its dramatic, mesmerizing level (had he been trying to hypnotize Rob?), spoke almost conversationally, partly to Rob, partly to the phalanx of youths flanking him. "People don't want freedom. Don't you realize that? Can you not tell? People want security, safety. Freedom is too dangerous. You don't want freedom, Robert. Hold still. What do you want now except to go back to the safety of your family? My friends here beside me, my young trusty followers, have found something better than freedom, have you not, my lads?"

"Right, Bishop," they answered in unison.

"Now hear this: young people today in applying for jobs are not looking for challenge. This is common, statistical knowledge. Right, my lads?"

"Right, Bishop."

"What the young man or woman applying for a job today is looking for is——"

"The lamp," someone said, and was noisily shushed.

The Bishop continued,

"——is fringe benefits——"

"Right, Bishop."

"A secure retirement policy——"

"Right, Bishop!"

"Adequate, nay more than adequate hospital and medical insurance——"

"Right, Bishop!"

"*And* the lamp," someone called out, and was again hushed. There was an uneasy shuffling of feet.

"And what happens when people are offered freedom?" The Bishop overrode the interruption and answered his own question. "They will kill whoever offers it. What happened to the only so-called free man who has ever walked the earth? We crucified him. And"——his voice dropped so that all the leather-jacketed youths had to lean closer to hear——"I have come to the conclusion that this was the only thing to do, nay, that this was the right thing to do. Right, boys?"

"Right, Bishop!"

"Man is not capable of freedom. If we are given freedom we will destroy ourselves. Has this not been proven to us often enough? The only way we can be freed from the slavery of freedom is by relinquishing freedom, as you have done, boys, in a reasonable and pleasurable way. Right, boys?"

"Right, Bishop!"

"I, I am offering you the alternative to freedom; I am offering you the ultimate freedom! I am offering the redemption of the city, and then the redemption of the world. All this is in my power. Right, boys?"

"Right, Bishop!"

"And I now offer it to you. Offer me your freedom, and I will free you from its dangers."

Dave and Emily, emerging from the tunnel with their three captors, heard these words.

——He's mad! Dave thought.

Rob struggled wildly to get loose from the Bishop's grasp. "Dave! Emily! Help me!"

Behind the Bishop a group of boys began to stamp softly, rhythmically. "The lamp, the lamp, we want the lamp." "A flight, a flight, the Bats want to fly."

The Bishop raised his thin hand for silence, speaking in his most authoritative voice. "Not yet, my lads! Patience! Your time will come! First we must offer the lamp to Robert and Emily and of course Davidson." His eyes sparkled feverishly in the brilliant floodlights. The dark cables were coiled about the platform, near the steps to the throne, like heaps of sleeping serpents.

Emily and Dave stood side by side, Emily's hand resting on Dave's arm, absorbing his tension. She listened, scowling, trying to hear what kind of a place they were in. She had remained, despite her fear, aware enough during the trip through the tunnel both to listen and to smell, and to command every muscle in her body to remember the circuitous route. When Dave had tried to whisper to her where they were being taken, she had filed his words away, undigested, so that they would not interrupt the discipline of her concentration. She had smelled for herself the stench of subway, and now she pulled Dave's words out of her subconscious, and into her mind's eye flashed a reasonably accurate picture of the unused subway station. She knew that the passage from which they had emerged was still behind her. She could tell from the echoes that the platform ended at her right, that beyond were tracks which ran into tunnels at either extreme of the subway platform, that the wall of the platform was to her left, that there were many bodies near the wall absorbing the echoes that would have helped her to judge sizes and distances more accurately.

She heard Dave's voice demanding, "What do you want?"

She heard Bishop Fall's voice in reply, "I want Austin's papers and I mean to get them."

259

Twenty

Dean de Henares stood in the ambulatory and realized that his Cathedral was not on fire. Cyprian, who had come in with him, whined. The Dean moved slowly from chapel to chapel, leaving a small trail of blood behind him, though he was not aware of this, seeing the candles lit on each altar, St. James, St. Ambrose, St. Martin of Tours, St. Saviour, St. Ansgar, the saints after which the school lavatories had irrevently been named and whom the Dean loved as his own family. He stood outside St. Ansgar's chapel, under an enormous crystal chandelier that glittered from the tiny light of the candles, and heard the broken side door by St. James open and slam shut. Cyprian, who had never before been allowed inside the Cathedral proper, barked.

"Tom!" the Dean called.

"Here!" the Canon called back. "What's up?"

Their voices echoed throughout the Cathedral.

"Wait!" The Dean made his way back around the ambulatory to where Tallis stood outside St. James chapel. "Somebody's lit the candles on all the chapel altars. And the lock to the St. James door is broken. There's a bent key still in it."

"Yes. I saw that. Do you have any idea what it's about?"

"Not the faintest."

"Mind your arm," Tallis said. "You're bleeding."

Now the Dean noticed the blood. "It's just a flesh wound. Can you tie it up for me? We'll find some linen in the sacristy."

"I could do a temporary job. But you'd better get to the hospital."

"Later," the Dean said, and started towards the sacristy. "Tom, who could have lit these candles, and why?"

It was Vicky, closely followed by Mr. Theo, who had rung the Gregorys' bell, opened the door.

"We've got to go back to the Cathedral," she kept saying excitedly, while Mr. Theo demanded explanations.

She tried to tell everybody exactly what had happened, but she was so close to hysteria that her father had to keep stopping her, questioning, making her go back. "And then I lit all the candles in all the chapels as a signal for Canon Tallis. We've got to go back to the Cathedral, Daddy! Emily and Dave are there somewhere, and Rob must be there, too, and we've got to go back to the Cathedral before anything else happens."

"Stay here, all of you," Dr. Austin said. "I'll go."

"No, Daddy! We've got to stay together, all of us! We've all got to go!"

For once Suzy was entirely on her elder sister's side. "Write a note to Dr. Gregory telling him where we are, Daddy. We've got to go, Vicky's right, and with Rochester. We've got to give Rochester something of Rob's and Emily's to smell, and something of Dave's if we can find it, and Rochester will take us to them."

"You'd never find them by yourself, Daddy!" Vicky cried. "The Cathedral's too huge! Suzy's right. Rochester's the only one who can tell us where to go."

Mrs. Austin said, "You can't leave us again. I agree with the children. Let's all go to the Cathedral together. I'll get some things for Rochester to smell."

Dr. Austin did not argue, but sat down by the telephone to write a brief note to Dr. Gregory. Mr. Theo kept sputtering because he was kept in the dark, no one ever told him anything, while Rabbi Levy tried to silence him long enough to explain.

Mrs. Austin brought a single scarlet mitten of Rob's that had fallen by his overshoes, and Emily's navy and red school scarf dangling from its peg. Dave had few possessions and these he did not leave around; she could find nothing of his to give to Mr. Rochester for its scent.

"Never mind," Dr. Austin said impatiently. "If he can lead us to Rob and Emily, Dave's bound to be there, too." He put the note on the mantelpiece, snapped Mr. Rochester's leash onto the choke collar.

The big dog pulled to get up the street so that Dr. Austin had a hard time holding him back. Mr. Theo and the Rabbi could not walk as quickly as the others, and the dog, straining to go, grunting in unhappiness at being restrained, and then choking as he pulled the chain tight, expressed the impatience of them all.

Vicky, who had been so determined that they stick together

at all costs, kept waiting for one of the old men to say, "Go ahead. We'll catch up with you." But neither of them spoke.

Dr. Austin drew Rochester up, sharply, so that the beast dropped to his haunches. "Mr. Theo, Rabbi Levy, you're both pushing too fast. Five minutes one way or the other at this point isn't worth a heart attack. Stand still and catch your breaths and then we'll walk more slowly."

Now Rabbi Levy did say, "Go ahead, Doctor. We'll follow."

But the Doctor spoke firmly. "No. If there's danger it's better if we all stay together."

They moved, more slowly now, up the street.

Suzy whispered to her sister, "People are staring at us."

Vicky realized that they were indeed drawing curious glances from the passers-by. She looked around rather wildly, then realized what an odd procession they made, led by the enormous dog grunting and straining at his leash, and brought up by the two old men: the Rabbi in his long dark coat that reached almost to the ground, his beard blowing wildly, his wide-brimmed hat on his head; Mr. Theo with his lion's mop of yellowed locks blowing, limping along beside the Rabbi and wincing because of his arthritic knees. Even by the liberal standards of upper Broadway they were an unusual sight. "Look at us!" she whispered back. "Wouldn't you stare, too?"

Mr. Rochester automatically turned east towards the Cathedral at 110th Street, pulling them all along with him. When they started across Amsterdam Avenue he began to bark uncontrollably, and it was all Dr. Austin could do to hold him back. They all looked up Amsterdam to the Cathedral.

Light streamed from the Octagon, from all the windows of the nave.

"Somebody saw my signal!" Vicky cried. "Somebody's there!"

Now they all began to run.

"Rub the lamp, Rob," the Bishop said. "Rub it and something lovely will happen."

"No! I don't want to! Let me go! You hurt!"

Dave restrained Emily. "Hold it, Em. You can't see where you're going and he's dangerous."

"Do something, then."

"Wait." Dave strained his eyes to see into the shadows. He thought he saw his father crouched near the end of a large coil of cable. Was there another figure beyond his father? He could not be sure.

The Bishop, holding Rob's hand in his steel talon, rubbed the little boy's fingers over the lamp.

Out of the shadows behind Amon Davidson emerged the huge, green-robed figure. "You called me?"

"Yes, Hythloday. Young master Robert has summoned you."

"And what are your wishes, my young master? Are you able to give orders to your humble servant?"

Rob suddenly sat up straight on the Bishop's throne. "Yes. I have no need of you. Go away."

There was a pause.

Emily could not see Rob, but she could hear the strength in his voice. She heard the breathing of the boys on either side of the Bishop, waiting to see what would happen. She heard the Bishop: "But I have need of him, Robert. You must not send him away."

Rob's voice was a thin fluting. "Canon Tallis said we were beyond that kind of wishing. Genie. Go away."

Emily held her breath. —Don't let him weaken. Make him be strong.

"Are you sure, young master, my dear, that you do not wish to reconsider? I could be of great service to you."

Now Emily's fingers clamped tightly on to Dave's arm. "I know who he is!"

But Dave was not listening. He was waiting to see what Rob would do.

"Go!" Rob ordered.

A genie has to play by the rules.

He bowed and disappeared into the shadows.

"Dave! I know who he is!" Emily repeated.

There was a murmuring from the waiting boys.

"Ah, do not despair, my lads!" the Bishop said. "This foolish child is not the only one who can rub the lamp."

The rhythmical stamping started again. "The lamp, the lamp, we want the lamp! A flight, a flight, the Bats want to fly!"

"*S*! Come here!" the Bishop commanded.

One of the boys detached himself from the group, went to the throne.

"Rub the lamp."

The boy took the tarnished piece of metal into his hands.

The genie reappeared from the shadows. "You called me?"

"Yeah. I called you. I want a flight."

"Wait!" the Bishop cried in a loud voice. "Robert must fly first. *G, K,* get him. Robert must fly! Give Robert a flight!"

"Come, young master," the genie said softly.

Emily screamed. "It's Dr. Hyde! He's the genie!"

For a second the Bishop loosened his hold on Rob and the little boy slithered down from the throne, but before he could run towards Dave and Emily the two youths had grabbed him and dragged him over to the genie.

Now at last all the pieces of the pattern fell into place for Dave. Emily was right: Hythloday and Dr. Hyde were one and the same. If Hyde used the Micro-Ray on Rob—

Amon Davidson shoved a low black couch out from the shadows into the glare of the floodlights. The two boys held the screaming Rob down on it. The green-robed figure approached.

"The lights," Dave heard Emily say. "Dave! Kill the lights!"

He flung himself towards the coil of cable where his father had been standing, scrabbled at the heavy black wiring, seeing, to his infinite relief, where the cable was plugged in. He gave a mighty yank.

Darkness came like a clap of thunder. He stumbled through it towards Rob's screaming, fell over the couch, over Rob, shouted "It's Dave, Rob," pulled the little boy up, away from the couch, away from Dr. Hyde and the milling boys shouting into the darkness.

"Here," Emily's voice came urgently through the confusion. "Here."

Holding Rob tightly, Dave pushed towards the voice, shoving at bodies that got in his way. He heard someone fall off the edge of the subway platform, yelling.

"Amon!" the Bishop shouted through the din. "The lights! The lights!"

"Dave!" Emily called. "Here!"

He was closer to her voice now. "We're coming."

"Here!" she kept calling in a low voice that carried through the rising tide of the Bats' anger and fear. "Here. Dave, here!"

He held Rob with his left hand. With his right hand he made a shoving, hitting path through the crowd.

"Here, Dave, here!"

His hand touched the softness of her hair. He felt her hand reach out for his face to identify him.

"Quick!" She grabbed at his jacket, turned and moved swiftly the few feet from where she had been standing, into the mouth of the tunnel, Dave and Rob stumbling after her.

The boys were in a panic now, in a rage that drowned the sound of Emily's voice. She moved her arms in wide, swimming gestures, felt walls on either side, knew they were safely in the tunnel, by her body's memory, by chance. "Rob! Are you all right?"

The little boy gave a sobbing hiccup in assent.

Behind them the subway platform was an inferno of darkness and noise.

"Light!" the Bishop was screaming. "Amon! Light! Hyde! Use the Micro-Ray!"

Emily, still pulling Dave by the jacket, headed deeper into the tunnel.

Twenty-One

Mr. Rochester, on his leash, sniffed the unfamiliar odor of the Cathedral. Dr. Austin held Rob's mitten and Emily's scarf to the dog's nose. "Find them, Rochester, take us to them," he urged.

The others stood a little back in order not to confuse the dog. The Dean, holding his wounded arm, had given Cyprian to Vicky to hold. Cyprian would have liked to play with Mr. Rochester, but Rochester was concerned only with sniffing, his nose down to the ground. Canon Tallis stood by Mrs. Austin. Suzy, between the two old men, felt herself trembling with reaction. She wondered if it had occurred to Vicky that perhaps everything might *not* turn out all right, that not all stories have a happy ending . . .

Vicky, restraining Cyprian, was trying to restrain her imagination as well. All kinds of possibilities, some "all right," some appalling, were whirring through her brain. Imaginary visions of funerals, happy reunions, burning cathedrals (for the Dean had told her that that had been his fear), shooting and howling mobs rushing up Morningside hill after them, her father vanquishing everybody with the Micro-Ray, Canon Tallis providing the answer to all problems, Rob all right but Emily hurt, Emily and Dave safe but Rob lost forever somewhere underground in the Cathedral—flickered kaleidoscopically through her mind. She moved closer to the Dean.

"Ought I to have stayed with Emily?"

"No. You did precisely the right thing. If you'd been taken, too, if you hadn't left us your signal, we wouldn't have any idea where anybody is now."

She felt better.

Mr. Rochester sniffed around the entrance to the organ loft, then crossed the ambulatory and sniffed at the iron gates that led to the circular stairs, began pawing, whining.

Dr. Austin tried the gate. "Can we get in?"

The Dean fumbled with his good hand in the capacious pocket of his monk's robe for his key ring, which was like Dave's. His left sleeve was dark with drying blood. Dr. Austin had checked Canon Tallis's hasty bandage and said that it would do until later. The Dean shook the keys on the ring, inserted one in the lock, opened the gate.

Rochester went through, sniffing, then started to descend. The stairs were dark. "Let me turn on the lights." The Dean moved to walk with Dr. Austin.

In answer to Mrs. Austin's unspoken question, Canon Tallis said, "We'll all go. But give them plenty of room. We don't want to be too close on their heels. It'll confuse Mr. Rochester."

Slowly they descended, the Dean turning on lights as they

went. He opened the door to the vast and cluttered shadows of the crypt.

Cyprian, with his squat, bowed legs, found the winding stairs difficult. He snorted with discomfort. Vicky petted and encouraged him. The two old men and Suzy were behind her; she and Cyprian were slowing them down.

"Can't you hurry?" Suzy asked.

"I'm trying to."

Cyprian wheezed anxiously.

The others were halfway through the crypt before he had managed the last of the stairs, and he pulled to join his master.

Mr. Rochester sniffed at some broken statuary.

"What is it, Rochester? What is it, old boy?" Dr. Austin asked him. "Find Rob. Find Emily. Rochester, come on."

The dog took an inordinately long time over a broken stone gargoyle, then moved on through the storeroom to the boiler-room door. The Dean unlocked it. His arm was paining him badly and sweat broke out in cold beads on his face.

Mr. Rochester pushed through the door. For a moment he stopped by one of the boilers, sniffing a large batteried lamp that had been left there. The Dean bent and picked it up. Sniffing excitedly, Rochester led them to the empty storeroom. Dr. Austin reached out to turn on a hanging lightbulb.

The stone to the tunnel was ajar. At the opening Mr. Rochester stopped and whined, then broke into barking. He looked at Dr. Austin, wagged his tail, looked at the dark hole to the tunnel, barked again, then sat down purposefully.

"Daddy!" Vicky cried. "That's the way Rochester sat on the dock at Grandfather's when Rob stowed away on the *Sister Anne* and we thought he was lost!"

270

"Is Rob there?" Dr. Austin asked the dog. "Rochester. Is Rob there?"

Mr. Rochester, sitting at the mouth of the tunnel, barked again. He made no attempt to go in, simply sat as though his duty were now done until Rob returned. Dr. Austin pulled at the leash to move him so that he himself could peer into the darkness, but Mr. Rochester refused to budge. Dr. Austin dropped the leash and, getting down on his hands and knees beside the dog, peered into the tunnel. All he could see was darkness.

Now the others began pressing into the little stone storeroom.

"Get back," the Doctor said sharply. "There's nothing to see. It's some kind of tunnel. Dean de Henares, what do you know about this?"

"Nothing," the Dean said. "To my knowledge this has been only a storeroom off the boiler room. Let me see." He crouched down beside Dr. Austin.

"What'll we do?" Suzy asked. "Mother, Daddy, what'll we do?"

Mrs. Austin had moved into an icy calm. She put her arm around her daughter. "We'll wait here. If Rochester thinks the children are there, and if he isn't going after them, if what he is doing is waiting, then that's what we must do."

Canon Tallis said, "You're right, Mrs. Austin. For any one of us to go blundering in there in the darkness with no idea of where that tunnel leads would be folly."

"Nevertheless," Dr. Austin stood up, "I'm going. Give me the lantern."

His wife tried to restrain him. "Wally, you can't see where you're going—you can't—"

"That's why I want the lantern."

"But Rochester didn't go in! He came this far and stopped. Rochester always knows when to wait."

"I'm not taking advice from a dog."

Tallis moved to stand beside him. "I think I would if I were you."

"Not when my children are in danger."

Tallis sighed, spoke quietly. "Very well, Doctor. But the tunnel may branch off in several directions. If there's any question, don't go on. You don't know what you may be blundering into."

Dr. Austin nodded, not promising anything, reached for the lantern, then plunged into the unknown darkness of the tunnel.

In the silence that followed, they were startled when Mr. Theo said, "I'm going to the organ."

"Theo—" Canon Tallis started.

"For Emily," Mr. Theo cut him off. "If she's anywhere, trying to get out, and she doesn't know where she is, if she hears the organ it will guide her."

"Go with him," Canon Tallis said to the Rabbi.

"I am perfectly all right by myself."

"Yes, Theo, but I want Rabbi Levy with you, anyhow. If anything happens, if you see anything—"

"I will play the Zephaniah trumpet solo if I need you," Mr. Theo said. "If I see something, but it doesn't seem to me to be dangerous, I will play that Händel diddlio you're so fond of. Meanwhile I'll play Emily's fugue. If things get out of hand I'll simply make noise. Come, Rabbi."

The two old men moved slowly out of the dank storeroom into the warmth of the boiler room.

"Theo!" the Dean called. "Take Cyprian!" He took the leash from Vicky and went after the old men. "Take care of them, Cyprian," he said.

"What's this all about?" Mrs. Austin suddenly demanded of the two churchmen.

Canon Tallis answered, "The day Emily was attacked, papers were stolen that contained almost all of the formulae essential to the control of the Micro-Ray. The most difficult equation of all, the key equation, was not found. My guess is that whoever attacked Emily gave the papers to Hyde and he thought he had enough information so he could make the Micro-Ray himself."

"Why?"

"Power," Tallis answered simply. "It would give him complete power over people. If you can control a person's brain, he's yours."

"Dear God," Mrs. Austin whispered. "Rob——"

"What was Hyde missing?" interrupted the Dean, leaning for support against the stone wall.

"The equation that would have told him how to cut without burning. How, for instance, to reach deep into the brain without touching the outer layers, and then to control the brain center without destroying it." ——The pleasure dome, he thought. This was one of the most malign perversions of knowledge he had encountered.

From high above them they could hear the roar of the organ. At first, so strange were the Cathedral acoustics, it was only a mass of sound; then the sound separated itself into melody, into point and counterpoint. The tremendous sound rolled the length of the nave and descended to them.

Vicky felt her skin prickling, first from the dreadful implications of Canon Tallis's words; then from the power of the music pulsing through granite and marble, flowing through the building like blood through its veins; and then because this would be a signal as visible to Emily as the burning candles had been to Canon Tallis and the Dean. If Emily could hear the music, no matter where she was, it would guide her back to safety.

Canon Tallis excused himself abruptly and pushed past the Dean out of the storeroom, strode across the boiler room and into the crypt.

"Where are you going?" the Dean asked.

"Be right back," the Canon called as he disappeared.

Dr. Austin returned.

"The tunnel branched . . ." he said in defeat.

Mr. Rochester whined.

They heard steps coming down the stairs, walking rapidly toward the storeroom.

Twenty-Two

Emily moved through the tunnel. Dave and Rob were slowing her down, and she was afraid the drag of Dave's hand on her shoulder would interfere with her body's tenuous memory of the trip to the subway station. She stopped, quivering with listening, with feeling through every pore for direction.

Far behind them they could hear the shouting of the boys, inchoate noises of rage, confusion, terror. She thought she heard the word, "Fire!" Ahead of them everything was soundless. But she could feel that the tunnel was widening. Then she heard the guiding roar of a subway train.

She stopped until the roar had gone by them, above, to their right; listened; sniffed; snapped her fingers; listened again.

"Can't you hurry?" Dave asked.

"Shut up. I am. There's a turn here. I have to think which way."

In the darkness Rob could sense her indecision. Behind them the shouting of the Bats increased.

275

Dave said, "I think one turn leads up into the junk shop. Try not to take that, Em. That's the tunnel the Bats use."

She stood there, listening.

Rob began to cry, a terrified, almost animal wail.

Dave said, sternly, calmly, "Rob, you've been very brave. You've been great. You mustn't let us down now. Rob, I'm counting on you. Hold my hand, but don't pull. You can do it, Rob. I trust you."

The little boy's wails dwindled to controlled sobs, then to sniffling. Dave's voice was tangible strength, assurance. Dave's hand was a promise of safety and love.

"Okay," Emily said, with sudden decision. "This way. Come on." She moved on again. Dave's hand on her shoulder seemed to be an insufferable weight. "Don't press down so hard!"

He tried to lighten his hold. He could feel her shoulder wriggling beneath his fingers, first as though simply to dislodge him, then in a rhythmical movement as though she were feeling ahead of her with her hands, trying to see through the darkness with her fingertips.

"Do you have to hold on?" she asked impatiently.

"Emily," he said, "when I am leading you, you have to hold on to me."

She didn't answer. Her shoulder continued its rhythmic movement. Her feet shuffled steadily along. He could hear her breathing.

She stopped.

"What's the matter?" Dave asked.

"The tunnel divides again here. Wait. I'm trying to remember which way."

Had she taken the correct turn before? Or was she

leading them into Phooka's Antiques, into the stronghold of the Bats?

"*Hush,*" she said, though they had not spoken. "I can't remember. . . . Hush. . . ."

Dave strained his ears. They had left the chaos and shouting of the Bats behind them. It seemed that he could hear the darkness that pressed around them, that he could hear the dank stench of fetid air. Rob's breathing was quick and shallow.

"Listen!" Emily cried. "Dave! Rob! Listen! This way!"

"What?" Dave asked. "Wait! I don't hear anything."

"Come on!" she cried. "It's the organ! I know which way to turn now. I can hear the organ! It's Mr. Theo!"

She moved surely now, with Dave and Rob stumbling behind her.

"Wait," Dave said, pulling back. He could hear nothing.

"Come *on,*" Emily cried impatiently.

"I hear it," Rob said. "Oh, Emily, I hear it!"

They moved through the narrow tunnel of darkness, and at last Dave could hear a deep roaring, like a distant lion. How could Emily have identified this as Mr. Theo at the organ?

The sound roared like waves through the tunnel. He began to be able to recognize melody, harmony, each sound echoing out and spreading into the next.

The music grew louder, clearer. Ahead of them he saw a faint light. "I can see now," he said. "I'll lead."

"No—let me—"

She pushed steadily ahead.

He took his restraining hand from her shoulder and she moved along the guideline of music to the light.

Rob stumbled, but Dave's strong hand steadied him.

Then they were out of the tunnel and Emily stumbled into the waiting arms of Dr. Gregory.

The small stone storeroom and the boiler room were both crowded with people. Dave shoved Rob towards Mrs. Austin, who gathered her child in her arms, weeping with joy and relief. There was a policeman in the storeroom, policemen in the boiler room. Dr. Austin said, "Dave!"

Dave saw the Dean, his left sleeve covered with dried blood, saw two strange men he realized must be Dr. Shasti and Dr. Shen-shu . . .

"Dave, wait here with us," the Dean said.

He realized that everybody except the Dean and Canon Tallis and two of the policemen were leaving the storeroom, the boiler room.

"Theo's been playing forever," the Dean said. "It seems as though we'd been drowning in Bach for centuries. I'm not sure I'll ever be able to listen to him again."

"I will." Dave took a deep breath. "If it hadn't been for Mr. Theo and Bach we mightn't be here."

"Now, Dave," Canon Tallis said when the others had gone, "while we're waiting, tell us exactly what has happened."

"Waiting?" Dave asked. "What for?"

"The—uh—Bishop and Hyde. We have a net out for them no matter where they try to go. They'll be arrested shortly. The police caught Q and he's told us everything."

"Mr. Dean, what happened to your arm?"

"Somebody winged it." The Dean brushed the question aside. "A, I think. Now, Dave, what happened?"

Dave gave a deep, unwitting sigh. The oath, under these circumstances, had already been broken. He held nothing back. Canon Tallis and the Dean listened, occasionally interrupting to ask a question.

"You're sure Rob wasn't hurt? Hyde didn't use the Micro-Ray on him?"

"No. Emily yelled about the lights and I'd seen where my father had them plugged in. That Rob: what a kid. I always knew about Emily, that she was special. But that Rob—" He turned to the Dean. "Can you give medals, Father? He deserves one. You should have heard him telling the genie to go away. And then after Hyde'd been after him with the laser, well, for him to pull himself together the way he did, and be able to go through the tunnel with us—he's a great kid. But you do see, don't you, why I couldn't talk before?"

"Yes, Dave. We see."

He had mentioned, during his narration of the night's events, his father's presence in the subway station and his pulling out the couch on which Rob had been flung. For some reason which he did not understand, the memory of his father's role in the Bishop's mad plans was the most difficult part of the whole thing to accept. He moved away from the pain to ask, "Then it was Dr. Hyde who was in the office that day? Who took the papers and attacked Emily?"

Canon Tallis said, "I'm certain of it."

"To *blind* a child—" Dave started.

"I don't think he intended to blind her," Canon Tallis said. "Remember, it was an imperfect Micro-Ray, and he's done what he can to make reparation, though nothing—" He broke off, gave a warning noise and gesture. Dave and the Dean froze into listening. Inside the tunnel they heard scuffling.

Then there emerged from the mouth of darkness a strange apparition, a man with an apricot wig half off his head, revealing a few wisps of white hair; a man whose clothes had been half torn from him, so that what remained covering his body gave the effect of a disheveled Roman toga.

The picture of Coriolanus in the Bishop's reception room.

"Henry Grandcourt," Canon Tallis said, "you have played your last role."

Twenty-Three

"I t was," the Bishop—no, thank God not the Bishop but Henry Grandcourt—said with pride, "my grandest role." His eyes flickered with fanatic brilliance. "And well played. You cannot deny that. The wig, the slight distorting of the mouth, what you thought was the natural aging of a man who mourned the death of his beloved brother: it took you a long time even to become suspicious, didn't it, Henares? I had you thinking it was Austin you were after, didn't I? And when you wanted to send for Tallis I played right along with you." He sneered at the Dean. "I took over your Cathedral right under your nose because I had a vision. You—*you* are the one who plays at being a priest. What have *you* done? While I—if I had been left alone I would have had the city, the entire city in the palm of my hand. I tried to persuade my brother, but he was too narrow to see it. Change frightened him. But Henry Grandcourt is not afraid of change. So a year ago I turned to Hyde. I offered him power. I

281

offered him my plan. And he followed me. He did as he was told. We knew that my brother didn't have long to live, so we waited, and made ready." The full actor's laugh, tinged now with madness, rolled through the Cathedral. "So when the first Norbert Fall died of his heart attack, Hyde was with me and signed the death certificate and my master plan went into action: the redemption of my failure. But don't think I didn't grieve over Norbert's death. Oh, I did weep for him. We were very close. I had studied him for years, his every gesture, his every word, until I could out-bishop any bishop. It was his wasted life I was redeeming as well as my own dreams. I did for Norbert what he could not do for himself. I became the bishop who will never be forgotten. Who else has ever begun to do what I have done? Who else has come this close to taking the city? My role, my great role . . ."

In the abandoned subway station, emptied now of the stamping Alphabats, of Dr. Hyde, who had been arrested as he emerged from the tunnel into the junk shop, of the madman who thought he had out-bishoped a bishop, Dave stood between the Dean and Canon Tallis. Two plain-clothesmen waited respectfully in the background. The floodlights were on again, revealing signs of smoke on the tiled walls. There was a smell of singeing in the air. On the partially burned couch lay a body covered with a blanket. The wildly aimed Micro-Ray had found one victim.

Dave moved from between the two priests and lifted the blanket. His father lay on the couch, his face distorted and angry in death as it had been in life. Dave leaned over him, trying to smooth out the features. Then he moved his fingers gently over his father's forehead and hair. He did not know that tears were streaming down his cheeks.

He replaced the blanket.

When the Dean's wound had been cleaned and dressed he refused to stay in the hospital but went back to the Deanery, where Dave was waiting in the library with Canon Tallis.

Juan de Henares went straight to the boy, holding out his good hand. "You'll stay with me now, Dave?"

Dave took the outstretched hand. "Yes, Father."

After Amon Davidson's funeral, Dave, dry-eyed, went home with the Dean, and accepted, without question, the room that was given him to be his own. Canon Tallis helped him bring his few things up the hill from the room he had shared with his father.

Dave listened, gravely, a half-empty duffel bag of clothes and assorted oddments slung over his shoulder, as the Canon, carrying a pile of books, told him, "Now, Dave, you can learn to have neither the sense of inferiority that undersells the human being—"

"Like the Alphabats?"

"Precisely. Nor the sense of superiority that pretends to have what isn't there."

"Like Henry Grandcourt?"

"Right. He made his life bearable by a pretense, because to face himself was a threat to him, rather than a challenge and a hope."

"A challenge and a hope?"

"Yes, Dave."

"Okay, Canon Tallis. I get the message. I accept."

They climbed the hill to the Cathedral.

Dave sat once more in the choir stalls of the Cathedral, this time not as a chorister but as a baritone with the lay clerks, singing a Requiem Mass for the repose of the soul of Norbert Fall. Joy was stronger than grief in his heart, for now the Bishop had been returned to him. Henry Grandcourt, the mad actor, had not, after all, played his great role as well as he thought, for he had acted as the Bishop would never have acted: acted: yes, that was it. Henry Grandcourt had *acted,* and the Bishop had *behaved,* and in a few months the actor's grand plan had crashed about his ears.

The music rose up to the lancet windows of the Octagon; it was cleansing, redeeming. The Cathedral accepted it, embraced it.

Now Norbert Fall could rest in peace.

They sat around the enormous dining table at the Austin apartment for Thanksgiving dinner: all of them: the Austins, with John home for the holidays; Emily and her father; Dr. Shasti and Dr. Shen-shu; Mr. Theo and Rabbi Levy; Canon Tallis and Dave and the Dean. Mr. Rochester lay with his head just over the doorsill which divided living and dining room. Cyprian, snoring, blocked the doorway to the kitchen.

"The tragedy," Dr. Shen-shu was saying, "is that Grandcourt was so nearly right."

Emily shook back her silky mane of dark hair. "I don't

want there to have been anything good about him. I want to hate him all the way."

"But you can't, can you?" her father asked. "The city *is* crying for redemption."

"But not that way!"

"How, then?" Dr. Gregory asked.

The Dean spread out his big hands, wincing a little because his arm still pained him when he forgot and moved it unthinkingly. "We have to do what we can do in whatever way we can, and that's all, even if it isn't enough, even if the city's growing too quickly for us. If that sounds defeatist, it's not. It's the way things get done."

"That's right," Dave said. "You can't *make* people happy, the way Henry Grandcourt was trying to do. Well, none of you could *make* me respond, could you?"

"Not and have you free to be Josiah Davidson. No."

"So in a way Grandcourt was better than I was."

"How better?" Vicky asked.

Dave looked at Canon Tallis, who said, "Grandcourt was following fallen angels, Vicky. His vision was distorted by pride. But I think what Dave means is that he was at least making a response to life."

"Yeah," Dave said, "and I was trying to get out of it."

"But you're okay now, aren't you?" Rob asked. "You're in it now, aren't you?"

"Yes, Rob. I'm in. All the way."

"And you're really going to stay with the Dean?"

"As long as he'll have me."

"He has to have you, doesn't he?" Rob asked earnestly.

"Isn't he in loco parenthesis?" As usual, he did not understand their laughter. With considerable reserve he said, "Well. As long as you're okay."

Dave said, "If I'm okay it's partly because of you, Rob. Because you were brave. And because of every one of you here."

Emily said, lightly, steering clear of emotion, "We all love you, Dave."

"Yeah. Thanks." He looked around the table with a quick smile, then ate busily. Through a mouthful of turkey he said, "What we could all do after dinner is go down to the music room and have a concert. Emily can play for us, and Mr. Theo, and Rob'll sing—"

"You, too, Dave—"

"Okay. And I'll play my horn . . . hey, what'd I do with my horn? Mr. Dean, have you got it?"

Emily said, "You left it on the mantlepiece downstairs."

Now Dave was able to look around the big table at all of them: Emily, who had allowed herself to need him, and her father, who was not so lost in the past as he seemed; the two doctors, the Indian and the Chinese, who had flown from Liverpool for Emily's sake; the two old men, so different except in their shared wisdom; the Dean, who could knock the chip off Dave's shoulder with the warmth of his laugh; the English Canon, who in so short a time had become a friend to them all; and the Austins: the Austins who talked too much, who were naïve, who in their innocence had freely offered him their love:

His people.

His family.

The L'Engle Cast

THE AUSTIN FAMILY

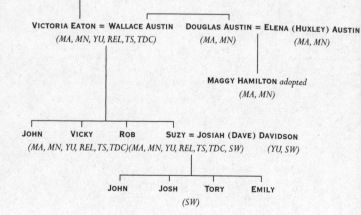

GRANDFATHER EATON = CARO EATON
(MA, MN, REL)

VICTORIA EATON = WALLACE AUSTIN   DOUGLAS AUSTIN = ELENA (HUXLEY) AUSTIN
(MA, MN, YU, REL, TS, TDC)   (MA, MN)   (MA, MN)

MAGGY HAMILTON *adopted*
(MA, MN)

JOHN   VICKY   ROB   SUZY = JOSIAH (DAVE) DAVIDSON
(MA, MN, YU, REL, TS, TDC)(MA, MN, YU, REL, TS, TDC, SW)   (YU, SW)

JOHN   JOSH   TORY   EMILY
(SW)

BOOKS FEATURING THE AUSTINS:

Meet the Austins (MA)	Troubling a Star (TS)
The Moon by Night (MN)	The Twenty-four Days
The Young Unicorns (YU)	Before Christmas (TDC)
A Ring of Endless Light (REL)	A Severed Wasp (SW)

f Characters

THE MURRY-O'KEEFE FAMILY

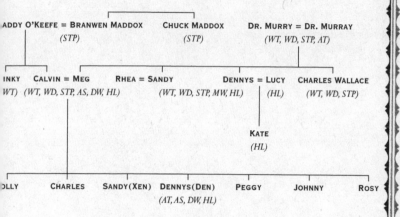

ADDY O'KEEFE = BRANWEN MADDOX   CHUCK MADDOX   DR. MURRY = DR. MURRAY
(STP)   *(STP)*   *(WT, WD, STP, AT)*

INKY   CALVIN = MEG   RHEA = SANDY   DENNYS = LUCY   CHARLES WALLACE
WT)   *(WT, WD, STP, AS, DW, HL)*   *(WT, WD, STP, MW, HL)*   *(HL)*   *(WT, WD, STP)*

KATE
(HL)

OLLY   CHARLES   SANDY(XEN)   DENNYS(DEN)   PEGGY   JOHNNY   ROSY
(AT, AS, DW, HL)

BOOKS FEATURING THE MURRY-O'KEEFES:

A Wrinkle in Time (WT)	*An Acceptable Time (AT)*
A Wind in the Door (WD)	*The Arm of the Starfish (AS)*
A Swiftly Tilting Planet (STP)	*Dragons in the Waters (DW)*
Many Waters (MW)	*A House Like Lotus (HL)*

CHARACTERS WHO APPEAR IN BOTH SERIES:

CANON TALLIS *(AS, YU, DW)*   MR. THEOTOCOPOULOUS *(YU, DW)*
ADAM EDDINGTON *(AS, REL, TS)*   EMILY GREGORY *(YU, DW, SW)*
ZACHARY GREY *(MN, REL, AT, HL)*

GO FISH

MADELEINE L'ENGLE

What did you want to be when you grew up?
A writer.

When did you realize you wanted to be a writer?
Right away. As soon as I was able to articulate, I knew I wanted to be a writer. And I read. I adored *Emily of New Moon* and some of the other L. M. Montgomery books and they impelled me because I loved them.

When did you start to write?
When I was five, I wrote a story about a little "gurl."

What was the first writing you had published?
When I was a child, a poem in *CHILD LIFE*. It was all about a lonely house and was very sentimental.

Where do you write your books?
Anywhere. I write in longhand first, and then type it. My first typewriter was my father's pre–World War I machine. It was the one he took with him to the war. It had certainly been around the world.

What is the best advice you have ever received about writing?
To just write.

What's your first childhood memory?
One early memory I have is going down to Florida for a couple of weeks in the summertime to visit my grandmother. The house was in the middle of a swamp, surrounded by alligators. I don't like alligators, but there they were, and I was afraid of them.

What is your favorite childhood memory?
Being in my room.

As a young person, whom did you look up to most?
My mother. She was a storyteller and I loved her stories. And she loved music and records. We played duets together on the piano.

What was your worst subject in school?
Math and Latin. I didn't like the Latin teacher.

What was your best subject in school?
English.

What activities did you participate in at school?
I was president of the student government in boarding school and editor of a literary magazine, and also belonged to the drama club.

Are you a morning person or a night owl?
Night owl.

What was your first job?
Working for the actress Eva Le Gallienne, right after college.

What is your idea of the best meal ever?
Cream of Wheat. I eat it with a spoon. I love it with butter and brown sugar.

Which do you like better: cats or dogs?
I like them both. I once had a wonderful dog named Touche. She was a silver medium-sized poodle, and quite beautiful. I wasn't allowed to take her on the subway, and I couldn't afford to get a taxi, so I put her around my neck, like a stole. And she pretended she was a stole. She was an actor.

What do you value most in your friends?
Love.

What is your favorite song?
"Drink to Me Only with Thine Eyes."

What time of the year do you like best?
I suppose autumn. I love the changing of the leaves.
I love the autumn goldenrod, the Queen Anne's lace.

Which of your characters is most like you?
None of them. They're all wiser than I am.

Austin Family Chronicles

MEET THE AUSTINS

For a family with four kids, two dogs, assorted cats, and a constant stream of family and friends dropping by, life in the Austin family home has always been remarkably steady and contented. When a family friend suddenly dies, the Austins open their home to an orphaned girl, Maggy Hamilton. The Austin children—Vicky, John, Suzy, and Rob—do their best to be generous and welcoming to Maggy. Vicky knows she should feel sorry for Maggy, but having sympathy for Maggy is no easy thing. Maggy is moody and spoiled; she breaks toys, wakes people in the middle of the night screaming, discourages homework, and generally causes chaos in the Austin household. How can one small child disrupt a family of six? Will life ever return to normal?

978-0-312-37931-5, $6.99 US/$7.99 Can.

THE MOON BY NIGHT

As if simply being fourteen-years-old weren't bad enough—what with the usual teenage angst and uncertainty—Vicky Austin's always comforting and reliable home life is changing completely. Her brother John is going off to college in the fall. Maggy has gone to live with her legal guardian. And the rest of Vicky's family is moving from their quiet house in the country to the heart of New York City. But before the big move, the entire Austin family is taking a meandering trip across the country in their station wagon, stopping to camp along the way, with no set schedule and not a single night of camping experience among them. Wild animal attacks. Life-threatening natural disasters. Cute boys on the prowl. Anything can happen in the great outdoors.

978-0-312-37932-2, $6.99 US/$7.99 Can.

THE YOUNG UNICORNS

The Austins are trying to settle into their new life in New York City, but their once close-knit family is pulling away from each other. Their father spends long hours working alone in his study. John is away at college. Rob is making friends with people in the neighborhood: newspaper vendors, dog walkers, even the local rabbi. Suzy is blossoming into a vivacious young woman. And Vicky has become closer to Emily Gregory, a blind and brilliant young musician, than to her sister Suzy. With the Austins going in different directions, they don't notice that something sinister is going on in their neighborhood—and it's centered around them. A mysterious genie appears before Rob and Emily. A stranger approaches Vicky in the park and calls her by name. Members of a local gang are following their father. The entire Austin family is in danger. If they don't start telling each other what's going on, someone just might get killed.

978-0-312-37933-9, $6.99 US/$7.99 Can.

A RING OF ENDLESS LIGHT

After a tumultuous year in New York City, the Austins are spending the summer on the small island where their grandfather lives. He's very sick, and watching his condition deteriorate as the summer passes is almost more than Vicky can bear. To complicate matters, she finds herself as the center of attention for three very different boys. Zachary Grey, the troubled and reckless boy Vicky met last summer, wants her all to himself as he grieves the loss of his mother. Leo Rodney has been just a friend for years, but the tragic loss of his father causes him to turn to Vicky for comfort—and romance. And then there's Adam Eddington. Adam is only asking Vicky to help with his research on dolphins. But Adam—and the dolphins— may just be what Vicky needs to get through this heartbreaking summer.
978-0-312-37935-3, $6.99 US/$7.99 Can.

TROUBLING A STAR

The Austins have settled back into their beloved home in the country after more than a year away. Though they had all missed the predictability and security of life in Thornhill, Vicky Austin is discovering that slipping back into her old life isn't easy. She's been changed by life in New York City and her travels around the country while her old friends seem to have stayed the same. So Vicky finds herself spending time with a new friend, Serena Eddington—the great-aunt of a boy Vicky met over the summer. Aunt Serena gives Vicky an incredible birthday gift—a month-long trip to Antarctica. It's the opportunity of a lifetime. But Vicky is nervous. She's never been away from her family before. Once she sets off though, she finds that's the least of her worries. She receives threatening letters. She's surrounded by suspicious characters. Vicky no longer knows who to trust. And she may not make it home alive.
978-0-312-37934-6, $6.99 US/$7.99 Can.

ALSO AVAILABLE:
A Wrinkle in Time, 978-0-312-36754-1
A Wind in the Door, 978-0-312-36854-8
A Swiftly Tilting Planet, 978-0-312-36856-2
Many Waters, 978-0-312-36857-9
An Acceptable Time, 978-0-312-36858-6

SQUARE
FISH

Available at your local bookstore, or visit
www.squarefishbooks.com.